The Cloak of Peacock Feathers

The Cloak of Peacock Feathers

Clair Jordain

First published in 2024

The rights of Clair Jordain have been identified as author of this work has been asserted in accordance with Section 77 of the Copyright, Designs and Patents Act 1988

This book is a work of fiction and any resemblance to actual persons, living or dead, is purely coincidental.

This book is sold subject to the condition that it shall not, by way of trade or otherwise, be lent, resold, hired out or otherwise circulated without the prior consent of the author in any form of binding or cover other than that in which it is published.

Copyright © 2024 Clair Jordain

All rights reserved.

ISBN:979-8-30153-173-6

DEDICATION

To my mother Muriel Jordain who gave me wings to fly
but the freedom to choose to walk.

AUTHOR'S NOTE – THE PEACOCK

The beauty of the peacock's feathers is legendary. The iridescence of the colours evokes a sense of wonder and well-being in all who see them. The figure and colours of the peacock have been used in religious and decorative art for centuries and span several continents and faiths.

In the Sufi religion it is believed that the peacock with its tail outstretched signifies the Self. In India it is also used as the symbol of love. Many cultures use the peacock to denote rebirth and immortality and connect the bird with the idea of paradise. Besides being used in Eastern religions, the peacock was also used by early Christians as a popular symbol for Christ. This links the concepts of resurrection and everlasting life in heaven - of change from one existence to another.

Other symbolisms include the observation that peacocks are serpent slayers. Serpents have been used throughout history to portray evil and temptation both internal and external. The feathers of the peacock were also thought to be able to preserve objects from decay and it was a time-honored practice to put its feathers on objects to preserve them and keep them safe.

Our story revolves around the symbolism of the cloak of peacock feathers with which our heroines have wrapped themselves to protect them from the world and to portray themselves as they want to be seen by others. Their cloaks grew out of the values and influences of their childhood built by their parents, close friends and experiences. But it is their choice, at the end of the day, what cloak they wear and in fact whether they choose to wear a cloak at all.

PROLOGUE

A young girl huddled in the corner of her bedroom. The light was off and the dried tears, which had run down her face like a small river, trying to find the easiest route to escape, were pulling at her skin. The noise of adults arguing downstairs had subsided and the quiet was more unnerving than the conflict. In the dim light of the evening, no one in the house wanted to switch on a light, no one wanted to see more clearly. In the dimness the world could be imagined differently, it could be the world of make believe and happiness.

The girl shuddered as the cold and fear started to combine until her shaking was uncontrollable. This added to her discomfort from the fear she already had, the fear of being remembered. If she sat perfectly still, perhaps no one would remember she was there. Perhaps she would survive the night without anyone shouting at her or breaking things. She prayed to a God she hardly believed in anymore. Please help me, please help us was her plea but she doubted it would ever be answered. Prayers were for people who had lives that could be changed, not a life like hers. Eventually she fell asleep out of emotional exhaustion and from crying so hard.

In the brightening of dawn, she awoke. The house was deathly quiet. She moved slowly and quietly, her catlike movements belaying her discomfort and fear. She opened the door to her room and looked out cautiously. No movements; no sounds except her father's incessant snoring. She had to risk it. She walked on tiptoe across the landing to the bathroom and once inside she quietly locked the door and felt a temporary relief at the relative safety the simple bolt gave her.

She then noticed her reflection in the mirror over the basin. Her face was smeared with the remnants of her silent screams, the screams she never dared to utter but which welled up inside her until she thought she would explode under their pressure.

She slowly ran some water in the basin and immersed her face in the cold wetness. It startled her at first but reminded her that she was alive. Her reflection in the mirror had now changed, she was able to see the face of a pretty ten-year-old girl. She saw her eyes, deep and swollen, which both hid her pain and announced it to the world all at the same time.

So, this is life, she thought. Is it the same for everyone? Can it change? She looked away. Not for her the reassurance of ever being able to control her life, of ever being able to have her say in matters, of ever being able to change things that needed to be changed. She was only a child. Perhaps that was all she would ever be. Perhaps she was destined to help others but never herself and perhaps she was destined to be forever alone in a crowd. One day she might be able to change her life, but not today. Today was a school day and a chance to escape for a while at least.

She left the bathroom and quickly dressed ready for school. She walked softly downstairs avoiding the creaking step and in the quiet kitchen she found some biscuits for her breakfast. Her parents were not yet awake, and she didn't want to bother them. She wanted to be alone.

She put on her treasured overcoat of peacock blues and greens, which was already really too small for her and sneaked out of the house. She was free. She wondered how many other children had had a life like hers. She considered if they grew up and took control of the lives, shaped them, changed them and made them their own.

She picked up speed and ran towards school, leaving her footprints in the mud on the verge beside the road, a reminder of her existence. The warm wind fingered her hair, and it felt good. She loosened her overcoat a little and a smile spread across her face. As if in response, the sun broke through the misty clouds overhead to keep her company.

CHAPTER 1

"I hate my body in summer clothes." Mellissa Wright was reading out loud from the agony column in the woman's magazine her friend Gillian Keene had just bought as they sat having a coffee in Brent Cross Shopping Centre. She was also with good friends Rachel Davis and Catherine Jones. The four friends were on a last-minute shopping trip to get ready for a two-week holiday to Majorca.

'Don't we all,' Gill sighed and stirred her coffee.

'Oh, I don't know. I think at least Cathy always looks good in anything she wears,' Rachel smiled at her friend who blushed in embarrassment. 'What does the mag say she should do about it, Mel?'

'Hang on, I haven't got to that bit yet. Here we are..." *I feel terrible in skimpy clothes. My arms are too fat"* ...blah, blah..."*my legs are too lumpy*" ...we've all been there.' Mel could feel for this woman's pain. She was so self-conscious of her size herself. *"Loose clothes can be practical and stylish"* ...so a tent it is then, girls... *"and choosing the right swimsuit can hide your faults well"* ...yeah, right! The only swimsuit that could hide my faults would be out of a museum. Up to the neck, down to the ankles and long sleeves for good measure – what a load of...'

'Now, Mel', Cathy was feeling uncomfortable with all this talk about bodies. 'We've all got our faults, but the best thing to do is not to dwell on them and anyway those sorts of swimsuits are available and they're not in a museum at all. I heard they're called modest swimwear which sounds great to me, and they stop you getting sunburnt.'

'But where's the fun in covering up all your good bits?' Gill was her usual provocative self.

'I don't want to flaunt my body for everyone to see…' Cathy said.

'Why not? You've got a body made for flaunting.' Mel thought of Cathy as stupid, immature and infuriatingly thin. She tolerated her only because Rachel seemed so fond of Cathy, who at 21yrs acted more like a naïve teenager. Rachel said she'd met her at an aerobics class and had taken her under her wing insisting on bringing her on all the women's outings together. Gill and Mel could never understand why. 'You might have a point there though, Cathy, it's something I might look into…'

'Not on my watch,' Gill was adamant.

'Oh, shut up Gill! What I wear is up to me,' and Mel pulled her green and blue jacket tighter around herself. This conversation was getting uncomfortable and she just wanted to go home.

'Ooh, we *are* in a bad mood today,' Gill said. 'What's eating you?'

'I'd just rather stay at home and save my money if you must know. I can't see what's so brilliant about going somewhere foreign that's so bloody hot you can't do anything and so bloody expensive you can't buy anything. That's what's eating me.'

'Baa humbug said Scrooge.' Gill said and they all burst out laughing making Mel feel so foolish.

'What are you saving your money for if not to enjoy yourself? For goodness' sake live a little Mel before you're too old. You're 25 not 65.' Gill said, 'my Gran has more go in her than you.'

'Then take her on holiday instead of me.'

'I would, she'd be a right laugh, but she's booked on a cruise, and I dread to think what she'll be getting up to. I'll have to have a word with her – you know the birds and the bees and all that.' Rachel and Mel laughed but Cathy gasped in disbelief.

'Gill! How can you talk about your Gran like that?'

'I can because I know she'd laugh with us. You know, since she met that Mr. Watkins at the Community Club, oh my, there's been no stopping her. What's important, though, is that she's living her life, which is what you're NOT doing, Melissa Wright.'

Mel had looked down into her half-finished latte, which had already formed a skin and was silent after Gill's tirade. The others also went silent.

'I know,' Mel finally agreed with her best friend. Then she noticed how puffy her ankles looked. *Walking around the shops for hours has done that. Oh, who am I kidding? They always look like that.* Then as she reached over to get another sugar for her coffee, she'd seen her arms wobble. *Oh my God, I've got the arms of an old woman. It's like that advert for that energy drink that gives you wings. I don't need it; I've already got mine.* This thought made her smile.

'There, you *can* smile unless that's just wind of course.' Gill smiled at her best friend. 'Let's enjoy getting togged out for the hols, Mel. No buts or excuses.'

'OK. So what monstrosities are you going to make me wear then?' said Mel pulling herself together. 'I don't think we've seen much that would suit a walking lava lamp so far.'

'Well…let's try that plus size shop that's just opened, I've heard they do a great line in lava lamp fashion. And if not, then there's always the tent shop down the end of Kilburn High Road.'

'Gill! Don't say things like that.'

'Why not, Cathy? said Mel, 'she's right. Get the bill

Rachel so we can get this over with, then we can stop for lunch,' Mel winked at the others. *If we get this over with quickly,* she thought, *I can reward myself with a Big Mac and fries* and she strode off along the mall before she lost her nerve.

CHAPTER 2

A week after the shopping trip, the women were packed and ready for their holiday. Mel had managed to get her act together and sort out some decent outfits. Secretly she was quite looking forward to the holiday, but she wasn't going to let on to the others.

Rachel had arranged for an Uber to take them to the airport, but it was already running late and this sent her into a complete panic. She hated any break from a planned itinerary. Her life was so ordered it almost ran by clockwork. Her uptight behaviour had exasperated Mel since their university days together but both Mel and Gill wished that one day Rachel would fall so hopelessly in love with someone that she'd just let them change all that. But two unhappy marriages later, Rachel was still Rachel and there didn't seem to be any signs that she was ever going to change. The others still hoped that one day she would understand that people didn't do things just to annoy her, much like the poor Uber driver was being accused of at that very moment.

'They do this on purpose, you know. No doubt tried to fit in another fare and is now going to make us late.' Rachel said.

'Don't worry Rachel. We've got plenty of time. You always arrange pick-ups far too early anyway.' Cathy pointed out quietly. Cathy had stayed at Rachel's the night before to avoid Cathy having to face her dad before she left.

'No letting the lower ranks get you down, Lieutenant.' Colonel Ben Davis, Rachel's father came into the hallway. 'Don't forget the importance of the mission. Good opportunity to suss out this Puerto de Soller as a place for future trips.'

Colonel Davis considered everything in terms of his job as a Royal Marines officer, even though he hadn't seen active duty for a while. He lived and breathed for the Corps but unfortunately expected everyone around him to think the same. His wife, Jessica, had long ago become resigned to his compulsions and after years of trying to alter him and enduring the inevitable rows that followed, she'd decided that the easiest way to survive was to go along with his obsessive ways for the sake of peace. Her life revolved around her friends' coffee mornings and getting togged up for official functions, reunion balls and charity events not to mention the health club she had recently joined which meant that she could get away from her husband as often as possible.

Rachel pulled herself together, 'I know, Sir! But I just hate dawdling.' Rachel had moved back into her parents' home when she and husband no. 2 had divorced and sold their apartment in Canary Wharf six months ago. Moving back into her childhood home had given her a sense of order and had helped her get through a particularly fractious divorce. After all, the Davis household had plenty of order if little else.

The Uber eventually arrived, and the driver seemed oblivious to the panic he was causing. They went on to pick up Mel and then Gill who lived just around the corner from each other in Kingsbury. Both women still lived at home as neither could afford the high cost of buying a property in London themselves. In any case, neither had ever really wanted to leave home.

There wasn't much traffic around at that time of the morning, so they still arrived at the airport with loads of time to spare.

'Thank you, we'll leave good feedback, no problem,' said Gill.

'After turning up late? I don't think so,' said Rachel.

'Look, he turned up, didn't he? And we got here, didn't we? So, stop fussing.' Gill was more than a little irritated by Rachel's attitude especially as it was still very early in the morning, and she hadn't had any coffee yet.

'Well, that went smoothly,' said Rachel as they got through security. I was expecting all sorts of trouble.'

'And now you're disappointed – admit it,' said Mel.

'Well, just a bit – but checking and rechecking everything obviously helped.'

'We knew you'd sort it all out. Well done, Rachel. Now for a cup of coffee I think,' Gill didn't get going in the mornings until she had had at least two cups of coffee.

Mel offered to go to the counter with Gill as she also wanted to see what there was on offer to eat as well.

'How much?' Everyone in Starbucks starred at Mel as she heard how much the bill was. 'We're only buying four cups of coffee and a muffin each not the whole plantation.'

'Thank you,' said Gill to the bemused cashier. 'I'll take the tray, shall I, Mel?

'Now listen all of you,' she said as they sat around a tiny table which they had managed to get in the crowded cafe. 'We're officially on holiday and I don't want any whingeing, whining or complaining...unless of course, it's from me.' Gill was great at breaking tense situations. Her job as a trauma nurse had taught her that.

'Enough said, Gill. I agree completely. I'll try my hardest.' Rachel said. 'Oh, look, there's our flight number on the board. Drink up quickly or we'll miss it and then what will happen. Where are the tickets? Where did I put them? And the passports? Get them ready for…'

'Shut up!' Gill shouted out and proceeded to drink her coffee very slowly just to annoy Rachel, after which they made their way to departures and the inevitable and endless wait to board the plane.

Rachel just thought, *they'd be lost without me, get on the wrong plane, lose their tickets, find themselves being body-searched by some hairy customs official with rubber gloves. They need me…they need me.*

The flight was surprisingly uneventful. Packed like sardines, there was little to do except snooze or read the inflight mag which was just a catalogue of overpriced items.

'Where's the taxi I ordered? Ah there it is, come on girls.' Rachel's organisation was faultless and the people-carrier she had ordered promptly drove them to their resort with the driver even pointing out landmarks along the way. 'Worth paying the extra,' Rachel said, 'we could have gone cattle-class in the coach, but I think this is worth every penny.'

The girls looked at the complex where they were staying openmouthed.

'This looks awfully stylish, Rachel, tell me again how come we came here?' said Mel.

'I told you, it was a thank you from Rodney Brown, you know, he's a client of mine, I sorted out a complicated tax problem for him, saved him thousands, actually and he wanted to thank me personally, off the books, so he said we could have his apartment here for two weeks free of charge. He owns the whole complex but keeps this one for entertaining, usually his latest bit on the side but less said about that the better. It couldn't have come at a better time to be honest what with my divorce being finalised last week. Rolly and I are officially no longer married and good riddance, cheating bastard!' Rachel swallowed hard. At 25yrs old with two divorces under her belt, this break was just what she needed.

'Don't let it get you down, Rachel,' Gill said, 'he wasn't worth it. I know he was loaded but really, he treated you like crap, sleeping with that woman from his firm and in your bed too, and he calls himself an investment banker? Wanker more like.'

'You're right, but this time I thought it was going to be forever. Oh, who am I kidding. I liked his money and his family connections and the lifestyle we had, even if it was only for two years. But I must have fucked it up as usual, just like I did with Pavol. That marriage only lasted two years as well. At this rate I'll have been married at least twenty times by the time I'm your Gran's age and she was only married once.'

'She found the right guy first time. You haven't.'

'I know. I thought Pavol was the one. Mel, you remember how giddy I was in university when he came around to fix our leaking tap in the bathroom, and how after that we were together so much, I thought I'd fail my degree. And after we married, I thought…well, I thought we would be together for always until out of the blue he said he wanted to start a family as he'd always wanted lots of kids. Since when? He'd never mentioned kids before and they hadn't featured in my plans at all, especially as I was only just starting out on my career. The massive row we had…well that was it. He went back to Poland. He said it was because things had changed in Britain since Brexit but really, I didn't help saying I'd rather die than live in some poxy little town in northern Poland with his parents. Why do I pick them? It must be me. I was such a bitch. Now I don't know what I want.'

'You and Pavol made your choices.' Gill said, 'and perhaps it was for the best to find out so early on that you had different priorities.'

'Yeah, I've heard he married a nice Jewish girl when he got to Poland, he'd met at synagogue and they've two kids already. Whoa, a lucky escape or what?' Rachel was asking herself this question more than anyone else. 'But you're right Gill. You're always right. Now less brooding and more celebrating. We're here to have a good time.'

'Absolutely!' Gill smiled. She wondered what Rachel was really thinking and if any of them would ever be truly content. She shivered and instinctively wrapped her jacket around her tightly to fend of the chill she had felt running down her back.

'Come see this!' Cathy was her usual excited self.

From the apartment balconies they could look out over the horseshoe bay of Puerto de Soller and beyond it the blue expanse of the Mediterranean Sea. Mel took in the view and approved. Rachel then went to check the facilities and approved. Cathy went to check the bedrooms and approved, and Gill just flopped down on the settee.

'Where's my drink then, slaves?' she said, 'I don't like to be kept waiting. And where are the eunuchs to fan me?'

'Where-ever you left them, your Highness!' was the reply, which was a far more civilised response than she'd expected.

'Who's for a stroll around the town to get our bearings and suss out everything?' asked Rachel.

'Sod that, where's the bar? Priorities girls, please,' Gill said.

CHAPTER 3

The girls unpacked quickly and headed straight for the pool side where Gill, Rachel and Cathy stripped off to their swimwear and started for the water. Melissa made her usual excuses and, covered by a full-length fine cotton kaftan, she tested one of the sun beds for strength, making sure no one was observing. *Good, nice and strong, don't want to make a fool of myself this early in the holiday,* she thought as she eased herself down onto it and started to read a novel she'd picked up at the airport. *This is probably the most excitement I'm going to have on this holiday.*

The sun shone down and began to melt away her anxiety. Its strong rays bore into her very soul, and she stopped tensing her muscles and let the warmth encase her. She felt so relaxed that she decided to take off her 'cotton tent' as the others called it and do a spot of sunbathing. *After all, a suntan does make you look slimmer,* she thought. Raising her kaftan over her head she became aware that everyone at the pool was staring at her as if she'd taken off a false limb or that they'd just discovered she actually had three breasts. She lay down quickly.

Gill noticed that Mel had stripped off and came back to the sunbeds. She whispered to her friend 'Well done you and about time before the sun decides to go somewhere else.'

'I feel everyone's staring at me. "Hello bathers, warning! Beached whale sighted – stay calm and keep clear."' Mel always mocked herself.

'Afraid not, Mel, they're staring at the leggy blonde behind you who just took her bikini top off. Did you think they were staring at you? If you took off your top they certainly would; she's got nothing compared to you, Mel. Silicone really can't compete with the real thing you know – it's so obvious. Trust me, she couldn't match up to any of us let alone you,' and she pushed her own girls up with her hands to exaggerate them. The blonde had overheard some of Gill's conversation and decided to move around to the other side of the pool in disgust.

'See, the competition is simply too much for her.' said Gill.

'I wish I'd got your self-confidence, Gill,' Mel whispered.

'I wish I'd got your pretty face.' Gill said, 'Want to do a swop?'

Mel had a timeless face that would never go out of fashion. Her skin was silky smooth and her eyes large and of the deepest green. Her hair was of the richest Tischen red and cascaded in waves down her back. Under all the fat and frump lay a curvy figure just aching to get out but Mel wouldn't let it. She always made sure she sabotaged even her hardest efforts to lose weight. No one was going to take her protective cloak from her – its softness that enveloped her very being was like a mother swan wrapping her cygnets in a feathery blanket.

Gill looked at her friend and remembered Mel hadn't always been so shy and lacking in confidence. She thought back to that Saturday morning fifteen years ago when she'd skipped happily along Church Lane from her own home, a large detached mock Tudor house set in immaculate gardens. Turning into Old Church Lane she headed towards Birchen Grove and the small nineteen-thirties semi where her best friend lived. She was going to call on Mel to see if she would come out to play. The sun was shining, and the summer holidays had only just begun. They had six weeks of fun and laughter ahead of them, playing around Welsh Harp and swimming in the reservoir even though they weren't supposed to, but everyone did. As she approached the front door of Mel's house, she'd sensed something was wrong. A feeling she'd had only once before, just a few months previously, when she'd arrived home and found her mother crying, only to be told that her grandfather had died. She remembered how heavy the air had felt and how time seemed to move slower. This had been the same feeling.

She'd slowly gone up to the front window that was slightly open and peered in, hoping to find out what was happening. Inside were the shadowy figures of Mel's parents. Her mother was sat in the armchair by the fireplace holding her head in her hands whilst her husband was pacing to and fro around the room. Gill suddenly noticed that Mel was just visible from behind the sofa, trying to be forgotten, intently looking at a mark on the carpet that seemed to be the centre of her universe, an emerging black hole all set to drag her down into its immense density and ultimate oblivion; the swirling fragments of her life spinning around in ever decreasing circles of surprise and despair. Gill had felt a lump in her throat and an overwhelming urge to reach out to her friend and drag her free from it.

She'd then moved her attention to Mel's dad and tried to hear what his ranting was about. 'I can't take this life anymore. I'm suffocating. Can't you see that? If you loved me, you'd understand. I need to breathe again. I'm still a young man and I need to feel that I still have a life. *She* gives me that feeling. *You* don't. You never have. All my dreams have turned to dust with you.'

'I'm sorry, my darling, I don't mean to be a tie on you.

I only ever wanted what was best for the family,' his wife said.

'Family? This isn't a family,' he said, and Gill felt the words plunge like a knife deep into Mel's heart. The child, who had doted on him, was now being discarded like a used toy no longer loved or needed. Mel had just sat there as if paralysed. Gill had wanted her to speak, to make him stop saying those things but Mel just remained silent and still. Rage had welled up in Gill's chest as she could do nothing but watch her best friend's life being destroyed and the sparkle in those deep green eyes, which had always been filled with love and laughter, flicker out.

When Mel's dad had left his family soon after for another woman, Gill knew that Mel had taken the rejection personally. After as Bob Wright had left, he had broken any contact with his old family. Sarah had found it difficult to find work after being out of the workplace for so long and also needing to look after Mel, so money was tight even though Mel's mum, Sarah, had inherited the house from her parents so at least they had a roof over their heads.

Mel's paternal grandmother has persuaded her son not to force Sarah to sell the house, but in return Sarah had had to agree that she would not force him to pay any maintenance for Mel. As a result, Mel's whole outlook on life changed. She became careful with money and equally careful with her feelings. Mel cocooned herself in the comfort of eating. Gill had thought how strange it was that something that kept you alive was also a drug – the worst kind of drug. One that you couldn't do without, was cheap and available everywhere. No wonder so many people turned to it when it was love they really needed.

Gill sighed as she thought of her friend.

'Must be time for lunch by now,' said Mel still uncomfortable about showing off so much flesh.

'We can always rely on you to keep track of mealtimes,' said Gill, 'Let's leave The Blonde to hold court here alone.'

She signaled to the others to get out of the pool. 'I don't know about the rest of you but I'm starving and hellish thirsty.'

'And us,' said Rachel and Cathy.

'Best save ourselves for this evening though,' advised Rachel when they sat down in the pool bar, 'we don't want to get sozzled and fall asleep in the sun. We're sure to wake up looking like lobsters.'

'You're right again as usual,' agreed Gill then proceeded to order four large glasses of cold lager anyway.

'I give up, you lot are impossible.' Rachel just shook her head in exasperation but drank hers without further complaint. 'Wow! This lager's really good. Can we have another.'

Eventually the women decided to head off for a stroll down the hill to the harbour and get some lunch. The resort nestled around a large bay with cliffs and hillsides hugging the coastline and had been built up around an old fishing port where some of the old quaintness had somehow remained. The main town was a few miles inland built there to protect the inhabitants from marauding pirates in former times. It had a quaint wooden tram connecting the port to the town which was now usually crammed full of tourists acting as if it was the last train out of a war zone whenever the tram arrived in the harbour where a few small fishing boats were still moored probably more for the amusement of the tourists than for commercial fishing by their owners. Several bars and restaurants had sprung up in the town for the temptation of visitors and souvenir shops selling junk aimed at the drunk or stupid were in abundance.

'All this tackiness. I hate it,' said Mel.

'Yes, but it's a necessary part of holiday life,' said Gill. 'Where would you be if you couldn't get your kiss-me-quick hats and stuffed donkeys?' She got up onto the bench they were sitting on and began to gesture wildly with her arms, 'there would be chaos, there would be anarchy, I tell you there would be mayhem and total widespread rioting. No, fellow tourists, let us not forget the reason why we are here. It is not to sample a foreign culture or history or even natural beauty. No, travelers, it is to get drunk, eat British food and find a good shag.'

'Gill!' Cathy gasped. 'That's not why we're here at all. At least not why I'm here. How about you Mel, and you Rachel? Tell me there's more than that to this holiday. I've risked my life to be here. Seriously, I'm not joking. When my dad finds out I've come here against his will he'll probably kill me…'

'That's a bit melodramatic, Cathy. You are over-age, and you can do what you like…' Mel tried to calm things down a little. She didn't like to see this much show of emotion in one place at one time.

'No, Mel, she's right,' Rachel butted in, 'He'll probably kill her or worse, imprison her in a tower for the rest of her life. But don't worry Cathy, we'll rescue you, won't we girls?'

'Of course! All for one and one for all. Touché Monsieur. Take that… and that.' Gill jumped down from the bench and lunged forward at Rachel as if she had a dueling sword in her hand to which Rachel retaliated deftly. A group of middle-aged Japanese tourists passed by and the look on their faces was a picture. Cathy just had to take a snap of them with her camera, but this only added to their surprise and disbelief over the behaviour of these strange English women.

The girls started to giggle at the absurdity of their actions and even Cathy lightened up. They continued their stroll along the harbour front and looked back to see the tourists still staring at them.

'My, I enjoyed that.' Gill said.

'And me, but I'm thirsty now. Can we stop somewhere?' Mel was on form.

'There's a bar just around the corner,' Rachel said, and

everyone stopped and looked at her in amazement. 'What? I just saw a sign back there advertising it, that's all.'

'Rachel, at times you're decidedly spooky, you know that?' Gill looked at her companion in a suspicious manner, but Rachel just smiled and led the way to what turned out to be a very pleasant little bar which served food, just where she'd said it would be.

CHAPTER 4

After an afternoon of browsing around the shops, the friends decided that a bar, which they'd found near the marina, was the ideal place to have some fun later in the evening. The combination of sun, sea and several lagers had thoroughly worn them out, but no one was going to admit this for fear of being branded 'old woman' by the others.

If lunch is for wimps, then what does that make a siesta? thought Mel who secretly craved a cool shower and a lie-down especially after all the walking about they had done. Instead, she chose to get some peace and quiet by sitting on the balcony of the apartment, surrounded by subtropical plants and white-washed walls. The smell of the orange trees nearby was almost intoxicating, and she breathed in deeply to fill her body with the sweet fresh fragrance. This is heaven she decided but then heard all hell break lose inside the apartment. Rachel had come into their room and announced that she'd written a timetable to help the group get ready to go out. Gill promptly set on her and this quickly escalated into a pillow fight of epic proportions.

Melissa was glad to be out of it. Her thoughts drifted away from the carnage inside and looked past the groves of citrus fruit and olives trees towards the sea. The intensity of the blues and greens of the water was overpowering and seemed to call her to immerse herself in its luxurious lustre.

She could feel herself drift into it and become enveloped in warmth, safety and love. She closed her eyes and felt its fluid wrap around her like the arms of her father had done when she was a little girl. She smiled as tears slowly crept down her cheeks.

She often dreamt of her father's hugs and embraces; they made her feel safe and loved and wanted, the three things she needed more than anything else in the world but instead she now pushed people away and built herself a mantle of protection - her precaution against ever allowing herself to be hurt by someone again. It was strange how she'd shun or destroy the very things she yearned for and needed.

'It's your turn in the bathroom, Mel,' called Gill from inside the room, 'better not dawdle. The Ayatollah is probably timing us.'

Melissa headed for the bathroom. 'How long have I got?'

'Forty-five minutes precisely,' said Gill.

Eventually all four women were ready and all of them looked stunning. Gill had chosen a strappy cross-over tie front dress in a tropical red floral design that Mel thought was far too short.

'That outfit's a bit OTT, isn't it? I know you've got a great body but steady on Gill. How are you ever going to stay in that?' said Mel.

'I don't intend to for long,' Gill winked back.

Mel smiled. 'No, I bet you don't.

'Mel, you know I'm all talk. I just like winding men up. It's only a bit of fun. Chill out!'

In contrast, Cathy was dressed in a flowing long floral cotton muslin dress, which draped her svelte figure beautifully. This also annoyed Mel, *she can wear anything and look great in it. It's just not fair,* she thought.

Melissa, feeling a little pressured to make an effort, had chosen to wear loose navy palazzo trousers with a long tunic designed to conceal anything. The outfit was made of a soft silky fabric with a convenient elasticated waist, which were Mel's eternal life saver. She'd teamed this up with gold-coloured accessories to highlight her hair. She felt comfortable but confident that it didn't show too much flesh. But just to make sure, she wrapped her favourite pashmina in a striking peacock design in blues, greens and gold, around her shoulders.

'Good choice, my dear, but don't you go anywhere without that shawl?' Gill said with a smile on her face.

'It could get breezy down by the harbour,' was Mel's reply and Gill let it rest at that.

Rachel, organised as ever, had a completely coordinated look with cropped linen trousers and jacket in pale pink with cream swirls. Under that she wore a cream silk camisole. Everything was immaculately pressed. Her accessories - bag, shoes and jewellery were also in cream. Together with her wavy short black hair she could have just walked off the catwalk in some Paris fashion house, but instead she was just being Rachel.

'You look very chic, come to think of it, we all do,' Gill said, so let's go get 'em!'

Laughing and joking they wandered down the hill to the harbour. Even Mel had started to become seduced by the Mediterranean air and was out to enjoy herself. They arrived at the bar relatively early and were able to choose the best table near the small dance floor which was also near to the bar. Rachel ordered a large jug of sangria and some tapas to nibble on and the group became the life and soul of the party. They laughed and danced until they were dizzy. Even Mel let her hair down, her mane fall voluptuously over her shoulders.

It was about midnight when a group of six young men

came in. The bar was busy, and they were looking around for somewhere to stand let alone sit.

'Hook 'em up and reel 'em in.' whispered Gill.

The men decided to stand by the bar. At first, they tried to make out they hadn't noticed the four women but there was no chance of that with Gill around.

'Do you come here often?' she playfully said in a very false posh voice. This got their attention and two of them wandered over to the girls' table.

'Where are you lot from then?' Rachel said probing the men for as much info as possible.

'North London.' Andy sidled next to Rachel who made room on the bench. 'How about you?'

'We're from London too. What part?'

'We all work in The Laboratory in Muswell Hill. Have you heard of it?'

'A laboratory? Are you lot scientists or something?' Gill's interest was piqued. 'I work in health care myself, I'm an A+E nurse, you know, sorting out all the drunks and kids who fall out of trees.'

'Sounds fun...or not.' Andy said, 'I suppose you could say we're in health care too but not really in the intense way you are. The Lab is a health and fitness club. Jon and I are fitness trainers, but we're also trained to do physio work as well, Vince and Steve over there work in the bar and Trev and Simon are maintenance guys.' Gill noticed that Vince hadn't taken his eyes off her since he'd walked in, and she was enjoying the attention no end. The others however seemed more interested in getting a drink. Mel took the opportunity to give these new arrivals the once over. Their deep tans, tight cotton jeans and equally tight white T-shirts showed their well-toned bodies off wonderfully.

'Cor! Are they hot or what?' Gill whispered to Mel. 'Which one do you fancy?'

'Well, they're all very nice I suppose' Mel said quietly. 'But I don't think any of them are interested in me.'

'Don't be so defeatist,' said Gill. 'They're gagging for it.'

'Well, if I must choose then I think I liked the one with dark curly hair and blue eyes. His name was Steve, wasn't it?'

'Good choice, Mel, consider it sorted.'

'No! Gill, don't do or say anything. Promise me you won't talk to him or say anything. Please.'

'O.K. Keep your knickers on – well for the time being at least. I promise. But make sure he notices you. He might as shy you, God forbid.'

Gill had her hooks into Vince in no time. He seemed older than the rest. *He's very full of his own self-importance,* thought Mel, but Gill didn't seem to notice. The mixture of sea-air, sangria and salsa had more than just intoxicated her, and it was not long before Gill was standing very close to Vince who had already put his arm around her in a protective or rather possessive way.

A few older local men, stood at the bar. They were having a good eye full of Gill's antics not to mention down her top every time she leaned closer to Vince to whisper into his ear. Mel wondered what she was saying but was able to guess most of the detail. Vince seemed to be reveling in the attention, but Mel noticed that he also seemed to be eyeing other girls in the bar. *It's as if he feels he doesn't have to impress Gill as he thinks she's a sure thing,* Mel thought, *he looks as if he's eying up his next conquest already.* Mel decided she didn't like Vince and certainly didn't trust him.

Cathy and Rachel had paired off with Jon and Andy, who were identical twin brothers. They were very polite and didn't seem at all like the others in their group. Mel noticed that Andy was attentively listening to Rachel as she went on and on about how she would reorganise the bar, the resort, the airline, in fact the world, in a much better way than they were at present. Mel was mesmerised watching their interactions, and she found herself feeling more than a little jealous.

I wonder what those guys are really thinking about Rach and Cath, though, thought Mel. *No doubt feigning interest to increase their chances of getting a leg over later. Oh, how cynical can you be, Melissa Wright, stop it!*

She looked around at the other guys in the group. Steve seemed to have his eye on Cathy but, as Jon had already staked his claim, he was just stood chatting to Trevor and Simon at the bar. Mel began to feel like a spare prick at an orgy. *I must do something positive,* she thought, *I must at least be polite.* She went up to the bar.

'Are you enjoying your holiday so far?' she asked the three unattached men.

At first, they ignored her but then turned slowly towards her and Steve sneered, 'Wha' d'ya say?'

'Are you enjoying your holiday so far?' Mel repeated.

'We only got here today, love, so how the hell should I know,' was his reply and he turned back to his friends.

Ah well, you did try old girl, thought Mel, *never mind, they can't help being pissing morons.* This thought made her smile.

'What are you looking at?' asked one of the morons, Trevor.

'Oh, nothing,' Mel was being more truthful than they really had the intelligence to appreciate.

She walked back to her seat and made a point of studying the menu listing the cocktails which the bar was able to offer. She noticed out of the corner of her eye that Steve, Trevor and Simon had downed their drinks and had started towards the entrance.

'Vince, a word,' said Steve. Vince walked over to where the three men were standing. 'Look, mate, there's nothing interesting here for us, so we're off to that club we passed on the way. Good luck with the tits.' He nodded towards Gill who thought he was being friendly, so she smiled at him.

'Steve, I know they aren't exactly fresh off Love Island but a shag's a shag. Wha' am I gonna do, if you lot leave? Her friend will be alone, and she'll probably go off with her. I think I'm on to a sure thing. She's hot for it.'

'Look, sounds like fun but I'm not interested in that fat bird, and she's already tried to make a pass at me. It'd be best all round if we pissed off. There's no other pussy in this place for us. We'll be better off in that club. Remember we saw that blonde with the big jugs going in as we passed. Now there's a prospect worth trying for,' Steve said, 'we'll see you when we see you, but if you get bored, you'll know where we are. Cheers mate.'

Mel and Gill looked at each other and shrugged their shoulders. 'What are they talking about? Bet it's us.'

'Yea probably is, but not in a good way, that's for sure,' Mel said as she picked at the remains of the tapas.

When she looked back, Steve, Trevor and Simon had gone.

CHAPTER 5

The departure of Steve and his friends had all happened so fast that Mel didn't know what to say. She sipped her wine and played with the remains of the tapas on the table. *Oh no, those two old men at the bar are looking at me,* they smiled at her, their broken stained teeth showing years of neglect. *I think I'm going to throw up, please let me just melt into a mush under the table, I don't want to be here, I'm sure they're feeling sorry for me, I've got to get out of here.*

She stood up 'I'm just going to the loo, Mel said not knowing if anyone heard her or not. She paused and looking back at her friends to check they were all fully occupied, she slipped out of the bar into the cool night air.

Mel stopped a few yards outside the bar and assessed her options. *So, what do I do now?* she thought, *I can find another bar and get drunk on my own, how sad is that, but knowing my luck I'll bump into Steve and the other morons and then they'll think I'm following them.* She walked down to the harbour wall instead and strolled along until she found a seat. She sat down and stared out across the harbour. The moon streamed over the water, shimmering between the boats and yachts moored there, the tinkle of their rigging sounding like children playing tiny instruments softly. *As if children ever play instruments softly*, she thought. She slouched deeper into the hard seat, and it dug into her shoulders as if trying to push her off.

'I don't blame you, I'd push me off too,' she said under her breath. *What the hell am I doing sat on my own in such a beautiful place, I'm bloody 25 years old*, she bent forward and put her head in her hands, *pull yourself together Melissa, please break this cycle of self-pity, I can't stand it any longer.* She took a deep breath and held back the tears behind her eyes.

The evening had started out so well but had deteriorated into the normal crap time. *I'll just go back to the apartment and feel sorry for myself there*, she decided and getting up gingerly in her strappy sandals which were already cutting into her swollen feet, she started up the dimly lit street, which led from the harbour back to the apartment complex at the top of the hill.

The evening was warm, but she felt a breeze building up. *Feels like it might rain later,'* she thought. 'Good, at least that might make it cooler tomorrow,' and she wrapped her pashmina around her and put her head down for the climb up the steep cobbled streets.

She was happy to be out in the fresh air and away from the failure she felt she had been in the bar. *You couldn't pull a Christmas cracker, you fat slob*, she thought and laughed. *Didn't Rachel promise this place would be full of eligible rich men. Where are they all? I know what it is - word's got out that I was coming, and they've all retreated to the mountains. "Run for the hills, chaps. It's the creature from the Black Lagoon, oh no, wait a bit, it's only Mel Lardy Arse from London!"* she giggled to herself as she passed the small shops and boutiques mainly catering for the tourists, now dimly lit.

She didn't notice the group of boys in their late teens come out of the bar behind her but suddenly she shivered as she somehow felt their presence. She looked over her shoulder quickly to see, hoping they didn't notice her and counted six young men. *Oh great! Half a dozen lager louts, just what I need, they don't even look old enough to be drinking.*

The street became more deserted. The boys noticed Mel walking alone, they decided to follow her. *How can I shake these pests off?* Thoughts were racing through her head mixing with the effects of the sangria. *Which way should I go? I don't know enough about this place, why didn't I pay more attention this afternoon when we were walking around. Oh shit! Why do I always rely on Rachel to know everything?* Even in the open street she felt trapped and alone.

Mel started to feel sick as her stomach churned and she began to sweat in panic, then her worst fears came true – one of the boys started to speak to her.

'Hello, gorgeous, had anything good lately?'

'Look at the love handles on her,' a second boy said.

'All the better to catch hold of.' The group laughed and Mel felt helpless.

She quickened her pace, but they easily caught up and closed the gap. Mel could smell the sweet orangey stink of stale beer on their breath. She saw a light coming from a side street and decided to go in search of help only to find it was little more than an alleyway. The light she had seen was in fact only the reflection of the moon on the whitewashed buildings, this new direction was quieter and more secluded.

'Where's she taking us?' the leader said, 'somewhere romantic.' The group chorused in agreement and sounded like a pack of baying hounds hunting their prey, she felt for the fox, she felt for the stag, their panic and pain, their desperation and a sheer will to survive.

Her legs ached. They weren't used to this level of activity, but she somehow kept on walking, clinging onto the rough stone of the walls to help her climb, trying not to show any signs of fear lest the hounds should quicken to the kill.

The alleyway grew narrower and windy and was so uneven she was sure she would trip on the cobbled steps. It levelled off as it turned to follow the contours of the hill. Then she saw it. The dead-end ahead.

CHAPTER 6

The alleyway opened into a small square with a central stone water trough. There were no lights in the houses in the square and no sounds from behind the thick wooden doors. She slowed down and her heart sank as tears welled up in her eyes. She stopped in the square; the gang of boys stopped too.

Then the leader came forward and put his arms around her waist. She smelt his sweat mixed with cheap aftershave and it made her feel sick. Her stomach churned and she held back a retching sensation.

'I like a woman you can get hold of. Softer to lie on, eh?' Laughter rose from the group as they encircled Mel. Her breath was quick and shallow. She felt as if she had transcended herself and was observing her nightmare from a safe distance. The boy moved his hands and touched her breasts. She winced and pushed him away.

'Whoa! Steady on, you know you want it really,' and he started to pull her tunic up. Mel struggled but he was too strong, he tore the soft material and exposed the delicate lace cups of her bra exposing her to the cool night air. She sobbed then heard another sound.

'That'll do lads!' A deep calm voice echoed around the

small square. The boys swirled around and came face to face with a mountain of a man in his early thirties. He stood well over six foot tall with broad shoulders and muscular arms. His presence was awesome. He filled the square with raw strength and a solid determination. 'I'll take it from here, shall I boys?' His words boomed over the drunks who seemed pitiful and weak in comparison like a bunch of hyenas coming face to face with a full-grown lion.

'Who the hell are you to tell us what to do? Fuck off!' the leader said. The man walked slowly over to him and taking him by the throat lifted him off the ground until they were eye to eye.

'Your yacht's due to leave in the morning, so you'd all better get back to the marina and sober up. I don't think your skipper would be very pleased to know what you've been up to, do you?'

'How do you know who our skipper is?'

'Oh, I know lots of people, including the local police captain. He hates lager louts even more than I do. Believe me, you don't want to know what he does to them. So off you go.' He dropped the unfortunate boy who fell hard on the cold stone floor and whimpered like a puppy. His mates picked him up and thought better of taking things further. The effects of the lager were wearing off as was their bravado.

When they were a safe distance, they turned and the leader shouted, 'you're a bloody loony mate, we were only having a bit of fun.'

'Didn't look much like fun to me. NOW CLEAR OFF!' His voice reverberated around the square and the boys yelped their way back up the alleyway and into the night like frightened dogs.

Mel stared at the man and tried to cover her exposed skin with her shawl. *Who the hell is he?* Her head was spinning and in her confusion she couldn't grasp what was happening. *Get a grip Mel. Sober up for God's sake. You've got to get away from here and away from him.*

She tried to retrace her steps, her feet screamed out as the cobbles conspired with her strappy sandals and after only a few steps she stumbled. The man reached out to catch her.

'No! get away from me,' she screamed thinking he was trying to stop her. She pushed herself away only to fall back, rolling over on her ankle and falling onto the cobbled street cracking her head on its cold unyielding surface. She lay on the floor moaning.

Mel went in and out of consciousness. *Who the hell is this stranger? Is he a local tough guy who gets what he wants, and no one dares stop him? I've gone from one nightmare to a worse one, straight out of the frying-pan into the fire, I feel sick and my bloody head hurts so much, I don't know what to do, should I fight him off or…* She drifted off again and all she could hear before she drifted off was his deep voice enveloping her before her world went dark.

When she came to again, she was in the man's arms. He was holding her as if she were a child's doll and the sensation of being carried so easily and gently shocked her. No one had ever been able to hold her up in his arms since she was a little girl. She remembered her dad carrying her from the car when she would fall asleep on long journeys. This memory made her feel safe, and she snuggled into the man's arms as if being enveloped by him would make everything better again. She smelt the warmth of his body and the smell of his perfume, heady and expensive. His clothes were crisp and soft and all she wanted was to sleep in his arms forever.

She suddenly pulled herself back from her delirium and realised that they were moving along the narrow streets of the resort. She froze unable to concentrate and conscious only of the throbbing in her head and the pain in her ankle. She opened her eyes and looked up at the man. She studied his face. He was rugged but had a kind look that eased her. His face showed signs of stubble, the sort a man gets after an evening out rather than neglect for days on end. His hair was short, dark and well cut. It looked soft and Mel wanted so much to touch it. His skin was tanned and portrayed someone who liked the outdoor life.

I wonder where he's taking me. Probably back to his house. Why? What is he going to do? she thought. She tried to remain conscious as long as she could, but she was too exhausted from her ordeal and the effects of too much sangria to fight anymore and she simply resigned herself to whatever was going to happen. *Well, if I'm unconscious at least I won't remember it,* she thought.

In her semi-conscious state, she felt herself float through the streets of the resort as if on a cloud. The wind brushed her hair and cooled her. Up above the streets she hovered and flowed around the narrow alleyways of the old town. White walls and blazing pots of geraniums floated passed her, and she could smell their acrid fragrance which somehow seemed fresh and natural.

Eventually she felt she was falling slowly down onto a soft pile of feathers wrapping themselves around her in luxury and freshness. She snuggled down and drifted off into a deep and peaceful sleep.

CHAPTER 7

'Where did Mel get too? I'm sure she was here a minute ago.' Gill slurred after too many glasses of wine. 'It's not like Mel to simply disappear,' she said. 'So where is she?'

'I think she went to the loo, Gill. But that was a while ago.' Rachel was so engrossed in her group's conversation that she didn't even look up. 'She'll be OK. Mel's Mel. She's always doing strange things. You know what she's like.'

Gill searched the toilets. Mel was not there so she went outside but still no sign of her. She was worried, she had always looked after Mel. They were more like sisters than friends.

'I'm sure she's OK. She's probably just slipped out for some fresh air. Don't worry,' said Cathy. Gill looked at her amazed. Cathy so was surprisingly calm it shocked her.

'I'm sure you're right. I'm overreacting. Vince, can we perhaps get some fresh air as well. Perhaps take a stroll somewhere? Maybe we'll find Mel on the way.' Gill thought she'd perhaps been over hasty in her concern, but it still niggled her. She was annoyed that she hadn't taken more notice of Mel instead of being so engrossed with

Vince whom she was beginning to get bored with, his conversation was limited to say the least, but he was very sexy, so she decided to hang onto him for a while longer at least.

'No problem.' Vince said with a twinkle in his eye. 'Let's go along the harbour.'

They left the bar and walked along the harbour. The moon shone on the water and the faint breeze encircled them like a lover's caress. Gill felt herself relax into Vince's shoulder as they strolled along away from the hustle and bustle of the bar. He softly kissed her head, and she felt good.

Eventually Vince turned into a side street and Gill was so relaxed by now that she didn't even question why they were changing direction. The side street was dimly lit and quiet. He held her closer, and she felt safe. They walked for ages until the street opened out towards the headland. The buildings disappeared and they stumbled along a cliff path that led to a few isolated houses. Gill imagined this was a lovely place to walk in the daylight but in the dark, she was just worried about breaking her neck. They came to a low wall bounding a small orchard.

'Let's stop a while.' Vince sat down on the wall and Gill joined him, sitting close to him. She wished she'd brought a jacket as the breeze was making her shiver. Vince put his arm protectively around her and caressed her head in his other hand as he softly kissed her. His kiss increased in intensity and Gill felt the urgency of his touch. His hand went down and caressed her shoulder and then her breast. Gill pulled away.

'Hey slow down, what if someone comes past? It's very open here. Let's just take this a bit slower.'

'No one comes along here at night. Nothing to be scared of,' and he kissed her hard. His tongue delved into her mouth, and she felt suffocated. This was not what she had planned. She liked the thrill of the chase, the buildup of tension but despite what she had said earlier to her friends about getting a good shag, she didn't really mean it. The wine was fuddling her head, and she was very confused about what she could do next to get out of this situation.

'Please stop! I don't want to do anything. Not here or now. Can we take this more slowly?'

'Why? You're obviously gagging for it. What's the problem now? You know you gave me a hard-on as soon as we met. Don't you think you should do something about it?' He pulled her hand towards his jeans and pressed it hard onto his groin. 'Mmmm, that's better. Don't you fancy a bit of that? Go on don't be shy.' And he rubbed her hand up and down.

'No thank you.' Gill tried to pull her hand away, but Vince held her hand in place and looked straight at her.

'I don't want to do anything,' said Gill, 'and your erection is your problem.' Gill was becoming a little intimidated at his persistence. 'I think I want to go back to the bar now thanks.' She tried to get up, but Vince caught hold of her arm and pulled her roughly down. She missed the wall and collapsed into a heap on the ground.

He looked down at her and sneered. 'Just where I like my women – on the ground at my feet' and he laughed. She went to get up only to find that he had still got hold of her arm and try as she might she was too drunk, and he was too strong for her to break free.

'You're not going anywhere, my lovely. You and I are going to have some fun. Why do you think I bought you drinks all night? As I see it, you owe me and here seems as good a place as any.'

He pulled her upwards and clasped his arms around her waist. He pressed his lean body against her. She felt vulnerable and scared. Her breathing became shallow and rapid, and she felt her face and neck become flushed. He bent to kiss her again, but she turned her head, and he landed in a pile of hair.

'So, you aren't interested in me now that the chips are

down. Different story for the last three hours, wasn't it?' said Vince. 'Not good enough for you, I dare say. Just a bit of rough to toy with?'

Gill stared at him. 'Who the hell did you think you are, talking to me like that? If I say no, then no is what I mean. Can't you understand plain English?'

The look on his face changed and he caught her arm and squeezed it tightly until she cried out in pain.

'Stop it! You're hurting me, you great oaf. I wouldn't want you if you were the last man on earth. You're just a pig. I'm going back.'

'You're going nowhere 'til I say, got that? Now get your knickers off.' He deftly spun her around until she was facing the low wall with his weight pressing against her from behind. He held her arm tightly and whispered in her ear. 'It's here, it's now and it's gonna be me. Understand?'

Gill started to panic. She shook her head to help get rid of the effects of the alcohol. Her heart started to race, and she frantically tried to think what she could do. Gill took in a few deep breaths and struggled hard, but Vince just tightened his grip on her arm. She became aware of his breath on the back of her neck. An hour ago, it would have sent shivers down her spine, now it filled her with loathing.

She'd heard of such things happening to other women and as a trauma nurse she had seen the results, but she'd never thought it would happen to her. Gill had always been the one in control of her relationships but this time she was suddenly very afraid. Vince clasped her throat with his other hand and started to suck at her neck.

'Just marking my territory,' he whispered. 'Make sure everyone knows Vince fucked you.' Gill was at a loss as to what to do. As he scarred her neck, she could only think of the humiliation it would bring when the others saw it. Love-bites were so common and dirty. She felt common and dirty. What would her friends think? How long would it take to disappear? Would it still be there when she got home? She tried to shout out in the vain hope that someone might be in earshot but Vince's hand clasped her neck tighter bending her head back so she could hardly breath.

Vince checked around to make sure that they were alone. The path was deserted. The streetlamp at the end of the path threw an eerie shadow over the scene. It's beam of light seemed dank and rancid and cast the couple with a jaundiced cover. The atmosphere was heavy, and the breeze had died down to leave a stillness like that just before the dawn of a great battle.

He reached inside her top and squeezed her breast hard. 'Nice tits,' he pinched her nipple hard. The pain made Gill gasp. He dug his nails into her soft flesh and tears started to fill Gill's eyes.

'Get on with it then!' Gill managed to say. She couldn't bear to wait for the inevitable any longer. 'I doubt you're any fuckin' good anyway and that's why you've got to take women by force.'

'Then let's see if the merchandise is worth the effort. A whore like you must have had hundreds already.'

Vince rolled up her tight skirt and tugged at her thong cutting it into her skin until it eventually yielded and broke free. She lost control and whimpered softly.

'So, you liked that, did you? I thought you would.'

'Can't we talk about this?' she said desperately. 'I'm sure we can work something out. Let's go back to my apartment. I'd feel better about this there. I don't feel good about doing this in the open.' She waited to see his reaction. Every breath she took was shallow and painful.

'Too late to talk whore, I'm going to show you what a real man can do to a whore like you,' and he kicked her right leg out to the side. He loosened his grip on her arm but only to free himself from his jeans. She felt him brush against her bare skin and she winced. He bent her forward over the stonewall pushing her head down, holding her by her hair. The wall was cold and rough, and her discomfort only added to her misery. As she looked down, she noticed a spider's web woven across the scattered stones. Trapped in its silk was a small fly, wriggling frantically to break free from its trap. Out of the corner of her eye she saw the spider slowly approach. She closed her eyes. She couldn't bear to watch the inevitable.

The realisation of the danger she was in suddenly became clear. 'What about protection? We need to use protection.'

'I don't think we'll bother with a Johnny. I like my whores natural. Brace yourself, bitch, cause you're getting what you wanted all evening.'

She was helpless to stop him as his hold on her hair tightened, pushing her forward until it scraped on the rough stone. He groaned as his excitement and her discomfort heightened.

He slumped over her almost crushing her under his spent weight. She struggled and pulled herself free of his impalement and immediately threw up then fell into a heap on the floor.

'You bastard! What have you done?' she screamed at him, finding her inner strength. He was wiping himself clean on her thong and then he zipped himself back up. Nonchalantly he looked at her. His disdain for her was so clear in his eyes.

'Thanks for the fuck, whore. Now piss off,' and he kicked her several times as she lay on the floor then he walked off down the path back to the town as if nothing had happened.

Gill lay there for what seemed ages. She was too frightened to move, every part of her body was hurting, she felt empty and violated. It was as if she had been turned inside out and put on display for everyone to gawk at. She didn't cry, she couldn't cry. She just felt numb. Cold enveloped her but she didn't shiver, she couldn't even feel it. She felt she would simply shatter into a thousand pieces if she moved and then get blown away on the breeze.

Eventually she heard someone coming along the path and panicked. She didn't want anyone to see her like this. All she felt was overwhelming shame and slowly got up, adjusted her clothes as best she could and retrieved her thong from the floor where it had been thrown. She threw it over the wall out of sight. She looked around and saw the two locals from the bar going home drunk.

'Oh shit!' she muttered.

They looked towards her and eventually recognition showed in their eyes. They came along the path and slowed down to look at her, shaking their heads as they passed and muttering something that she didn't understand. They were neither surprised nor concerned. They ambled onwards towards their homes and their simple lives, chatting about all the foreign women who simply drank too much, cavorted around half-naked and then showed surprise when things got out of hand with lads who couldn't hold their drink and weren't mature enough to control themselves.

Gill had stayed very still as the two men passed as if it would make her invisible. Afterwards she turned and followed the path back towards the town. She decided to chance taking a side road she hoped would lead to the apartment and avoid her being seen by anyone. She found a bench on the side of the hill near the apartment and sat down to catch her thoughts. She saw a few late revelers in the distance singing and playing. *I bet they're off to bed to sleep,* she thought, *but will I ever sleep again?* She took a deep breath and mustered all her strength.

'Gillian Keane, get a grip and move your arse! No use feeling sorry for yourself. Get home, take a bath, get that pig's stink off you,' she said harshly to herself getting wearily up from the bench.

Once back inside her bedroom, she was relieved and also concerned to find that Mel wasn't there. She ran a deep hot bath and soaked herself - its warm tenderness enveloping her broken body. She relaxed and for the first time since her ordeal, she started to cry. Tears streamed down her face, and she sobbed as she tried to forget the pain, the humiliation and the hate that had caused all this to happen.

She dried herself carefully and inspected her fragile body for marks and damage. Luckily the human body is a resilient object and the worst one showing was the mark on her neck. Easily explained she thought trying to convince herself of the fact. She was sore and bruised but had no cuts. The bruises from the kicks would appear soon enough. She would heal, at least physically, but who knows how she would ever heal her deeper wounds.

CHAPTER 8

The sea breeze wandered in through the open window of the villa and Mel shivered as the salty air blew softly over her face. The sensation woke her from her stupor, and she slowly opened her eyes not knowing what she would see. Her surroundings were bright and clean, the walls were white and the drapes, which hung at the windows and fluttered in the breeze, were a bright yellow and blue. Looking around the room, she saw it was simply furnished. She noticed she was laid down on a large settee. Her head ached and her ankle started to make its plight known to her.

She then noticed that she was not alone. In the open plan kitchen area to one side, she saw him. He had his back to her, so she felt safe observing him. His heavy torso seemed to fill the space he occupied. He had a vest and shorts on which showed off his muscular body. *Was this the man who rescued me?* she thought, *'He's not a typical knight in shining armour but then what is a knight in this modern day and age supposed to look like anyway?'* He was preparing something and seemed engrossed in his chore. He began to hum a cheery tune and Mel found herself faintly amused by it. He suddenly turned around and realised that Mel had been looking at him for some time.

'Hello, you're awake. Good morning, how are we?'

'Who are you?' Mel said, 'and where am I? What did you do to me?'

'Hey, one question at a time. My name's Iain Ferguson and I brought you here to my villa as you passed out after your ordeal with those morons. I didn't know where else to take you and as we were close my villa, it made sense to come here. As for 'what did I do to you?' I just put you on the couch after checking your pulse and taking your shoes off. I think you may have sprained your ankle a bit when you fell. Is it hurting?'

'Yes, it is and my head, and in fact all of me, feels like death'

'Oh, the beginnings of the almighty hangover. Too much sangria no doubt. I never understand why tourists drink it when they aren't used to it. I've made a hangover cure for you just in case.' He brought a long glass over to Mel and helped her sit up. The glass he gave her was filled with a disgusting looking liquid, but he insisted she drank it.

'Argh, it's revolting. Are you trying to poison me?'

'No, not really, you did enough of that yourself last night. Alcohol is a poison you know. Can't see the need for it to be drunk in excess, myself. A good glass of wine or an aperitif maybe but guzzling cheap booze down your neck as if it is going out of fashion just in order to have a good time, that's sad, really sad.'

'I rarely drink, I'll have you know. I was just trying to get into the swing of things and have a good night out with my friends.'

'Where were your friends?' asked Iain.

'They… well…they were busy with some people they had met, and I was tired, so I thought I'd go home, that's all. Not a crime, is it?' Mel said defensively.

'Well, it very nearly turned into one, but not of your doing that's for sure. A girl should be able to walk home on her own if she wants to, but unfortunately male hormones don't always see it like that.'

Mel suddenly remembered the ordeal in full. She looked down and felt emotion well up inside her. She thought of the near escape she had had, the gang of boys and their taunts. She then remembered the man who had saved her from all that and looked up into Iain's eyes and he understood her realisation and fear. Tears started to roll down her cheeks - a release of all the tension of the previous night. Natures pressure valve letting off steam. She looked down again not sure how to feel or how to cope with the emotions whirling around her.

'I'm sorry. I'll go now, I think. Thank you for all your help.' She went to get up, but the effects of the hangover and her injured ankle stopped her.

'Don't move! I'll get a cold compress for that ankle. We can put a bandage on it to help support it later. Let the hangover cure work a bit first before attempting to run any marathons.'

'OK. You're the boss,' she said trying to lighten the mood, 'I feel so helpless and stupid being here, it was bad enough getting myself into that mess last night, now I feel even more of a fool, I hope I'm not putting you out.'

'You're just fine where you are. It looks as if you have only twisted your ankle. You should be OK in no time. If you like we can try and get a message to your friends. Do you want to call them?'

'What a sensible idea. Are you some sort of modern-day Good Samaritan or something? I'm not used to people being nice to me except my friend Gill that is. Gill! She'll be frantic about where I am, what time is it? I must let her know I'm OK, yes, I will ring her.' Iain passed her handbag, and she called Gill's mobile.

'I don't expect a reply, I bet she's still in bed, she must have drunk more than me, so God knows when she'll wake up. I'll message her, she never picks up her voice messages.' Mel messaged to let her friend know she was

OK and would be back later and then collapsed back into the settee.

'No matter, at least you let her know you're OK, so she won't worry when she does surface. Would you like some breakfast?'

'This hangover cure is working wonders. You should patent it. I feel much better already.'

'Afraid I got it out of a book on hangover cures written by a barman at the Savoy Hotel, good book, quite a lifesaver really, though I don't drink much anymore,' Iain said, 'so breakfast it is then. Fry up?' He smiled at Melissa as she suddenly looked up at him with a look of horror on her face and they both started to laugh.

After eating several slices of toast Mel decided she ought to be getting back to the apartment, but she found that really, she didn't want to leave.

'Well, I must be getting along anyway.' Iain said. 'Have loads to do today and time is always against me. The people here are wonderful, but the laid-back attitude still gets some getting used to.' Iain started to clear away, and Mel knew this was her cue to leave even though her feelings for this man, whom she had only just met, were confusing her.

Iain went into another room and Mel started to shake her head, 'what's the matter with you? You know nothing about this man. What are you thinking of?' she muttered out loud to herself.

'What was that? Self-abuse and on my sofa.' Iain had returned to the sitting room and had heard the tail end of Mel's self-remonstration. 'What do you need to think about then?'

'I'm…not sure really. Just me being silly. I think I had better leave now if my head will let me. I was wondering… um…if you were going to be around saving damsels in distress this evening as well'

'Let me see…Yes, very probably but you aren't planning on getting yourself into any more tight spots, are you?'

'Certainly not, I just thought I'd ask,' she turned towards the door flushed with embarrassment. *God, what he must think about me asking him that, I'm not even interested...or am I?*

'Do you know your way back?' Iain called out to Mel as she opened the door and looking outside, she realised she didn't have a clue where she was.

'Um, probably not.'

'Hang on a minute then and I'll walk you back to the town. Just let me get a few things together. Are you going to be OK on that ankle?'

'Yea, I'll manage, it's not that bad, not as bad as my head anyway.'

They walked slowly down the cobbled streets away from the imposing villa. Mel tried to get her bearings but found that just concentrating on walking was as much as she could manage. Iain suggested she hold onto his arm to steady herself and she willingly obliged.

'I can't fall for this guy. It's just not on.' Mel mused under her breath, knowing that she was lying through her teeth.

'Are you wired for sound or something? Or are you genuinely talking to yourself? Either way – seriously odd if you ask me'

Oh great, Mel thought, *now he thinks I'm a nutter or a spy, that's a great start to a relationship, just stop thinking, it'll be safer.*

They arrived at the street which led to the apartment complex in which Mel was staying. It looked different this morning compared to yesterday. There was a tranquility and yet a bustle all happening at the same time. She looked at her watch and noticed that it was still really early – well early for someone who was on holiday and hung-over from the night before. Some cafés were beginning to open whilst others hadn't even bothered yet. There was a deserted feel about the place as if some terrible disaster had happened, but they hadn't bothered to tell her.

'I'll leave you here then if that is OK. I think you were heading up there until you took that turning into the dead end. I'll see you around, maybe. Bye!' Iain said in a matter-of-fact way, which took Mel by surprise. Last night she had felt he was interested in her, why else would he have put himself out for her and then carry her to his villa and take care of her. His coolness now didn't make sense.

'Yes, that would be nice. Perhaps this evening. Where will you be?'

'Oh, here, there and everywhere as usual. Nowhere in particular. I'll see you around,' and he wandered off down the street towards the harbour.

Mel stood there motionless and not a little embarrassed. She imagined that everyone within ear shot had been listening and her rejection had cut deep to the bone. She never took rejection well and this seemed to hurt more than usual.

Why do I bother? she thought, *I'm better off just giving up and staying home all day. Who's he to reject me anyway? Only just the sexiest man to have crossed my path in ages and it seems he doesn't even want to know, God, what a failure I am, where's Gill when you need her? I need something to eat.*

Mel started to walk then stopped again. *Christ my foot hurts! Where the hell is the apartment? Oh yes, up that street, the same one as last night. Well, here goes!* She took a deep breath and started the climb up the hill to the complex.

The walk this morning was more interesting than last night and certainly less fraught, though she kept looking behind her just in case she was being followed. *Nothing like a good dose of paranoia to get you moving in the mornings,* she thought and in no time, she had reached the complex despite her ankle and made her way through the army of cleaners pretending to tidy up before the inmates finally got up and messed the place up again.

Mel decided to sit on a low wall surrounding the pool area for a while before facing the onslaught of questions about where she'd been. She wasn't entirely sure what was going on herself, so she had to get things straight before her interrogation. *I owe them an explanation but what am I going to say? I nearly faced a fate worse than death, then I was rescued by a knight in shining armour who in the cold light of day, doesn't seem to be really interested in me at all. Yeah, that should do it. What a great start to a holiday, I wish I had never come.*

But in the back of her mind, Iain was causing her more concern than that of explaining things to her flat mates. He had got to her somehow, she didn't know how or why but he was in her thoughts, and she couldn't shake herself free of him. *Why am I interested in a man who is obviously not interested in me? And why do I keep thinking about him? I don't fancy him. I don't. He's not my type. Mel Wright, you're a blatant liar, you know how he makes you feel. Oh, bloody hell, girl, what are we going to do? He's everything you've ever wanted - strong, polite, good looking. I do not want him.* She sighed. *I do.'*

This emotional ping-pong she was playing made her even more hungry. She eventually admitted to herself what was bothering her. Mel – the cool collected one, who never let anyone near her emotionally, had been got at by a man who didn't even care.

She got up, bought herself a Coke and chocolate bar from the vending machines by the pool and wandered through the complex grounds to sit among the citrus trees and think. She shut her eyes and allowed the sun to soak into her and ease her feelings. *I just need to think, that's all.*

CHAPTER 9

'What a great night,' Cathy yawned as she emerged from her room. 'I really enjoyed myself. Didn't you?' She looked around the room. Gill seemed preoccupied. 'Where did you get to anyway or shouldn't we ask? Rachel and I were worried.'

'No need to worry, Cathy,' Gill felt only numbness and confusion, her gaze never lifting from the magazine she was pretending to read. She looked haggard and tired, and Cathy noticed that her eyes looked swollen.

'Didn't you sleep well or something?' she innocently asked.

'You could say that,' Gill moved from the settee and went back into her room. She couldn't face telling Cathy about her nightmare, about how her world had fallen apart. She was tired, but the fear of sleep had kept her awake all night, huddled in the corner of the bedroom, holding her knees close to her chest and rocking back and forth like some frightened child. How could she tell Cathy that? Not sweet and innocent Cathy.

Cathy felt uneasy about Gill. This might have upset her, but she had learnt to ignore such feelings. By making out that possible problems did not exist, she had managed to survive, in what was to her, a puzzling world. Her parents had always tried to shield her from the realities of life whilst at the same time warning her about the dangers lurking at every turn. Her ensuing confusion about reality and life made it difficult for Cathy to cope sometimes so ignoring contradictions and confusing information was her way of dealing with these moments. Working with young children also helped. Their lives were full of fantasy and imagination, and Cathy enjoyed going along being around such free minds.

'I'll just take Rachel a cup of tea then,' she said to the empty room.

Rachel wasn't up yet which was as much a surprise to her as to everyone else. She felt strangely at ease and yet also perplexed all at the same time and the feeling had rendered her somehow paralysed. She was lying in her bed staring blankly at the ceiling when Cathy came in with two cups of hot tea.

Rachel grunted at her roommate and Cathy tentatively entered Rachel's sacred sanctuary of order and preciseness on her side of the room to put the tea down. Everything had been put away or was in its place even though they were only staying in the apartment for two weeks. This was in stark contrast to the space of all the other girls where clothes and belongings were already strewn around especially over the floor and remnants of snacks and half-finished cups of tea and coffee were beginning to find their way into even the most unlikely places. In contrast, Rachel's space was a haven of peace. It could have just had a makeover by the House Doctor off the TV such was its level of logic and poise.

'Good morning, Rachel. I feel great. How about you? Aren't Jon and Andy just wonderful,' Cathy chattered aimlessly as usual. She swung herself around as if dancing with some invisible lover in a theatrical production fresh out of a thirties' movie.

Rachel observed her friend. Cathy was indeed beautiful, and her figure, although some might say a bit skinny, was in perfect proportion. Her satin chemise showed off her outline in an alluring and yet innocent way which made Rachel want to reach out and run her hand along Cathy's silhouette. She felt herself becoming entranced by the thought of touching her friend and shook her head to regain control of her emotions and desires.

'Don't you think so then?' said Cathy almost stunned by her friend's disinterest in the two boys with whom they had had such a great time last night.

'Oh, yes. I agree. They were very interesting and nice to look at too. I was thinking of something I had forgotten to organise. Sorry, I didn't mean to upset you.'

'That's alright.' Cathy said cheerfully. 'I knew you couldn't really have thought they were anything but gorgeous,' she hugged an imaginary lover, 'what shall we do today? We arranged to meet the boys later, didn't we? I can't wait. I'm so excited.'

'At noon by the harbour for lunch I believe was the final arrangement. It's 11am now so we will have to get a move on. Cathy you're first in the bathroom. Where are the others? Did they both make it home last night? Where did Mel get too anyway?'

'I don't know. But I'm sure she's OK. What shall I wear? Rachel, help me, I need you and your sensible mind. I'm always in such a tizz,' she sighed, 'silly me.'

'You're not silly, Cathy. You're just perfect as you are. Don't ever change. Promise me?'

'I promise, Rachel. Don't be sad. Today is going to be just great. I know it.'

Cathy disappeared into the bathroom and Rachel was left on her own with her thoughts which were disturbing her greatly. She remembered last night very well even though she had had a great deal to drink. She remembered holding Cathy's hand most of the evening and even putting her arm around her at one point but it hadn't seemed to upset Cathy but what had the two boys thought of it? Did they think Cathy and her were really a couple? Rachel stopped as her next thought really confused her. Would it have been so bad if they had, she found herself thinking and shook her head to try to clear this idea from her head.

'I like boys,' she said out loud as if to convince herself of the fact. 'I really do but ...'and her voice dropped, 'I also want to touch her. What am I? A monster. A freak. God, what am I doing?'

Rachel did what she always did in such moments of crisis in her life. She drank her tea and made a list, this time of where they could go that afternoon. This calmed her by the time Cathy emerged from the bathroom, fresh and glowing after her shower only covered in a fluffy white towel. This was not what Rachel needed just at that moment, so she dived out of bed and straight into the bathroom and locked the door. A long shower reformed her composure and by twenty to twelve they were both ready to go down to the town for a fun filled day with Jon and Andy.

CHAPTER 10

'Wake up slob,' Vince prodded Steve in the ribs, 'more totty to tame, get a move on, I'm feeling horny already and starving hungry, let's find a greasy Joe's and have a blow out.'

'What the hell? What time it is? My mouth tastes like Ghandi's flip-flop.'

'Oh, who didn't get his leg over last night then? Just haven't got what it takes, mate. Leave it to the old pros to show you how, eh?'

Steve opened one eye. 'You got laid? Good on you, mate. I thought she looked like she was gagging for it. Any good?'

'So-so. Not very cooperative at first but I soon loosened her up.' Vince winked at his mate and they both burst out laughing.

'So, tell us more then.' Steve insisted that his friend spilled the beans on his sexual conquests.

'Well, she wanted to look for that fat friends of hers, so I agreed, being the gentleman I am,' Vince smirked, 'I managed to steer her up towards the headland, you know, we'd sussed it out as a possible 'romantic place' yesterday. Really quiet at night. Not a soul there. And just dark enough that I didn't have to see her face too well. At first, she made out that she didn't want sex...'

'Didn't want sex? She was all over you. Why do you think I left? You had the surest thing in the room. Her only decent looking mate was only interested in Jon, I can't think why, he's such a ponce, and the others really looked like dogs especially that fat one. You know she made a play for me. Yuk, I nearly threw up at the thought of it. Be like fucking a whale.' Steve made out he was throwing up.

'Yeah, enough of your woes, mate, as I said she wasn't too keen at first, said she didn't want to do it in the open. So, I turned on my charm and 'persuaded' her. Not a bad screw but I don't think I'll waste my time there again. I'm going for a dump and a shower, ' Vince went into the bathroom and after a quick shower came back into the bedroom to continued where he had left off. 'You know, this holiday's shaping up better than I'd thought, I was sure it was going to be bloody boring especially as the Thompson Twins had arranged it, this hotel's a bit shit but handy for the bars I suppose, so can't really complain.'

'You, not complain? Now I've heard everything,' Steve smiled at his friend.

'OK, but you have to admit this resort isn't exactly Magaluf is it? There's hardly any pussy to speak of.'

'Well, you did OK last night. Think about me and the lads, we didn't get anything.'

'So, we'd better suss out some lucky girls for this evening, and this time you'd better pull your todger out and get a lay as well, I can't do everything for you, you know.' At this jibe, Steve let rip with a huge loud fart. 'And the same to you, mate. Now move your fat arse. I'm starving.'

After much cajoling Vince managed to get Steve out of bed and into the bathroom. Walking along the harbour, they found a café, which according to the copious pictures of plates of food seemed to be open for All Day English breakfasts.

'Another fine export from Britain.' Steve remarked with a mouth full of sausage. 'Doing our cholesterol the world of good not to mention my head. Oi, look there's that bimbo from the beach yesterday over there. Now I wouldn't mind me some of that.'

'Not bad, Steve. I like your taste. Wonder if she likes two at a time.'

'Vince you're a complete animal at times.'

'What do you mean at times? I'm obviously not trying hard enough. Now eat up, she's getting ready to go, let's follow her and maybe get chatting, I fancy eyeing those tits again, I could sink my teeth into those melons anytime.'

The men headed off after the blonde, on the way they bumped into Jon and Andy.

'Oh, here come the Thompson Twins. How's it hanging or isn't it, no doubt?' Vince said in his usual sarcastic way.

'Hello Vince, nice to see you too. Going after more poor unsuspecting women?' Andy said.

'What else is there, mate?' Steve picked his nose and flicked at the twins.

'You're gross. If you must know we're going to see Rachel and Cathy...' Jon said.

'Oh Cathy! Oh Cathy! Give her one for me you lucky bastard. Catch you later or not,' Vince and Steve hurried off to stake their claim with the blonde.

'What a pair of morons, Jon,' Andy said. 'If we hadn't met the girls, we could be going around with them for the rest of the holiday – what a nightmare.'

'Think of it as an anthropological experiment – *studying the wild retard in his own environment*,' Jon said, and the two boys laughed out loud. 'Steady now, there's the girls, best behaviour now.'

'There they are,' Cathy was so excited that she couldn't contain herself. The boys stood at the harbour wall, their strong bodies silhouetted in the bright sunshine. *Wow, they looked like Greek God's,* thought Rachel. She followed Cathy as she raced towards Jon and Andy with innocent enthusiasm.

'Hi! You came then?' Cathy said.

'Of course, why wouldn't we? We've been looking forward to this afternoon all morning. How are you?' Jon said with genuineness in his voice.

'Oh, I don't know, just that last night was so great, I thought it must have been something I made up,' Cathy giggled. Jon took her hand and pulled her towards him and gave her a big affectionate hug. The other two looked at each other. Andy held out his hand and Rachel took it slowly but firmly in hers. It made her feel grounded, and she liked that.

The weather was glorious, as the two couples walked along the harbour wall. There was no need to speak, words seemed superfluous and intrusive. At the end of the wall, they stopped and both boys turned to the girls and bent down and softly kissed them. The kiss was so warming it could have melted the Polar icecap, it was even melting Rachel. She felt herself go limp and Andy held her closer to him. He was pleased he was having such an effect on his little ice maiden.

Cathy and Jon snuggled closer together as a breeze started up and the girls shivered slightly.

'You're cold. Let's find somewhere sheltered to have lunch. We can discuss what to do this afternoon,' suggested Jon.

'Good idea,' Rachel said, 'There is a small taverna close to here, which the guidebook says is very good and reasonable.'

'Sounds good to me,' said Andy.

'Let's go!' Rachel led Andy followed by the others and they chatted easily as she used her guide map to find the restaurant. They managed to get a table overlooking the water and Rachel ordered a mixture of traditional foods for the group like some mother hen looking after her brood. No one seemed to worry about her doing this. Andy thought it was endearing, he liked her confidence and sense of order.

The chemistry between the four was so natural to any casual observer that the group seemed like perfection itself. Happy, young and beautiful. The picture of the ideal holiday setting.

Rachel looked across at Andy who noticed her attention and smiled at her. She felt a little confused if not perturbed at her inner wranglings. Andy was so good-looking, fit and healthy, intelligent and in fact everything a girl could wish for. Rachel felt herself warm towards him as they chatted, and she observed him interact with his brother and Cathy. He was so easy going in sharp contrast to her obsessive control. He simply went with the flow of events around him. She found herself admiring this as a quality rather than a fatal weakness, she wanted to be more like him and almost envied him. As they sat next to each other she reached out and held his hand under the table, never moving her gaze from his face, desperate to judge his reaction and expression. He simply squeezed her hand gently and held it as if it were a precious jewel. She knew then that even though she loved Cathy and wanted her close, she also wanted Andy and could see herself falling in love with him so easily.

'Shall we go for a walk?' Rachel said, 'the headland is said to be very beautiful. We could buy a few cans of Coke and just walk till we've had enough.'

'With no set itinerary?' Cathy was shocked at Rachel's apparent laid-back attitude to the day. 'Won't we get lost?'

'No. I don't think so. Shall we go then?' Rachel was shocked at her own reaction to Cathy's comment. *All that trying to be so organised shit, it just doesn't seem to matter anymore,* she thought, *nothing seems to matter anymore as long as I'm holding Andy's hand, nothing else matters as all.* She squeezed his hand, and they looked at each other simply smiled and walked on.

They wound their way around the back streets of the resort and found the path which led to the headland. After a gentle stroll they stopped at a low wall and rested. Cathy looked over the wall and noticed something on the ground.

'What's that?' she said.

'It looks like…well it looks like underwear. How gross.' Rachel said. 'Who'd take their knickers off up here? Some people are so common.'

'Probably some tourists who got carried away with drink.' Andy said. 'Not unusual in places I'm afraid.'

'Gosh! I can't imagine taking my underwear off in a place like this. And why leave it here afterwards?' Cathy said innocently

'They look really grubby, perhaps they couldn't be bothered to put them back on…' Rachel said

'Or perhaps they were just too drunk to remember them,' Andy interrupted. 'Oh dear, it seems they also threw up, best we move on I think.'

They moved off towards the headland and tried to put the sordid scene out of their minds. The views when they reached the promontory were breathtaking and reminded them that Majorca wasn't all tourist bars and high-rise hotels. The group stood and looked out across the rich blue Mediterranean Sea. The intensity of the colours of the sky and the sea and the vegetation made such a canvas that it was hard not to allow their minds to drift into a peaceful calmness.

'I can understand why so many people have wanted to sell up in Britain and move here to live, at least before Brexit, that is. This is fabulous. The air seems so clean and the water – I could just jump off this cliff into it right now,' Rachel breathed in deeply and closed her eyes savouring the sweet scents that wafted past them from nearby citrus groves and mixed with the saltiness of the water evaporating from the sea below.

'Don't tempt us, I could get used to this far too easily,'

Jon said. The two boys looked at each other. The empathy between them was so evident that Rachel and Cathy felt really left out of the moment. Rachel thought of her own secret thoughts and was glad that no one else could read them, not yet anyway.

'Let's go along the coast for a few miles and then cut inland back to the resort,' Rachel couldn't help herself make suggestions but everyone else agreed.

Eventually they found a café bar in a small village.

'We can have a nice cold drink, I'm so hot, I think it's more shaded at that table,' Cathy said, her fair complexion suffering from the heat.

As they sat outside at a small table, they noticed the locals passing by.

'Everyone seems to know everyone else, I can't imagine living somewhere like that,' Rachel said, 'it must be like living in a goldfish bowl where everyone knows your business,' she felt vulnerable, she liked her privacy and her secrecy which living in a city gave her. 'I like London. Somehow, I feel safe there.'

'But think what you lose living in a city.' Cathy looked at the world from a different perspective. 'People care about each other here. They're all probably related and went to school together, grew up together, married people they'd known all their lives, and then saw their own children going to school with their neighbours' children…'

'Uck! How boring! And you call that living? Shoot me now. If that was all there was to life, I couldn't stand it.' Rachel was back on form.

'Yeah, but think of all the regimentation, the knowing your life before you have lived it, everything preordained for you even possibly the person you would marry, wouldn't you like that?' Andy felt obliged to test Rachel and her commitment to being organised.

'Are you serious? I would hate it. No adventure, no excitement, no hope.'

The group mused on this last comment of Rachel's.

Had she hit a nerve or was it that they were confused about their own feelings concerning life and love? They finished their drinks and started back towards the resort, the sky was changing colour as if to mirror their mood and had become a mixture of striking red and orange as the sun had started to drop down towards the sea and the clouds were now streaking across the sky mixing with the hues of scarlet and gold to form an eerie hue. The effect was dramatic but a little unnerving and the pace of the group quickened.

They arrived back at the hillside apartment complex.

'We need a lie down and a freshen up and we'd better check on the other two before they send out a search party for us,' Rachel gave Andy a quick kiss on the cheek, 'let's meet up later for drinks and perhaps dinner somewhere. Today has been one of those special days, I'm sure Cathy agrees,'

'I do, it was wonderful,' she turned to Jon, 'I'd like to see you later, that would be…well…' she skipped off into the complex humming a tune no-one could recognise, which made them all smile.

'The air or something in this place is pretty odd.' Rachel said to Cathy once they were back in the apartment. 'I feel like a new person. It scares me, but I really think I like it.'

'Me too,' spoke Cathy quietly, for her changed views and ideas on life were faintly troubling her.

CHAPTER 11

Mel finally arrived back at the apartment after Rachel and Cathy had left for their lunch with the boys and headed straight for the shower. She didn't even notice Gill still in her dressing gown laid on the bed. After a long refreshing shower, Mel came out of the bathroom and started to dry her hair. In the growing heat of the Mediterranean day her hair was soon blowing in waves of Titian gold over her shoulders. She looked across and saw Gill lying motionless on the bed.

'How did last night go then?' she wondered what everyone had got up to after she left. Gill just continued to lie on the bed and ignored Mel.

'Gill, what's up with you?'

'Nothing!' Gill eventually said, 'I just want some peace and quiet.'

'What? Peace and quiet aren't words in your vocabulary so are you going to tell me or I am going to have to beat it out of you?'

'Piss off, Mel and leave me alone.'

Mel stood and looked at Gill in amazement. She considered that something really major must be bugging Gill for her to speak to her like that.

'I'm sorry, have I done something? Are you pissed off with me because I left the bar?'

'You weren't sorry last night,' Gill said.

'I'm sorry, I didn't think you'd be bothered, you were having such a good time, I thought I'd make myself scarce so as not to cramp anyone's style, least of all yours,' Mel was taken aback, 'I did leave a message earlier, didn't you get it?'

'No, I haven't looked at my phone,'

'That's not like you. You live on your phone. Tell me, what's really the matter?' Mel had known Gill long enough to recognise that there something much more serious going on. 'Are Rachel and Cathy OK? Nothing's happened, has it?'

Gill ignored Mel and turned her back on her friend. Mel was perplexed but not put off. Something very wrong was up. Mel just stood in their room and stared at her. Gill felt uncomfortable and eventually looked up at Mel.

'Please go away.'

'No. I won't. Not until you tell me what's bugging you. Is it just because I left the bar early?'

'Oh, for Christ's sake, no! It's nothing to do with you or 'Dippy' or 'Uptight' either.'

Mel came over and sat next to Gill who pulled her dressing gown tighter around herself and curled up into a ball on the bed. Mel could see that her friend was in pain, and she wanted to help. Gill had always refused help in the past, preferring to handle things in her own way, but this time Mel could see that Gill wasn't handling this at all well.

'Gill.' Mel said quietly. 'I love you; you know that. You're my best friend in the whole world. You've always been there for me. Now let *me* help you. What's happened to you Gill?' Mel started to think about the events of last night. *The change in Gill must have happened after I'd left the bar,* she thought, *was it that I'd stayed out all night at Iain's? I couldn't help that. Or had it something to do with...?*

'Did Vince upset you?'

'I don't want to talk, Mel, please understand that.'

'I don't understand and that's the problem. Did he do anything which you didn't like? He was a big man, and you had had a lot to drink...' The realisation of the situation unfolded in Mel's mind, and she drew in a sharp breath as the realisation became clearer. 'He didn't force himself on you, did he?'

Gill looked up and Mel saw the tears welling up in her friend's eyes. Gill just lay there; the tears trickled down her cheeks like a silent scream. Mel stared back at her blankly unable to fully comprehend the enormity of the situation.

'He raped me, Mel. On the cliff path, right out in the open and I couldn't do anything about it. He forced himself on me. He called me scum and then kicked me. He said I asked for it like a dirty whore. Mel, I never did. I liked him. I thought he was nice. I was having such a good time last night. Why, Mel, why?'

Mel felt her heart race at her friend's confession, and she bent forward to hug her, but Gill drew back.

'I'm not clean anymore, Mel. Don't touch me. I can still smell him on me. I don't want anyone to touch me ever again,' Gill curled herself up into an even tighter ball.

'I'm sorry,' Mel said quietly. 'I don't know what else to do. You were always the one who knows what to do in a crisis. We all rely on you, too much perhaps. But giving you a hug is what I think I should do. I don't think you're dirty. I love you. Don't push me away.' Mel bent forward again and tenderly put her arms around Gill. Gill lay motionless and let her friend envelope her in love and comfort. The effect was one of surrender to all the emotions she had pent up for what seemed like days but were in fact only hours. The tears that had begun to trickle grew into a torrent and she turned to bury her head in Mel's shoulder and cried. Her crying was hard and deep and expressed the despair and self-loathing she had been bottling up and trying to push from her mind. The release of all the emotion was so powerful that Mel started to cry in response. The two girls let their salty tears melt away the misery like rainwater on old snow.

'What do you want to do?' Mel said eventually.

'I don't want to do anything.' Gill replied. 'I just want to die.'

'Hmmm, sorry, not an option in the Gill's 'Guide to the Universe'. Not allowed, fifty pound fine.' Mel tried to lighten the situation but saw that this was not the time or the place. Somehow when Gill did it, it came across as funny. Mel felt she was just being annoying. 'I don't know what to say. I want to help. I feel so helpless…'

'You feel helpless? Think how I feel. I can't close my eyes without seeing him and hearing him. All the venom he spat at me. Why? I just don't understand why. I must have been a real bitch or something to deserve that. He really hated me.' Gill shook her head as if it would help her understand her humiliation and Vince's cruelty towards her. 'I have thought about it all night and lived it over and over in my mind. Mel, I can't understand and that is what makes me so angry and hurt. The bruises will go but the hate. I can't cope with the hate.'

'Whatever happened, it wasn't your fault. Rape shows *he* has a problem; *not* you. Understand? You are wonderful and we all love you.' Mel paused. She didn't want to broach the subject but felt she had to. 'Do you want to tell the police?'

'Oh God no, they would just laugh at me and tell me I deserved it. Remember we're in Spain now – land of the macho man. Rape is probably a national sport!'

'Gill, that's not true. Spain is as civilized as the rest of Europe. We could go to the police station together, now if you like.'

'NO, N. O. spells no, I just want to forget it.'

'Did he use a…you know… a condom?'

Gill's silence told volumes.

'Oh God, Gill. We must get you to a doctor.'

'No, I'll get a test done when we get home but I feel sure it will be OK.'

'But you never know these days.'

'Thanks for trying to cheer me up, Mel, you're doing a great job.'

'Sorry! We'll do what you want but promise you will take care of yourself. I'll always be here for you and the others will be too - even if they are mega annoying at times.'

Gill knew she was surrounded by good friends, and this was perhaps a fact she had overlooked in her misery. She was relieved that Mel had pressed her for an explanation. She was sorry she had shouted at Mel. Poor Mel, it was usually Mel who needed her help. Now she needed Mel's help, and that would take some getting used to.

'Can you fix me a sandwich or something, I'm starving, and something to drink – just a Coke or something. I'll take a quick shower, and then will you come for a walk with me? I don't think I can face going out alone, but I need some fresh air. I need to blow away a few cobwebs.'

'Great idea. I've knackered my ankle - that's a long story - but I can hobble along somehow. A walk would be good, and I've got lots to tell you as well. Hurry up then. There isn't any food in, so we'll have to get a sandwich at the café bar downstairs. You have your shower. It'll do you the power of good.' Mel turned to go but then turned back and said 'everything will be OK, Gill. We'll get through this together like friends do.'

The sun shone down on Gill's face as they walked arm in arm along through the complex grounds. The scenery was very beautiful, and Gill soaked up the warmth. The freshness of the place was like a tonic to her, and she started to unwind and relax.

'This has changed me, Mel. I don't feel like I'm the same person.'

'You probably aren't. Any life experience changes us,

the more dramatic, the greater the change, I feel changed too, it must be this place or something. It's spooky.'

'I feel my strength coming back since we talked. Thank you, Mel, for being there for me. I'm feeling new or different emotions now. I want to beat the crap out of him. Can I Mel? Would that be acceptable?'

'Absolutely! And I'll hold your coat while you do it, how's that? Actually, come to think of it, I think I've got an idea. Do you mind if I tell someone else about this?'

Gill turned to Mel with dread in her eyes. 'Oh, Mel I feel so ashamed, I couldn't bear anyone else knowing. Please don't tell anyone. Can't we just keep this to ourselves for now?'

'OK, if that's what you want.'

Mel then retold the story of the problem she had encountered with teenage hormones and how she had met Iain. Gill smiled and even laughed in places as Mel hyped up the story.

'Seems we both had exciting evenings all round. Dippy was very chirpy this morning, so I guess she had a good time. I envy her innocence but thank God these things didn't happen to her. She's still a child in so many ways. I don't see how she could have survived it. I feel bad enough. As for Uptight, she didn't surface at all this morning until it was time for them to go to meet the two guys they were with. I hope they don't turn out like Vince.'

'Nor that Steve, he was just pig ignorant, I think Jon and Andy are OK though, they seemed to be from a different planet than the jerk twins,' Mel and Gill laughed, it was good to see her friend relaxing enough to enjoy a joke, especially at the expense of those two loathsome men.

'I think I want to get back now,' Gill said. 'The air has done me good, but I still ache all over.'

'My ankle still hurts too, it may be better if I rest it too, but I think I'll lie by the pool for a while. I need to think too.'

'Carry on, but I'll stay in the apartment today. I need some time on my own to compose myself before Dippy and Uptight get back. They are sure to want an explanation about last night and I haven't worked out what I want to tell them yet. Please don't mention anything to them if you see them.'

'Course not. You call the shots, Gill. But remember I'll be looking out for what I think's best for you. Just don't do anything stupid will you?'

'No, I promise. I do appreciate your help. Thank you, Mel.'

'No, thank you for letting me help you. I appreciate how hard it was to tell me, but I love it that you confided in me and let me help. It's usually you who has to help me.'

They arrived back at the apartment. Mel bathed and bandaged her ankle before going back down to the pool side. She had an idea but needed to work it out how to tell Iain even though she had promised not to as she felt he'd know what to do. Besides, it would be the perfect opportunity to talk to him again. Her knight in shining armour could also be Gill's as well.

The other two girls eventually arrived home from their day out with Jon and Andy but only stayed in long enough to change before they headed off again for dinner. Gill kept in the bathroom and avoided having to talk to them. They were so wrapped up in their own affairs that they didn't seem to notice. Mel and Gill grabbed a takeaway from a kebab house just outside the apartment complex and stayed in all evening before having the early night that they both needed.

Mel's ankle had eased by the following morning, so she decided to walk to Iain's villa. After a few wrong turns she eventually arrived only to find he wasn't in. She was a little disappointed to have missed him but the wait for a reply to her note she left was unbearable. She spent the rest of the day mooching around the complex trying to cajole Gill into venturing out of the apartment. Eventually she had managed to get her to go down to the pool but only if she promised to not leave her alone.

'This is the life, the sun is so soothing and warm. It's easy to forget it can fry you to a frazzle as well,' Mel said to Gill in late afternoon. 'I hope I haven't burned. I shall look such a prat.'

'You should be careful. Your complexion always burns,' Gill still found it in her to be the caring person but somehow found it more of an effort. Her inner upsets took up much of her energy and she often drifted away into her own little world, her dreams were only short however as she brought herself abruptly back to earth with a flashback to Vince.

Gill wished that Father James was here to listen and comfort her as he had done for the whole family on more than one occasion. She felt guilty about not having been to mass for a while. She regretted it now. She needed to have the familiarity of her childhood around her. She needed to fall back on her beliefs and her community but only Mel was here. Gill felt she was a burden on her friend for the first time in her life. Gill, the one who always coped and was always the one to carry her friends and family through troubled times. Gill who was the backbone of the trauma unit where she worked, always calm under pressure and ready to go the extra mile. *I couldn't bear to think about going back to work,* she thought, *everyone will be looking at me, knowing my shame, my weakness, how can I do my job? How can I take on the world's troubles if I can't deal with my own?*

Mel's mobile began to ring and startled Gill whose nerves were already on edge.

'Sorry I missed you yesterday afternoon,' Iain said, 'but I had some business to attend to in Palma, I'm impressed you remembered where I lived.'

Mel just smiled – why wouldn't she remember?

CHAPTER 12

Iain hadn't been sure if he was pleased or annoyed when her found the note from Mel slipped under his villa door. He was fiercely defensive of his privacy but at the same time he did like Mel, and this annoyed him even more. How many times had he said he wouldn't get involved with tourists? They were only heartache. They came to the Med for some fun and then left two weeks later forgetting all about the people they left behind to go back to their ordinary lives. He had been left behind too often to let it happen again. But he was lonely. There was only so much of the ex-pat scene he could take and if it wasn't for some useful contacts he had made for his business deals, he would have chosen to ignore them completely.

'I thought perhaps we could meet up later maybe for a drink or something?' Mel said hesitantly. In the back of her mind, she thought that she might be jumping the gun a bit. She felt in some ways that Iain was keeping her at arm's length – not pushing her away but not inviting her in either.

'Yes, I suppose that would be nice.' He replied. 'Shall we say eight o'clock by the harbour wall? I'll wear a red carnation just in case you don't recognise me.'

'Oh, I shall recognise you alright, no worries there. I never forget a face I like.' Mel could not believe her audacity. *What am I doing*, she thought, *I've never made such a bold remark to a man before. I must be drunk or something.*

'Fine, I'll see you then. Goodbye,' and he rang off.

'Not much of a one for conversation then.' Gill said.

'No, you're right. I can't quite make him out. He's quite an enigma.'

'Wow! An enigma, eh? How posh,' Gill said, and they both laughed.

For the rest of the afternoon Mel was impossible to be with and Gill barricaded herself on the balcony of the apartment to get away from her.

'Mel, stop fussing, I've never seen you so flustered about a date. You usually think of it as an ordeal and can only look forward to when it's all over, what has come over you? You're not going to do something daft like…fall in love are you?'

'Piffle! I will never let a man get that close to me, you know that. I don't want all that agro and heartache. Love? - What's love got to do with it?'

'Cue for a song. *What's love got to do, got to do with it? What's love but just a second-hand emotion.*' Gill's singing was distinctly out of tune. 'Tina - eat your heart out.'

'Nothing much wrong with you now, is there,' Mel said and regretted it as soon as the words came out. Gill stopped singing and went back to pretending to read her magazine. 'I'm sorry, Gill. I didn't mean that. You sing all you like, it'll keep any cockroaches away, after all. I'm just a bit nervous and I'm rabbiting on, sorry, I'm just scared about meeting Iain again and it's thrown me into a tizz, I don't know why. It doesn't make sense, none of this holiday makes any bloody sense.'

'Couldn't agree more with you there, Mel, no sense at all, this place must have some sort of magic spell on us or something, I just wish mine were a bit nicer that's all, it's the 'no sense' that makes everything nonsense.'

'Yeah,' said Mel absentmindedly, 'I know what you mean, I feel I've begun to lose control of what's happening around me, I feel like I'm floating but I can't stop it. I try, but I just can't get back to where I was. I liked being isolated, aloof, in control of my relationships. It made me feel safe. Why does it have to change?'

'Why indeed,' Gill said, 'why indeed? It seems we're both going through changes, which are out of our control. I never thought what happened to me would've ever done but it did. I keep trying to go back in time and convince myself that I was OK the way I was, but something is missing now. I want to be the old Gill, but would that be enough now? I don't know. I DON'T KNOW!' Gill raised her voice and shouted into the air. Her frustration was obvious. Mel felt helpless to do anything about it and as if nailed to the floor she could not even move to comfort her friend. It was as if she was in a state of suspended animation.

'I don't know either, perhaps we aren't supposed to understand.' Mel confused herself by this statement. 'Enough philosophy for today, I think I'll wear my black outfit, what do you think?'

'Great, hides yourself very well, good choice.'

'You're right, but what the hell. I like wearing it and I'm nervous enough already not to add a new daring outfit to the list of things to worry about. I think I had better be going soon, are you sure you'll be OK? I don't know where Cathy and Rachel are or when they'll be back.'

'No problem. I need some time on my own to think. I like our conversations, Mel. They really help.'

'They do? Good, I'm glad. When you work out what it was we said, let me know. There, how do I look?'

'Stunning, go get him tiger!'

'Yeah, right, see you later, I won't be late, I've a feeling about that.'

CHAPTER 13

Mel felt a bit guilty about leaving Gill but also had an uncontrollable urge to see Iain again. She walked in a semi trance down to the harbour as if drawn towards him. She felt unnerved but couldn't stop the flow of events which were happening all around her. Cathy was coming out of her shell, Rachel was lightening up, Gill was starting to cope with her experience with Vince and here she was, Mel Wright, excited about a date which she actually had set up. *The world's turning upside down*, she mused, *but what the heck, I think I'm enjoying myself,* Mel smiled as she rounded the last corner before she reached the harbour. Her smile made her look radiant, and Iain couldn't help but notice.

She is gorgeous, he thought, *but she seems very keen, I worry that she's reacting to the kindness I showed her, I wonder if she's coming on to me out of gratitude.*

'Hello Iain. Hope I haven't kept you waiting. Had a bit of a problem with my friend Gill but I'll tell you more about that later. Where shall we go?'

'Hello Melissa, I haven't been here long, so no problem. I thought we'd go to a quiet bar off the main drag, fewer tourists there and the wine's much better, shall we go?'

He doesn't waste any time with pleasantries, does he? thought

Mel, it's as if he doesn't really want to be with me, then why agree to see me? Men are such confusing creatures, no wonder I've never had much time for them, in fact, I feel like going home right now, she nearly turned around right there, *but I can't, I need to be with him, get a grip Mel, work on him, win him over, you can do this.*

'Fine, let's go,' she said 'a glass of wine would be great right now. Lead the way.'

They walked along the harbour past all the usual nightlife designed especially for tourists, tacky, rough and overpriced, and after a few minutes Iain turned off into a narrow alley. Thoughts about the first night flooded back into Mel's mind.

What am I doing here? she panicked, *I must be mad, I don't really know anything about this bloke, he could be a criminal on the run with a wife and three kids back in Britain, he could be a beach bum simply house sitting that villa. Why did I come? I should have stayed with Gill, I should never have come on this holiday in the first place.*

'Here we are. What do you think? Doesn't look like much from the outside,' said Iain. 'That's to put the tourists off. My friend Juan runs it and I'm sure he'll find us a nice table and rustle up some homemade food. Are you hungry?'

'Always,' Mel said before she could stop herself and then bit her lip to stop herself saying anything else stupid. 'I mean, I like authentic cuisine, can't get it very often in tourist resorts, can you?'

'Only if you know where to look. Come on, I'm famished too'

The bar was small and dimly lit. There were about five other people inside. The occupants stopped and turned to look at the new arrivals; to suss them out and check they weren't lager louts or worse - loud American tourists. They seemed to recognise Iain, some waved to him while others simply acknowledged his presence with a brief nod of the head. Iain went up to the bar and Mel trotted closely behind a little intimidated by the surroundings.

'*Hola amigo,*' a short dark middle-aged man shouted from behind the bar. 'Nice to see you Iain. *Com va?*' Juan and Iain shook hands warmly, '*bona sera, senorita?* Please to follow me. I have just the table for you. Some wine Iain? I have a new red from Miguel, I think you will like it. He has done well this time.'

'If your brother made it, then I shall like it, Juan. How have you been keeping? Sorry I haven't been in lately but business, you know how it is.'

The table Juan had chosen for them was in a secluded part of the bar, away from the regulars who stayed around all evening drinking, playing cards and chatting about how they would right the wrongs of the world – *Demà*, tomorrow. The place was clean but very rustic and Mel was warming to its charm.

When Juan brought a bottle and three glasses over to their table Iain enquired, 'Can you rustle up some food, Juan? Whatever you have in will be fine.'

'No problem, I will see what Maria can do for you.' Juan poured some wine into the glasses and, raising his, flashed an enquiring glance towards Iain to see his reaction to the wine. *He's obviously well thought of by Juan.* She thought. Mel felt a sense of pride come over her as she considered who and what Iain really was. *At least, if he's liked by the locals that must count for something and perhaps the beach bum theory was a little premature.* Mel watched Iain taste the wine, not like a wine snob you might find in a Sloane Square wine bar but as someone who truly appreciated a good wine for its own sake. He closed his eyes and savoured the flavour. Mel could see he was genuinely enjoying it and after several seconds he opened his eyes and looked at Juan.

'*Bo*! Good! That's excellent. I want some. Ask Miguel to drop a case over and send one to my Madrid offices, I'll try to get some interest in it for him. Is he taking it to the *Festa* in September?'

'He will if you say it is good enough.'

'It's definitely good enough.'

'*Gràcies*, Iain. He will be very pleased. I will tell Maria you are here. She is going to tell you off for staying away for so long.'

'Can't be helped, but I've missed you both. Let me introduce you to Melissa. She's staying here for a couple of weeks…'

'Or maybe longer?' Juan cheekily enquired.

Iain seemed to ignore this comment, and this embarrassed Mel more than if he had answered. When he did eventually reply it was as cryptic as it was short.

'Who knows?' Juan took his cue to leave the two alone and went to tell Maria the good news that Iain was here and hungry and with a woman.

'That was kind of you to praise his brother's wine so much.'

'The wine is good – very good. Miguel works so hard to try to make the best wine in Majorca. He wants to be known for making wine better than Franjo Roja. It's a bit of friendly rivalry, I think. And if this area gets known for good wine, good food will follow, we'll get a better class of tourist coming here, then property and land prices will rise, so you see it's all self-interest really, I'm afraid.'

'I can't believe that. I think you genuinely care for these people.'

'Perhaps I do.'

'So, what is it you actually do for a living then?' Mel enquired.

'Oh, this and that. Nothing in particular, really.'

'But it must be more exciting than me…'

'Why?'

'Well, because it must. I work in a bank and that sums it up really.' Mel was curious about her White Knight and pressed him further, 'What do you do?'

'I deal in things…antiques, property, wine - whatever – all very legitimate in case you're worried, I simply have a knack of spotting a good deal and making the most of a good situation, I've been out here for five years now, I own my own villa, have a nice car which I don't seem to use much other than going back and forth to the airport, and a good circle of friends, I like it here. The weather's marvelous of course and the scenery is great, better when the tourists have gone mind you.'

'Tourists like me, I take it.'

'Well, there are some obnoxious people who come here on holiday. I blame the cheap airfares and package holiday firms. They are ruining all the best places on the Med. It's really hard to find an unspoilt place nowadays.' Iain tried to tactfully explain his earlier comment but felt he was probably failing to do so miserably. Speaking his mind was always getting him into trouble especially with women. 'I can only speak as I find that's all. Don't be offended by it. It's not pointing at you particularly.'

'No, no, of course not,' said Mel with just the hint of sarcasm in her voice and she looked directly at him until he smiled and said 'OK, I admit it. I don't like tourists. They spoil everything and then bugger off back home and don't give a damn about what havoc they've caused.'

'So how many tourists have you been out with who then "buggered off"?'

'Too many,' said Iain taking a large gulp of wine and feeling a bit uncomfortable talking about himself in such a way.

Totally out of character, Mel found herself leaning forward as if to divulge some deep secret and saying, 'Well to be quite frank, I'm not into 'buggering' be it off or otherwise, so you're safe.'

Iain started to laugh. He saw how absurdly immature he had been. He was acting as if his world had fallen apart because some girl or other had left and forgotten him. He was using the tourist trap bit as an excuse for not owning up to how much it hurt to be rejected. It was like a deal not going through, which he hated even more.

'Point taken and noted for future information.'

The food arrived and Juan explained enthusiastically what each course was. 'Maria made these panadas this morning, the pastry it melts in your mouth, and then there is some Frito Mallorquin she had from yesterday, it is so good the next day, don't you think?' Both Iain and Mel just nodded as they tucked into the feast Maria had magically produced for them. 'Leave room for the dessert.'

'Don't tell me she has made…'

'You know Maria, there is always time for her to make it for you.'

'She spoils me and my waistline.' He turned to Mel who was intrigued, 'Best leave some room, dessert will be to die for.'

Maria had excelled herself as usual and after what seemed an eternity, they had finished the meal including some freshly baked Ensaimada for dessert. They sat back in their chairs both feeling like stuffed pigs.

'That pastry was so light, it just melted in my mouth, I will have to go on a diet when I get home. I won't be able to get into any of my suits for work at this rate,' Mel sighed, all she really wanted to do was fall asleep.

'I shall just have to work out more, I love running early in the mornings or doing a workout in the gym. By the way, why have you made yourself fat anyway?'

'Gee thanks! Nothing like a direct question,' Mel said taken aback by the bluntness of the enquiry. 'I just like my food, that's all.'

'Yeah, Juan likes his food, he's not fat but then he's happy. You're a beautiful young woman, why do you need to carry around all that excess baggage?'

She had never felt comfortable about talking about her size. It was a part of her that she preferred to hide from. Even Gill never really talked about why Mel was fat, it was an unspoken pact.

'Perhaps it's to protect myself against a cruel world,' she eventually managed to control her emotions long enough to reply, 'or something just as melodramatic. I don't know.

Who does know…or more to the point who admits why?' Mel was feeling very uncomfortable talking about this subject with Iain who was effectively destroying her self-image by the minute. 'Can we talk about something else? I don't feel right discussing this with a date.'

Iain looked at Mel with disapproval and softly said. 'You don't need fat to protect yourself; you need self-confidence and a belief in yourself. Fat doesn't give you that. It just holds you back and drags you down.'

'And you'd know of course.'

'Yes, I would,' he replied in his soft deep voice again. He looked straight at her. She could see an understanding in his eyes, and it perplexed her.

'Why would you?' Mel said.

'Because I used to be fat. I was for most of my childhood. Then I simply decided it wasn't who I wanted to be anymore. So, I change it…'

'You're right, it's what I should do too, but it isn't that easy…'

'The time has to be right, I get that, but it's something to think about, isn't it?

'Yes.' Mel looked down at her wine glass. He was right but being told was painful. It was as if he had stripped her bare and then made her look at herself in a big mirror. A sort of mirror that only told the truth rather than the ones she had at home which when she looked in them, told her only lies, it was easy when you practiced hard enough. Her nakedness upset her, and she could feel her eyes burn as she desperately held back tears of emotions long repressed and ignored. *This man has got to me,* she thought, *how did that happen? No one ever gets inside my head like this, I've to get out of here, I've got to get my privacy back…I want to go home.'*

'Will you please excuse me? I think I'd like to get back to my friends now.' Mel said and Iain knew he had gone too far too soon.

'I'm sorry, if I've upset you, I never meant to, please understand that. But if it helps,' he hesitated, 'I only wanted to help...'

'Help? Is that what you really do for a living then? Rescue young women and then destroy them yourself? I really felt changed being around you, I really liked you...'

'And I like you.'

'Funny way of showing it, Iain. What school did you attend to learn how to treat girls then? Attila the Hun School for Young Gentlemen?'

This last comment caused both of them to start laughing at its absurdity, it also helped to release the tension.

'Let's go back to my place for a coffee,' Iain offered her an olive branch and she was so glad. 'And I think I have some humble pie in the fridge for me to eat as well.'

'Fair deal. Does it taste nice? Can I have some too?'

'OK. We'll share it, but I get the biggest piece – no arguments,' Iain paid the bill and said his farewells to Juan and Maria. 'We'll see you again soon,' he promised them, 'And don't forget that wine.'

'OK Iain. Val!' Juan then turned to Mel. '*Bona nit*! Look after him - he needs it,'

'*Val*!' Melissa replied to Juan, '*Bona nit*!'

'*Bona*! – You see, Iain, she will fit in around here very well.'

Iain smiled politely but said nothing.

They walked in silence up to Iain's villa. The moon was full and shone down in an eerie light over the bay. The view from the villa was breathtaking and Mel stood on the terrace and breathed deeply trying to take in all the atmosphere and romance of the scene. The headiness of jasmine was all about her, and she thought of days gone by and ancient times when damsels in distress were two a penny and knights in shining armour really did exist. This thought however brought her feet back to the ground with a thud as she thought of Gill.

'Iain, can I trust you with a secret and ask your advice?'

Mel summoned her courage. 'I want to talk to you about my friend Gill. She doesn't want anyone to know yet, but I feel something has to be done before someone else gets hurt.'

'Fire away. Always here to help.'

'The other night when you found me, I had left my friends in a bar near the harbour. They'd all found dates for the evening, and I felt I'd prefer to just go home. Later in the evening, one of my friends, Gill, went out to look for me with the man she'd met...well...he took advantage of the situation. No let's be honest here, he raped her, up on the headland path, she's OK physically, just some bruises etc. but she's really messed up in her mind. I think that this guy had probably done this before and will no doubt do it again. The things he said to her seemed to point to the fact that he has a serious problem with his attitude to women. I don't know what to do.'

'Has Gill been to the police about this?'

'No, she doesn't think they'll be interested. She thinks they'll just be macho guys who won't take her seriously.'

Iain grimaced at this comment but knew that the perception of Spanish police amongst British tourists wasn't as good as it should have been.

'Has she seen a doctor?' he said.

'No, she won't do that either, she says she'll go to see her doctor when we get back to in London. I'll make sure she does.'

'Then what do you want to see happen?'

'I want him to feel her pain. I want him to be taught a lesson that you can't treat girls like that and get away with it. I want the crap beaten out of him, I suppose, and I'd do it myself if I could.'

'Oh, I see, rational thinking...'

'Bugger rational thinking, was he thinking rationally when he violated her and kicked her and abused her?' Mel turned away feeling herself lose control with all the emotion she was feeling – anger, frustration, uselessness.

'I'm sorry, I shouldn't have told you, please forget I ever mentioned it.'

'But you have told me so I can't forget it. You're right, we have to do something before he does it again as he surely will. These people have problems, and this behaviour isn't going to go away by itself. He needs 'educating'.'

Mel turned towards. 'Thank you for understanding.' She moved towards him and kissed him softly on the lips. Her heart jumped as he responded, and they embraced each other firmly for what seemed a lifetime.

Iain took a deep breath. 'I never thought we'd do that, I'll admit that I have been resisting your advances, I don't like holiday romances, they never last.'

'Never say never, you don't know what might happen, don't be so quick to judge people by the actions of a small sample. That's statistically unsound, you know.'

'True, but not as easy a habit to break as it sounds. Let's discuss this later. My head's reeling and I need time to think. How about a cup of coffee and then we can discuss your friend's problem?'

'Good idea. Milk, no sugar, thanks.'

They sipped their coffee on the terrace. Mel felt so relaxed for the first time in years. She was sitting overlooking a beautiful scene, sipping good coffee with an incredibly sexy and wonderful man planning their revenge on Vince. What more could a girl want?

After a discussion about Vince, Iain announced 'Let me make some enquiries. I've to go to Madrid tomorrow on business for a few days, but I think I know just the people to help us. Leave it with me, someone will call you with arrangements and I'll call you when I get back. I'd better get you home now so you can rest that ankle. Have a few days lounging around the pool with Gill. That will do the pair of you the world of good.'

Mel was a little stunned that he hadn't asked her to stay

but also flattered in an old-fashioned sort of way.

'How gentlemanly,' observed Gill when Mel arrived home unexpectedly and described her evening. Mel was careful not to mention her conversation with Iain about Vince at least not yet.

CHAPTER 14

It was Thursday evening, and the streets of the resort were crowded with people out to have fun.

'That's him,' Melissa pointed out Vince with his mates going into a bar.

'I will take it from here, see you later, maybe we can have a drink and toast the plan's success.'

Luisa knew what to do. She ambled over to the bar. 'Excuse me,' she said brushing herself against Vince seductively, 'is there room for a little one?'

Vince turned slowly and smelt her expensive perfume which was intoxicating. He looked her up and down and couldn't believe his luck. 'Anytime, love, can I get you a drink?' *This girl's mine*, he smiled at her in a sickly way.

Luisa was slim and beautiful with classic Mediterranean looks – long black hair flowing in waves over her bronzed skin. She looked at Vince through dark deep sultry eyes outlined with long full lashes. She had an elegance about her which was only heightened as she stood next to the uncultured figure of Vince. Her dress was immaculate and made of softest silk which flowed over her body like cream and her outline made her the attention of everyone in the bar - both men and women.

'That would be lovely. Martini Bianchi, please,' she looked him straight in the eyes and smiled a soft half smile which spoke a thousand words and all of them within Vince's limited vocabulary.

'What's your accent? It sounds Spanish.'

'It is, I am from Madrid, I come here for the summer, Majorcan weather is so much nicer than the mainland. Have you been here before?'

'No. First time for me and the boys but I'm getting to like it more by the minute.'

Steve groaned to his mates. 'He's done it again, he's such a jammy bastard, why didn't she push past me? Anyone would think I had BO or something,' he sniffed under his arms just to make sure.

After she'd finished her drink, Luisa turned to Vince and whispered in his ear, 'Can we go somewhere more private?' she nodded towards the other lads. Her implications were crystal clear to Vince.

'We're just going outside for some fresh air and a walk, see you losers later, OK?' Vince winked to his mates.

'Yeah sure, later.' Steve said and turned towards the bar to order another drink, this time a double.

Once outside, Luisa held Vince's hand and guided him towards a back street. Once off the main drag, she hurried them along the winding street until they came to a small car park.

'Over here,' she said beckoning to Vince who was no slouch when it came to being invited to dark places by beautiful women. This dark place however held a few surprises for him.

A man dressed in a uniform came forward out of the shadows and walked towards Vince.

'Excuse me, Senõr, but I would like you to accompany me to the Police Station. Come this way, please.'

'What d'you mean? Police station? Why? What've I done?'

'We need you to help us with our enquiries about

certain events which have happened over the last few days. Please come quietly, Senõr, we do not want any trouble, do we,' and the policeman put his arm lightly on Vince's arm. Vince looked around for Luisa, but she had slipped away into the darkness as if she had never been there. Vince was disorientated by these events and having had several lagers by now he felt his head crying out for explanations.

'Whatever you say mate,' he managed to say, 'I'm sure there's been some mistake, but we can sort that out easily enough'

The policeman ignored Vince's conversation and led him to a waiting car. They eventually arrived at a small police station and Vince was led into a dimly lit room without any windows. It was cold in the room, and this served to sober him up. He looked around and saw evidence of someone having been in the room before him. The floor was dirty and stained and littered with cigarette ends and there was a distinct smell of fear. Vince shuddered. He had no idea why he was there, but decided the best course to avoid trouble was to cooperate fully and then get the hell out of there.

'Last Saturday you spent the evening in the Cabana Bar by the harbour, did you not?' A plain clothed man had entered the room and without introducing himself had started his interrogation.

'Yeah, we were there.'

'And you left the Bar at about 2am?'

'Yeah. I did.'

'Were you alone?'

'No, I was with a girl.'

'I see. And where did you go from there?' The man walked around the room and talked without expression in his voice.

'We went for a walk along the headland. It was a great night, and we needed the air. Say, what's all this about?'

'Just answer the questions, Senõr. What happened to the girl?'

'I don't know. We walked for a while and then I thought we'd sit down and admire the view, but she was restless and said she had to get back to her friends.'

'I see. And you never saw her again?'

'No, I haven't, what's happened?' Vince was starting to get nervous. Why were they asking questions about that slag Gill? It was true he hadn't seen her since that night but then he wasn't looking for her either.

There was a pause. The man stubbed out his cigarette and left the room. This un-nerved Vince and he could feel the sweat rising on his skin. He started to panic and wished he hadn't come to the station so willingly. His mind started to flood with stories of how Spanish police treated young Brits.

'Can I go now?' he asked the other man who stood between him and the door. 'I don't know anything anymore.' The policeman remained motionless and silent. His eyes were fixed on an imaginary spot somewhere on the other side of the room. It was as if he were a statue. Vince wondered whether anyone would try to stop him if he just got up and walked out. He wanted to try out this theory, but fear seemed to have taken away the use of his legs. The door reopened and the first uniformed man came in.

'Get up. Follow me.'

Vince dutifully got up and followed the man down several corridors and found he was being taken to the cells. His heart raced and his skin started to creep with uncertainty.

'In here.' The man beckoned Vince to enter a cell, which seemed dimly lit and stank of stale urine and other human waste. The door closed behind him.

'Hey! What's going on? I demand to speak to a solicitor, I want to call the British Embassy, I demand you let me out of here.'

'Demand all you like, mate. You're here for the night now.' A voice with a British accent came from the dimness and startled Vince.

'That's right. It's just the three of us. How cosy,' a second British voice joined the conversation. Vince went cold. He eventually composed himself and reminded himself that he was quite capable of handling himself if he needed to.

'Best we get to know each other better then, eh, mate?' the first voice said. "My name's 'Worst Nightmare' and my friend's called 'Big Boy' and we're the 'Buggery Twins'. Pleased to meet you.'

'Stay away from me. I warn you, I'm a black belt…'

'Ooh, a black belt, very impressive. Black belt in what? No, let me guess, I know – fucking defenseless little girls, we know exactly who you are mate and we're here to teach you some better behaviour.'

'What are you talking about? I've never touched girls. I like a shag like the rest of us but only women, I swear! Who told you different? They're lying, there's some mistake, it isn't me you want…'

'Oh, but it is,' Big Boy interrupted, 'now where shall we begin?'

CHAPTER 15

Vince woke up and found himself lying on the side of a dirt track. He looked around and couldn't place where he was. He tried to get up but his whole body ached, and pain shot through him. He gave up and tried to catch his breath. What had happened to him? At first, he couldn't remember last night's events but then it all came flooding back to him and he immediately threw up, hurling vomit in all directions and managing to get himself covered in the process. He lay there and wished he were dead. His body might have been in pain, but it was nothing to the pain in his mind. He had been used like some disposable tissue, used as a receptacle for God knows who or what. He felt himself retch again but there was nothing left to throw up and this made him feel worse.

He lay there for what seemed like ages. The sun started to come up and eventually blazed down on him. He felt so thirsty and hungry but the thought of putting food in his mouth made him feel nauseous. He tried to get up again and this time overcame the pain and got to his feet. He noticed he was on a hillside overlooking the bay where the resort was. He started to walk slowly and painfully down the track and eventually came to the road that led into town. He looked at his watch, but it wasn't there. He reached into his pocket for his phone but that was also missing. He didn't bother looking for any more of his belongings. There would be no point.

He walked along the streets of the town. Only local people, going about their daily business seemed to be up and about, all the tourists were still in bed, warm, safe and comfortable. He passed the bar where he had spent that first night on holiday and stopped. *Why did the police ask me about Gill? She's alright. I only shagged her, for God's sake.'*

It then hit him. All he had done to her was what had been done to him last night except last night there'd been two of them and they had done much more besides. He sat down on a low wall and put his head in his hands. *What was it all about? Those guys talked about girls?... I've been set up and somehow that slag Gill's involved. She had to be...but why and how? The police were involved but they didn't arrest me or charge me, they simply put me in that cell with those two perverts and ...then they let me go.'* He started to feel angry. 'Revenge, the bitch got her revenge on me, the fucking bitch.' The pain in his abdomen brought him back to reality and he got up and continued walking back to his hotel.

'What the hell happened to you?' Steve said in his usual caring way.

'Nothing.' Vince snapped back. 'I'm going to take a bath. Don't disturb me.'

'Hey, what happened with that girl? She came back past the bar no time after you'd left, where've you been? Don't say she said no as well, you're losing the old touch, Vince my boy, join the ranks of the great un-shagged.'

'Piss off!' Vince slammed the bathroom door shut.

He gingerly took off his clothes. His body was riddled with pain as if he had been run over by a stream roller. He looked at himself in the mirror as he ran a hot bath. At nearly thirty he was in good shape, but he felt like death. His eyes seemed hollow and empty as if all the stuffing had been pulled out of him. He leant his hands on the basin and looking down he began to sob. He couldn't believe he was doing it, but he couldn't stop himself either. The tears rolled down his rugged unshaven face and landed on his hands which were cut and bleeding from trying to defend himself. He picked one hand up and turning it over to look at it more closely and then noticed it was shaking.

'What the hell is the matter with you, Thorn?' He said as his anger welled up from deep inside. He picked up a bottle of after-shave that was on the shelf and smashed it hard on the floor.

'Oi! I hope that wasn't mine,' Steve's voice bellowed from the bedroom, 'that was a present from me Mum.'

A present from his Mum. Vince thought of his own Mum and felt wretched. She had always been good to him. Tried to protect him from his dad who was always drunk or just plain angry. She even took most of the beatings for him as well. He remembered that. Why did she do that? He never understood and it only made his contempt of women grow. He had held her in contempt for her kindnesses to him. He spurned her affection and in his turn he treated her as badly as his father had done. Like father like son. It was becoming plain to Vince now just what had motivated his mother to act as she did, but he had been too blind and angry to see it when she was alive. She had loved him. She hadn't liked being beaten or ignored or abused. She had taken it out of love for a boy who hurt her just as much as the man she had married. Vince sank into the hot bath and wept, for himself, for his mother and for all his wasted life.

CHAPTER 16

'We're going to Palma today by train, want to join us?' Cathy said, 'I love trains, oh, this is going to be so exciting, it's a wooden one, you know, over a hundred years old, please say you'll come Gill, I hate it that you stay in all the time.'

'I'm OK, Cathy, you go and enjoy yourself and bring me back a souvenir.'

Gill's confidence had had a huge hole knocked in it. She felt that she had been stripped of her outer coating - the one she used to protect herself. It had left her bare and vulnerable just as if her entire skin had been removed to expose raw nerves and sinews open to the infections of the world. By shutting herself away, she thought that her wounds would heal quicker, that she would be able to cope once more with being just Gill.

'Aren't you coming down to the town to see us off at least, Gill?' Cathy was being very insistent and starting to get on Gill's nerves even though she knew she meant well.

'Not today, Cathy, I don't feel too well, best stay here and rest I think, you have a great time, I may go out tomorrow.' But of course, tomorrow was never going to come, not as far as Gill was concerned. *How can I join in with other people?* she thought, *why should I put on a pretense of being normal? I just want to fade away, I don't deserve to exist, I feel so worthless.*

What troubled Gill the most was she knew that she might just need someone's help. Gill had always been the one who helped, not the one who was helped. Her mother was the same and between them they had become known as the saving angels – always there for others, never too tired or too troubled to deny anyone their support. They went to the aid of anyone who asked or seemed to need them. Perhaps this was why Gill had chosen a profession as a trauma nurse where she could protect the weak and vulnerable but now what she wanted most of all was to be left alone. She resented the constant interruptions of the others asking her for her opinion on things or trying to get her to join in their activities. Even Mel for whom she was always available to support and protect was getting on her nerves. So, Gill decided to shut herself away in a world of her own, ignoring the others whenever she could.

Gill's withdrawal didn't help Rachel either who needed someone other than Cathy to talk to about her own inner wrangling. Despite being occupied with Andy, Rachel was also tormented by fears of a different kind. Her pain grew each day as she became more and more infatuated with Cathy. Her obsession almost overwhelmed her sometimes. Sharing a room with her object of desire was a torment and she took to hurting herself whenever she had a lustful thought about the girl who was innocence itself. Causing herself pain by pinching or biting herself redirected her thoughts at least for a moment.

She muttered to herself under the drowning sound of the shower. 'Why can't I stop it? Why do I have to? I love her, I want her. Is that so bad? Why? Why? Why indeed? I need to feel her touch, her caress, her warmth next to me…please stop this torture, I can't take it any more…'

'Are you OK in there? Stop talking to yourself and hurry up, we've got to meet the boys in half an hour, remember?' Cathy cheerfully shouted through the closed bathroom door, oblivious to the torment which Rachel was going through inside, oblivious to the part she played in it all. Cathy was the innocent and also the cause, innocently, of Rachel's torment.

Andy seemed to be patient and understanding about Rachel's behaviour, but he was also confused. She seemed fine when there were just the two of them but as soon as Cathy and Jon appeared Rachel changed and became quiet and preoccupied. He sensed she was a very passionate person but felt that years of self-restraint had left her uptight and inward about her feelings and desires. But he found her even more irresistible because of this. In a perverse way, he saw it as a challenge to make her admit her feelings for him. He was sure she did find him attractive and fun to be with. He knew he wanted her in his life and not just for a holiday fling.

Rachel was trying valiantly to appear in control - to keep up the façade. *Stiff upper lip and all that*, she thought, *Dad would be proud of me, except he wouldn't understand why, any more than I do. I envy him his no-nonsense world, this is one of those curtain-therapy moments*, she laughed to herself, *I can hear him now, "pull yourself girl!" then he'd change the subject and that would be that, conversation over.* Rachel sighed as she thought of him and then looked over at Cathy and sighed again, not knowing what to do or which way to turn for help.

Cathy had her own problems. Her relationship with Jon was deepening. *I've never felt like this before, it's frightening me*, she thought, *I feel so confused, it goes against everything Dad taught me, other people don't seem to have a problem with this sort of thing, I'm so stupid, why can't this be OK for me too? If it's dirty and sinful then why do I want it, want Jon so very much? It can't be wrong,* she thought of what it would be like to be with Jon, *he's a good man, I know he likes me, at least, I think he likes me,* she looked at Jon as the train to Palma rumbled along the single track which cut through the mountains. Jon turned and smiled at her and squeezed her hand which made her feel both elated and confused at the same time.

During the day, she made frequent trips to the Ladies to give herself a chance to calm down. This happened so often that Rachel even asked if she had cystitis.

Most of the other girls' problems went unnoticed by Mel. She divided her time between visiting Iain, spending time fussing over Gill and walking through the hillsides behind the resort. Her inner turmoil was causing her discomfort but not pain. She felt she was coming out of a great freeze and like toes which have been frozen from playing too long in the snow, the gradual return of feeling caused a tingling sensation which bordered on painful but brought with it a relief that sometimes overwhelmed her.

Her time with Iain was a mixed blessing, as sometimes he seemed interested but other times cold and distant. She was also careful not to ignore her friend Gill in her time of need. This appeared to the other two girls as if they were being ignored or shunned and could only think it was jealousy due to their having found such great guys to spend their time with. But Mel wasn't really giving the two girls a second thought. She was so wrapped up in her changing feelings towards Iain. She felt like holding back, like walking away and forgetting the whole affair but somehow, he drew her to him. He wasn't doing anything positive to cement their relationship or cause Mel to want him so much, on the contrary he was only ever helpful and charming. This confused Mel. He never tried to seduce her or take advantage of her in any way. He would always greet her enthusiastically when she called but never called her himself. She was doing all the running and found herself running faster and faster in her almost relentless pursuit of this man who was very affectionate when they were together but who seemed not to be bothered if she called or not.

Gill had noticed the changes in her best friend.
'Who'd have thought you'd become quite the man-chaser, Mellissa Wright. What's come over you?'
'I hadn't noticed I was chasing him,' Mel said but looked away from Gill. 'I like him and want to spend time with him. He's very charming…'
'Yeah, and so laid back about the two of you as to be almost horizontal. But at least he isn't a predator and that's refreshing,' Gill's eyes glazed over as the hurt came flooding back to her and she turned over on the sunbed to compose herself. The struggle to overcome her feelings of despair and worthlessness was exhausting her. She would sometimes breath out as far as she could and hope she never breathed in again. But this never worked for more than a few seconds. Even though Gill tried to deny it, her inner strength was still there. She knew she was building herself again, reinventing herself. The Gill, which it had taken two and half decades to perfect, was gone in a pile of ashes, out of these ashes, like a phoenix, she was determined to rise, new, pure, unsullied and stronger than ever.

CHAPTER 17

Change was not just confined to the four girls. The men, involved with them, were also going through changes that unsettled them. Each had been touched in some way by their encounters with the young women they had met just over a week ago. Hard determined men who had built their lives on solid ideas shaped by peers and family alike.

Vince's change was perhaps the most dramatic. Steve could not understand him at all. His mate had become someone else, if he didn't know better, he would have sworn he had been taken over by aliens.

'What the hell's gotten into you? We're supposed to be on holiday to get a great tan, drink ourselves silly and get laid as often as possible, that's what holidays are about, remember? Since you met that Spanish bird, you've been a pain in the arse.'

Vince winced, 'I'm just not in the mood, stop nagging me, you're like a mother hen sometimes Steve, I need a drink, coming or what?'

'You can get drunk on your own mate, if you're going to be such a miserable git, at least me and the boys are trying to have a good time on this holiday. God knows we saved up long enough, but it's the last time I'm going to let

The Thompson Twins organise anything, I only came along because it was cheap, and they convinced me it was going to be fun. All sun, sea and rich women or something like that, and what did we end up with? A fucking awful cheap hotel, hardly any night life and where's the women? That's what I want to know, and now to top it all, you're playing the grouch. I'm going to find Trev and Simon, at least they're up for anything and for quiet blokes, they can bloody well drink anyone under the table, in a word, they're more fun you are, God help us! See you around.' Steve left their room and headed off to find his mates.

All in all, the holiday was turning into a disaster, but Steve was determined he would get at least one shag out of it. 'There must be at least one shag in this place,' he said to the other two at the English pub bar along the front from the hotel, 'we just haven't been looking in the right places.'

'Better try the morgue then,' was Trevor's reply as he downed another cold lager in one.

Vince made his way down to the hotel bar, a dreary place that was dimly lit even at midday. He was still troubled by the thoughts he'd started to have after his ordeal with the Buggery Twins. Memories that had started to flood back to Vince caused him to wake up in cold sweats over the past few nights. He tried to blot them out with drink, but nothing seemed to help. He just kept hearing the sound of his mother sobbing after his father had been on one of his sessions. He could remember coming downstairs one night and finding her curled up on the floor in the corner of the kitchen, blood streaming from her nose and her face showing the beginnings of a black eye. He remembered just standing there and wondering why she had let him do it. What was wrong with her? Had she no self-respect? He also remembered the loathing he had for her for allowing herself to be treated that way. It was at that moment that he had shown all his contempt for her by telling her that she had probably deserved it and then going back upstairs to bed.

Vince had been sixteen when she had eventually found a way out of her miserable existence. The family doctor had recorded death by misadventure, but he knew that she had meant to end it. The doctor had treated her cuts and bruises too often not to understand her pain and torment, and when he had broken the news to Vince and his father about her death, he had seen only too clearly the cold empty looks in their eyes.

'So, who's going to look after us now then?' was all that Vince's father had said, 'the selfish bitch!' He had returned to watching the football on the TV. Vince had remembered standing there, thinking much the same thing but afterwards found out that the harsh reality of living with his father was that he was now going to be the punch bag instead of her. Vince had packed his bags the day of the funeral and had not been back since.

Jon and Andy had had much different lives. Their father was a sports coach and their mother a teacher. They had grown up with outdoor pursuits and long holidays to learn the values of family life. As twins they had lived as one, dressing and acting as well as looking the same and loving to confuse people who couldn't tell them apart. They had even chosen the same subjects at school and the same course at university. After they had graduated, they had been lucky enough to get jobs in the same health club in Muswell Hill in North London, not far from their parents' home, but the harsh reality of working with people like Vince had made them realise just how lucky they had been.

Meeting the two girls had turned their holiday around. Jon was completely smitten by Cathy. He found her like a breath of fresh air, so pure and honest. Andy had not been so sure about Rachel, but Jon had begged him to give it a try. Andy had found that the more he knew about Rachel, the more he actually liked her. She was good-looking and always immaculately dressed. She was intelligent and so organised - perhaps a bit too organised at times. He sensed she was a passionate creature. He just didn't know if she felt the same about him, as she was so often preoccupied.

Meanwhile in the kitchen of his villa, Iain thought about Mel's growing affection for him. The trouble was, even after their little chat in Juan's, he was still not sure he wanted a relationship. *I've got commitments, I've got to travel a lot, spend a lot of time on business, especially if I want to keep ahead of the pack.* He paused and picked up a bottle of the wine Miguel, Juan's brother, had sent over and looking at it, he thought about the love that had gone into making it and put it back down on the counter, a*nd I especially don't need to be tied down with a long-distance relationship, I really don't.*

Even though Iain thought Mel was very pretty, he knew she obviously had problems which she covered up by eating too much. Food was Mel's addiction but what about his? *Well, I work too hard and too long and it makes me a lot of money,* he smiled, *but money doesn't keep you warm at night and doesn't keep you company when things go wrong and why have money if you don't have anyone to spend it with?.*

CHAPTER 18

Rachel lay on her bed. The heat and glare of the Spanish summer had got to her, and she felt faint and drowsy. This together with the emotional ups and downs of this holiday had left Rachel worn out. She hoped that the dimness of the bedroom would relax and calm her nerves. She had become hyper-active at one point earlier in the day when they had missed the train back from Palma and had to exchange their tickets for the next one, getting the last four seats available. This small event had made her feel that she was losing control, which had sent her into a panic.

She was also panicking about her feelings towards Cathy which had intensified over the last few days. That and spending time with Jon and Andy only served to further confuse her and cause her to develop a permanent stress headache. *I like Andy a lot,* she tried to convince herself, *I might even fall in love with him...but then there's Cathy, sweet innocent Cathy, she needs me.* Rachel turned over on the bed and held her head in her hands. 'What shall I do? What can I do?' she said out loud.

'What can you do about what, Rach?' Cathy entered the room and was looking at her friend in confusion. 'Don't tell me the heat is making you talk to yourself now.'

'I was just thinking about what we could do tomorrow.' Rachel composed herself quickly, not wanting Cathy to see her torment. 'This heat is almost unbearable. Why did we come here in the first place?'

'For the good weather, what else? You know how we Brits are — we always complain about the weather no matter what it's like. It's our national pastime. Well, I'm going to take a cool bath. How about you? Let's share one, eh? I can't leave you here moping around,' and she went into the bathroom and started to run a bath before starting to undress. As she slid her T-shirt over her head Rachel became mesmerised by her body. Cathy's slim silhouette stretched as she pulled the soft jersey cotton from her body, her firm skin looked so touchable that Rachel found herself aching to reach out and caress its softness and run her hand over her curved outline. Cathy seemed oblivious to all the attention she had excited in her roommate and continued to unbutton her cotton skirt and let it fall to the floor around her ankles. Her legs were smooth and just developing a good tan. She was wearing crisp white cotton underwear beautifully matching with a lace trim. They seemed virginal and Rachel thought how appropriate they were for such a divine and innocent creature as Cathy. Rachel stood up and went over to her friend.

'Let me help you with that,' she said and undid Cathy's bra from behind, feeling her softness.

'Thanks, Rach. You're so considerate. I really love sharing with you,' and she turned to Rachel and embraced her, her firm breasts pressing against Rachel's ample chest with only Rachel's thin cotton shirt between them. Rachel didn't know how to respond but put her arms around Cathy and hugged her closer, wanting the two of them to melt into each other and become as one.

'I'll check the water. You get undressed. This'll be so refreshing and such fun.' Cathy said in her usual bubbly voice.

'Yes, it will be. I'll get ready.' Rachel was almost in a

state of hyperventilation as she tried furiously to push thoughts out of her mind. *It's wrong to spoil such innocence. It's almost immoral,* she thought. *I'd be taking advantage of her trust.* She couldn't control the thoughts racing through her mind. 'I have to stop this, but I can't,' Rachel blurted out loud.

'What was that? I can't hear with the water running' Cathy called from the next room.

'Nothing Cathy, I just got my bra caught, that's all.'

'Oh, let me help you then, that's what friends are for' and she proceeded to help her friend undress. Rachel felt helpless to stop her or to help her, so she just let her continue. Had she been a man her feelings would have been very evident, but Rachel's only sign of her increasing arousal was her shortness of breath and her feeling of weakness.

Rachel stood naked before her friend.

'There, all done, let's dive in.'

'Sounds good to me,' Rachel managed to utter and followed Cathy to the bathroom. Cathy had lit some tea-lights and switched the light off. 'This'll make it cooler than having that bright light on in here. Lucky the room doesn't have a window.'

The two girls felt the coolness of the water envelope them. It gave temporary relief to Rachel who bathed herself in its cleanness and started to unwind herself from the tightly strung ball she had become. The room was sensual but in a calming way and the flicker of the tea lights gave a soft glow. The two girls looked at each other. Cathy knew that somehow Rachel had awakened in her feeling of belonging and love, which she so needed. She felt a certain attraction to Rachel but didn't really understand the true implications of it. She only knew that Rachel meant a great deal to her. On this holiday she had had several feelings towards people that she had not had previously. Jon had also become very important to her, and she loved being with him and holding his hand and when he kissed her, she felt a glow rise from deep within her.

'How does it feel when Andy kisses you?' Cathy asked

'It's very nice. He is a good kisser, I guess.'

'What makes him a good kisser then?'

'Well, he's gentle and sensual and seems to want to kiss me. He doesn't seem to be using a kiss to get something else. He just seems genuine when he touches me. I guess that makes a good kisser, but how about Jon? Spill the beans on him then.'

'Well, I don't really have much to compare him with, but he does make me feel all tingly when he kisses me.' Cathy giggled just like a schoolgirl talking to her mates about that first encounter with a boy.

'Sounds nice. What does he do when he kisses you?' Rachel enquired

'He holds me close as if he knows I might fall over or something. That's nice. I like that. Then he moves closer with his face and closes his eyes.'

'Do you close your eyes?'

'I do eventually, when I feel the tingling start, I don't want any distractions when he touches my lips and presses very gently against them. I never know really what to do, I feel such a clot at times, I wish I had had more experience, at my age no one believes me when I say I haven't had any experience with boys. I feel really stupid.'

'You're not stupid, Cathy, you're perfect, and any man who gets you to keep for his own will be a very lucky man indeed. I would envy him.'

'Really? Wow, you are such a good friend. I wish sometimes you were a boy, and we could be a couple. I think you would be such a good lover.'

'You never know. Be careful what you wish – it could come true. And Rachel boldly but cautiously put her hand on Cathy's thigh.

The two girls looked at each other and communicated only by their eyes. Rachel dared to move her hand further up Cathy's thigh and feeling no repulsion or resistance from her, Rachel caressed her soft wet skin. Cathy continued to look at Rachel as if in a trance before moving until they sat entwined in each other. Cathy held out her hand and caressed Rachel's cheek. She moved her hand down with whisper lightness until her hand hovered over Rachel's breast.

'Shall we get out?' Rachel eventually managed to say, and they went into the bedroom. As they lay down on the bed, Rachel wrapped her arms around Cathy protectively while Cathy entwined her leg between Rachel's and snuggled close to her friend.

'Are you OK about this, Cathy. I don't want to do anything which you are not happy about.'

'I'm fine. I feel safe with you, Rachel. I want us to be close. I think I have for some time but didn't know what it was I was thinking.'

Cathy looked at Rachel who bent her head forwards and touched her lips, they pressed their naked bodies together, still wet from the bath, their wetness spread over them like a soft wave on the beach. They only wanted to melt together as one, soaked in their attraction and passion for each other.

A faint knock on the door went unheard by the lovers and Mel popped her head around the door to tell the girls that Gill and she were back from the pool and to ask if they wanted to come down to the bar. She was met with a sight, which was she found totally unexpected.

'Oh! Sorry!' said Mel and closed the door quickly.

'What's the matter?' said Gill when Mel walked into the kitchen. 'You look as if you have seen a ghost.'

'Not a ghost…very real…very real, but very unexpected. I think I need a drink, and a sit down.'

'Mel, are you alright? Are Rachel and Cathy alright? What's going on?'

'Something which has been brewing for some time, I'm

afraid Gill,' came the reply from the doorway of the girls' room. Rachel and Cathy stood covered in their dressing gowns and walked over to Mel.

'Sorry if we shocked you,' said Rachel, 'but we didn't hear you knock. What did you want?'

'Well, that seems irrelevant now but perhaps an explanation instead.'

'For what? We were only fulfilling our needs, that's all, in the privacy of our own room.'

'How long has this been the case then, Rachel?' Mel enquired.

'Wait a minute, how long has what been the case? What the hell's going on? Have you two been doing drugs because if you have you can bugger off out of this apartment right now.' Gill had become totally confused but felt it was serious and was annoyed that everyone else seemed to know exactly what was happening except her.

'Calm down, Gill,' Rachel retorted. 'It's not drugs.'

'Then do you mind telling me what the hell it is?'

'Gill...well, Rachel and Cathy were ...um...touching one another...' Mel tried to explain but the words failed her.

'We were making love,' Cathy's voice cut through the tension like a cool breeze and calmed everyone down.

Gill looked at her, then at Rachel, then at Mel then flopped down onto one of the bar stools in the kitchen. 'I need a sit down.'

'How about we all sit down.' Cathy announced. Her sense of practicality was overwhelming, and everyone complied with her idea.

'Has this been going on long?' enquired Mel.

'About an hour if you count the bath.' Cathy seemed to have become a completely changed woman and was taking the scene remarkably calmly. 'We do love each other, and we weren't hurting anyone, please don't get upset Mel - or you Gill, we're still the same as we were but, well, we have found out something else about ourselves.'

'Did you have to find out when we were just next door?' Mel couldn't get the image of the two of them together out of her mind. All she could see was the sight of two female bodies intertwined. It would have been bad enough if it had been one of the girls and a bloke but somehow this twist on things made Mel feel very vulnerable and uncomfortable. 'Do the boys know about this?'

'Not yet,' said Rachel, 'But I suspect we'll tell them something eventually. We still love them as well. It is possible to swing both ways, you know.'

'So, I've heard but never this close to home,' Gill had regained her composure. 'Why did it happen?'

'Why does anything happen?' Rachel said indignantly. 'It's natural, you know, to have feelings towards fellow human beings, we aren't hurting anyone, just like Cathy said. We aren't saying join us for a group leso gang bang or anything…'

'No, true. But this is still a shock and see it from Mel and my point of view. It's unnerving, Rachel, one minute we think we're all after the same thing then we find you two are finding it a little nearer home. I feel a bit intimidated, frankly, but I know that that's my problem and not yours. This will take some time to sink in and for us to be able to feel at ease about it. You're our friends and we only want what's best for you, so if this makes you happy, then great, but it is a shock to us as we had no idea….'

'Neither did we really until this holiday. This place is certainly causing some upheavals all around. You've become morose and inward Gill and Mel has become more elusive than the scarlet pimpernel,' Rachel said. 'I don't know what's in the water, but I think we should stop washing in it let alone drinking it.'

'You're right,' Gill said, 'we have all changed, perhaps for the better' she looked down and added 'and perhaps for the worse.'

'Gill, don't blame yourself, you had nothing to do with

what happened to you,' said Mel to defend and protect her friend.

'No, perhaps not, but I do have everything to do with how I've reacted to it.'

'Reacted to what?' Rachel picked up that there something that the other two girls were not saying. 'What's happened, Gill?'

'She doesn't want to talk about ...'

'Yes, I do, Mel. Thank you for trying to protect me but if I don't admit this to others, how am I ever going to admit it to myself. Vince raped me, on our first night here on holiday and I've had a hard time coming to terms with it.' Gill stopped speaking and walked over to the window.

The strain of having announced what had happened to her was very intense and the physical act of moving helped her to dissipate her tension. Rachel and Cathy looked at each with disbelief. Gill who was so together and in control and sure of herself had changed. To hear why was shocking. The two girls looked at Mel who sighed and not knowing what to say or do, simply looked away.

It was Cathy who eventually broke the silence. 'Well, I think we all need several cocktails after all that. Pool side bar it is then.'

Gill smiled as she looked out over the bay. *Cathy's changed,* she thought. *It's usually me who says let's go for a drink and here I've been upstaged by dear little Cathy.*

'Great idea, Cathy.' Gill said. 'Come on you two lovebirds, get dressed or we may be charged with running a leso brothel or something. You're right, there are strange things happening to all of us, but whether that's good or bad, I don't know. That's up to us.' She strode towards her bedroom and turning she added, 'but one thing we must be sure of and that is no matter what happens, no one and nothing must ever break us up as friends. Is that a deal?'

'It's a deal,' the others said together.

'We're never going to live this down, are we?' said Cathy.

'Not a chance,' Mel said. 'And last one down, buys the drinks.'

'Oh, a challenge, I love a challenge,' Rachel said, and the four girls almost fell over themselves to see who could get ready first.

CHAPTER 19

The following evening Rachel and Cathy went out to meet the boys as usual, Rachel was up to her usual antics of organising and as this was going to be their last evening together before they went home, she had arranged something extra special.

'We'll be off now. Have a great evening. See you two later,' Rachel whisked Andy away to give each couple a chance to have some time alone together.

'Are you warm enough? The breeze has really picked up this evening.' Jon said as they walked along the front.

'I'm fine thanks. I think I'm shivering a bit, but it's more from nerves than anything else.' Cathy said, 'I'm not used to being alone with a boy.' She looked at the ground.

'There's nothing to be scared of. I wouldn't hurt you for all the world. I love you.'

He moved closer to Cathy and put his arm around her protectively. She snuggled closer to him and nuzzled her face in his chest. He smelt good – warm and safe, her heart skipped a beat. *Wow!* she thought, *this only happens in romantic novels but it's happening for real...unless I've got a heart problem, oh dear,* she touched her chest reflexively.

'When did you say you have to be back at the apartment?' asked Jon

'Tomorrow,' Cathy said.

'Oh! So, this was decided when?'

'Rachel arranged it all this afternoon. Didn't Andy tell you? Perhaps she forgot to tell him as well.' Cathy laughed, 'that's Rachel for you.'

'Well, where are you going to stay?'

'I suppose I'll have to stay in Andy's bed if that's alright with you. I feel silly now that you didn't know, I've even brought my nightie and toothbrush, does it seem rude of me? I'm sorry.'

'No, no problem if you're OK with it. Well, it gives us a complete evening to do with as we please. What do you fancy?'

Cathy smiled. If only she could say what she was really thinking and answer 'YOU!' She turned away from Jon to hide her anxiety. 'I don't mind. Just being with you is fun.'

'How about going back to the hotel bar for a change. It should be fairly quiet there,

'Yeah, that sounds great.'

The hotel bar however was crowded with a large group of young men from a factory somewhere in the Midlands on one side of the room and an equally large group of young women from a Merseyside hospital on the other. The ensuing chaos was deafening as the two groups vied for the loudest karaoke song and monopolised the whole bar.

'On second thoughts, let's take some drinks back to the room and see if there are any good films on TV,' Jon said.

Jon and Andy's room was quite spacious if basic, it had two double beds, an ensuite bathroom and a large TV with satellite channels.

'I'll just use the loo. See what's on the TV. A film might be good even if we have to pay to view, it's our last night so let's splash out,' Jon said and disappeared into the bathroom to gather his thoughts. *Here I am in a bedroom with the most beautiful girl I've met in ages, what the hell am I going to do? She's so adorable, but so innocent. Control, Jonathan, old boy, control. Yeah, right!'* He splashed cold water on his face and looked at himself in the mirror. *You can handle this.*

Cathy found the remote control and flicked through until she found the pay to view channels. She had rarely looked at these channels as her father did not approve of the commerciality of such things let alone the content of much of it. He had always said that if you had to pay for it, then it was bound to be bad for you or immoral or corrupt. Cathy smiled at the absurdity of his logic sometimes and shook her head in her own disapproval of him. 'He will not spoil my holiday. He will not spoil my holiday,' she repeated over and over under her breath, she was sick of his ideas influencing her own, suffocating her every time she found him creeping into her thoughts. 'You're twenty-one years old and it's about time that you formed your own opinions, Cath, my girl,' she mumbled until she had half convinced herself it was true.

The selection of films was not extensive; there were a few Disney type things for the kids, an American thriller, a slushy movie she had seen with her Mum last year in the cinema (unknown to her father) and then at least five sex films. The clientele of the hotel was evident. She browsed the write-ups of these films and started to laugh at the absurdity of the story lines. Then she came across one which did seem to at least have a story, so she pressed the preview button and before her was a scene she didn't quite know how to handle.

'Is that even possible?' she said to herself, just as Jon came out of the bathroom and shocked by the display of group sex on the screen, tilted his head and replied,

'I'm not sure, but I guess it could be.'

Cathy dropped the controls in surprise and embarrassment. 'Oh, I didn't hear you. I was just looking through the movie list. Sorry.'

'Don't be sorry. We're both adults and sometimes these films can be quite funny, if a little hard to believe. We can watch whatever you want.' Jon looked at Cathy who returned his gaze. Inside her head a battle raged. She was curious and did want to see this film, but those voices were shouting to her that this was evil, wrong, dirty. She looked straight at Jon and tried to read his mind. Did he have thoughts like hers? Did he have to fight his conscience like she did? Or was he free to think and do what he wanted? Was that because he was boy? Or because he had control of his thoughts and his life? The inner turmoil was tearing her apart and the look of panic had set on her face.

'We can watch whatever you like, Cathy. It's only the two of us. You look scared to death. A film like that though may have some effects on me, I can't deny that.'

'Can we talk a bit instead?' Cathy said.

'Yes of course,' Jon sat down next to Cathy on the bed.

'I...like you a lot, no...I love you, oh dear, I find it hard to express myself sometimes. I feel things with you that I've never felt before, and I am scared,' Cathy got up and started to pace around the room. This was going to be harder than she had thought. 'I'm scared of what we might do, I'm scared of what I might do. I need your help. I'm still learning to handle all this emotional stuff. I feel like a kid sometimes, I'm so thick when it comes to love and all that. I've never been with a man, and I'm scared and a bit annoyed about that too. Can you understand?' she came and sat down next to Jon.

'Yes, I can. I can assure you I'm not the sort of man who jumps into bed with every girl who comes his way. In my job, I often have women falling all over me but frankly I'm not interested, I want to have a relationship which means something, I'd like our relationship to mean something. You're so special,' he held her hand, 'I can't believe my luck sometimes when you look at me and smile and when you kiss me – wow! I would wait forever for you. I love you, Cathy. You're all I have ever dreamed of.'

They sat in silence for a minute to let all that had been said sink in before Cathy said quietly, 'Kiss me!' and she leaned forward to touch Jon's lips with her own. 'I...think I'm ready.' She softly giggled her girlish giggle that Jon found so endearing.

They discarded their clothes in silence and lay naked under the thin covers of the bed. Jon dimmed the lights and switched off the TV. The couple lay close and silent, their breathing was the only sound they could hear. They looked at each other and held their gazes as they explored each other's skin and felt the curves and textures of each other bodies.

Cathy recalled her experience with Rachel the previous evening and felt that they were both exciting but somehow different. Their touch was personal, and she wondered if that was just because they were different sexes or if all lovers felt different.

Jon gently touched Cathy as she shivered with anxiety at the prospect of what they were about to do. He sensed that she was ready and looked directly at her.

'Are you OK? Do you want me to go on? There's no pressure,' he reassured her.

She nodded. Thoughts flowed through her mind, she heard her father's voice, she thought of Gill, she thought about Rachel and then she pulled herself back to her thoughts about Jon. Here was a man she had known for less than two weeks whom she now shared her body with and gave herself to so openly, but she didn't seem to care worry anymore.

'Oh Cathy, I love you so much, I want to be with you like this for ever,' Jon breathed into Cathy's ear.

Jon wrapped his arm around Cathy beckoning her to snuggle up to him. He kissed her head.

'I hope I'm always the one, I want to be there for you always, to protect you,' Jon smiled at Cathy.

Cathy smiled. 'I'd like that too.'

In the morning, they didn't feel the awkwardness of the one nightstand, the embarrassment of having known someone yet not knowing them at all. They spent morning together and then it was time for Cathy head off to the airport with the others. She looked back at Jon as he waved goodbye to her from the complex as their taxi rambled away along the narrow streets and eventually arrived at the airport.

Cathy had come on this holiday as a scared and naïve girl but was flying home as a woman who knew that life was there for living after all. All she had to do was fight for what she wanted. That was not going to be easy, and she knew that she still had many rivers to cross and most of them were going to be deep and fast flowing.

CHAPTER 20

The flight home was very uneventful. The girls had their minds on other things of greater importance. They seemed to know that each had to have time to think and that this was as good a time as ever. Gill looked around her on the plane.

What were these passengers thinking about? Did they have fears and secrets as well which they desperately wanted to hide and forget? Did they have dreams and nightmares as she did? She sighed loudly and Mel turned to look at her.

'I'm OK,' Gill reassured her friend but deep down inside it still hurt, and she knew it was going to take a long time to heal her hurt, no matter how brave a face she put on it.

Mel went back to her magazine but looked at the pages with empty non-seeing eyes. She drifted away back to Iain. Was she in love with him or was it just an infatuation? She wasn't sure and the uncertainty was tearing her apart. Why couldn't she just let herself enjoy the feeling, experience the love and affection of another person? She wanted to stop the plane and make it turn back there and then but her logical mind took over again and spoke sense to her. Who was she kidding that anyone would ever really love her? It was a holiday romance pure and simple, fading by the minute as the miles opened up between them and the hot summer sun set over the horizon.

Rachel and Cathy spent the time in contemplation but held each other's hand for comfort and to help them realise that their relationship was real but not permanent. Was theirs a holiday romance too? A moment of folly, loss of control and infatuation. These were two women searching for something and someone to fill a void in their lives.

But what was the role for Jon and Andy? Rachel thought of Andy and their night together. The sex had been good – very good and she knew that he was a genuine and honest man who really wanted to be with her, but she was so confused with her own feelings. This confusion caused Rachel to squeeze Cathy's hand. Cathy looked at her friend and smiled.

'It'll be OK, Rachel. Everything'll be OK,' she squeezed Rachel's hand in return.

Eventually the plane landed, and the girls passed through the airport rigmarole in a trance. They picked up the Uber which Rachel had ordered and one by one they were deposited back in their own reality.

As Mel stood outside her home, the house looked drab and uncared for. Mel had not noticed this before but was now acutely aware of it. She was almost ashamed of it.

Well, I'm home at last, she thought, *back to the real world. But is this real or is it a fiction I've invented?* Mel took a deep breath and opened the front door, 'Mum, I'm home! Put the kettle on. I could die for a cup of tea.'

'Oh Mel, so good to have you home again. I'm quite lost without you, I think there's some milk in the fridge,' her mother said sounding enthusiastic, but her voice trailed off and Mel looked into her eyes and saw a vacant look that had become more evident over the last few years.

'Mum, have you been drinking again?'

'Oh, don't fuss so, I only have a little sherry to cheer myself up now and again.' *Now and again? Really?* Mel thought, knowing that it was getting more and more frequent lately. The signs were only too evident, the forgetfulness, the way the house had been left to fend for itself, her mother's constant tiredness. For some reason Mel felt she was losing her, that she was drifting away into another existence. Mel went to the fridge to get the milk only to find that the only offering smelt so bad that it almost made her throw up.

'I'll go down the shop and get some fresh. I think this is a bit past its best and it's nice to have fresh milk in tea, don't you think? Have you any food in for tonight? Doesn't seem to be anything in the fridge, I'll see what I can get. How about that?'

Mel's mother nodded in an absent way and went back into the sitting room and slumped herself down in her favourite chair. She stared across at the empty companion chair in the suite, the chair that had always been her husband's and had never been sat in since he left. Each week it was meticulously dusted and the cushions plumped up as if he were going to appear at any minute and sink down into it. Mel had pleaded with her mother on several occasions to allow her to buy a new suite and brighten up the house, but she had always met with an obstinate refusal. 'This is our family home, Mel. It's fine as it is' was always the reply, and that statement formed the end of any discussion on the subject.

Mel had noticed that since she had graduated and joined the bank, her mother had started to deteriorate. It was as if she no longer felt that she was as useful to her daughter. Her little girl, whom she had struggled to raise, to provide for by herself, was now a woman and she knew that one day she wouldn't need her at all. For someone who had devoted her life to her child this was a hard reality to come to terms with and not one she was coping with well.

Mel walked out into the fresh air and breathed deeply. The atmosphere in her home was becoming unbearable and it was a relief to be back outside. She walked briskly to the M&S Simply Food across the main road at the petrol station and bought milk and bread and two bars of chocolate as a treat.

Shall I get fried chicken from the takeaway on the corner or walk down the hill to get a McDonald's? She stopped and sighed, *I'd rather a Big Mac but then I'll have walk up the frigging hill again. Shit! It shouldn't be this hard to get something to eat. But Mum likes the Filet'o'Fish Meal, so suck it up and get one for her, she needs cheering up. Besides, I need one of those suck-yourself-inside-out milk shakes like my life depends on it.* She strode off down the hill like a woman on a mission and after having to wait forever to get the food, she returned up the hill although much slower, her knees and feet screaming at her by the time she got home.

Gill returned home to an empty house which was a novelty to her as her house was always bustling with friends, neighbours and relatives popping round to chat or scrounge something from her mother. The silence was eerie but welcome and Gill went straight up to her room and unpacked. She had noticed that she had become very fastidious since her ordeal, and it worried her that she might be turning into Rachel. She folded away the clean clothes which her mother had washed whilst she was away and put all her dirty holiday washing in the basket sorting the colours as her mother had asked all the inmates of the house to do in vain for years. Gill even put her suitcase away in the loft and then flopped down on the bed exhausted.

She gazed up at the ceiling, the same ceiling she had looked at since she was a child and wondered where she should go from here. Her world had changed, her world had been destroyed by one man's need to control and hurt. She was still angry about his motives and her own reactions; why hadn't she seen it coming? Why hadn't she been able to stop him? It was all her fault after all, and she began to flashback to that night and re-live it over and over again in the vain hope that eventually if she did this enough times it would change what had happened. She sat up and looked at her reflection in her dressing table mirror, the mirror she had used to help her first experiments with make-up, the mirror in which she had practiced her seductive look to impress the boys in school, the mirror she had gazed into when she first fell in love. This mirror had seen her life but had never judged her as she was now doing to herself.

'Mirror, mirror on the wall, who the hell am I anymore?' and she slammed her fists down on the glass top of the dressing table with such anger and frustration that it was a miracle it didn't break. It did hurt her hands though, and she winced with the pain, but realised it released her from the pain within for just a moment, long enough to breathe a fresh breath, a breath not contaminated by her inner turmoil and grief. She looked at her hands, they were red where the impact had taken place and now glowed with heat from their ordeal.

'Is that you Gill?' the reassuring voice of her mother drifted up from downstairs. Gill looked back at her reflection in the mirror, smiled and winked at herself and ran downstairs to greet her mother. Life had to seem to be normal. That was the Keane way after all.

Cathy walked in through her front door as quietly as she could. Her mother heard her enter however and popped her head around the kitchen door. 'Don't worry, he's not home from work yet. Did you enjoy your holiday?'

'Yes, thank you Mum. It was great, we met some really nice people and the resort was wonderful.'

Cathy's mum looked at her daughter and seemed to be reading between the lines. The woman who stood before her wasn't the girl who had left two weeks ago. She could only speculate as to what had happened to change her but prayed her husband would not be so astute as to notice. He was working a double shift today so he would be very tired when he got home, and she hoped that this would distract him from paying Cathy any real attention. She had lived on tenterhooks for years, waiting for the moment when Cathy would walk through the door a woman. She knew it would happen. In this world it was inevitable, not like her own world.

As a girl, Martha Lucus had been closeted away from harm, from reality, in a cotton-wool world and then unwrapped and presented for her husband on her wedding night, an ordeal she would never wish her daughter to experience. Her ignorance of men, life and sex had made the day, which she was supposed to remember with fondness for the rest of her life, an unpleasant and painful initiation into womanhood and married life.

Her husband for all his preaching was not a gentle man and his rough domineering of her innocence that night had cut her in more ways than one. He had preached to her about the sins of the body the whole time he was touching and what seemed to her examining, her body, making sure she was as pure as she had been made out to be. Then he had lain on top of her crushing her until she could hardly breathe and had forced himself inside her as a prize he had won and was now branding as his own. She had been thankful when it had lasted only a short while and he had rolled off her, kissed her forehead and told her she was a good girl, and that God would forgive her sins of lust and temptation. He also explained that it was her duty as his wife to endure this whenever it pleased him as this would also please God and she would bear him children for God's work.

She had lain in the darkness and had tried so hard to keep the tears from welling up in her eyes, trying desperately not to let them escape and trickle down her cheeks. She felt in her such hurt and humiliation that she had to hang on to any thread of pride and self-worth she had left.

She had always prayed that Cathy would find true happiness with a man, who would take care of her and be gentle and kind. She so much wanted to know if this was going to be the case, but dare she ask?

'Did you meet anyone in particular, then?'

'Oh, some people, that's all, Mum, just some people.' Cathy didn't feel easy talking to her mum about what had happened. She loved her mum and trusted her more than she did anyone else in the family, but she was also keenly aware that her mother took her vows to her husband very seriously and she couldn't be sure she wouldn't tell him any secret that Cathy chose to reveal. Her secrets from the holiday were too important and too personal to be ever told to her father. She lived in fear of him at the best of times, but if he knew what she and Jon had done let alone what she and Rachel had done, Cathy was not sure he would not kill her on the spot and claim that it was God's will and punishment.

'Very nice dear. I do so love you making new friends. Do they come from around here?'

"Yes, Barnet. They work at The Laboratory Health Club in Muswell Hill, they're fitness instructors, well at least Jon is, he's a graduate Mum.'

'That's nice, dear.'

'Rachel and I hope to see them again sometime. I must go and unpack now. When's dinner this evening if Dad's at work?'

'We can eat whenever you like, I've cooked a roast chicken with fresh baked bread and a salad, I know it's your favourite.'

'Thanks Mum, I've missed your cooking.' Cathy knew the way to make her mother happy and complimenting her on her cooking was a sure way to make her smile. Martha smiled as Cathy bounced out of the room.

Rachel paused before going into her house. She was still confused about everything that had happened on the holiday. Her feelings for both Cathy and Andy were at odds and she didn't know if she could survive the normal interrogation or 'debriefing' as her father put it, which was obligatory whenever anyone came home from being away. The whole family would have to sit down and listen whilst he asked endless questions about the trip, locations, people, activities. Rachel and her sister dreaded going away sometimes simply because the coming home would be such an ordeal. Rachel just wished that her father could lighten up and leave his work where it belonged. But her father had become so deeply obsessed with his work that he was also becoming a bore to his mates let alone a pain to his family. Rachel wondered why men often feel they have to live for their jobs. It didn't make sense to Rachel who had picked up several of his traits from having spent so long in his company. He would spend hours lecturing her in neatness, duty, organisation, planning until she couldn't switch off. She knew this infuriated her friends, but just couldn't help herself.

She took a deep breath and went into the house.

'Welcome back, Lieutenant,' her father bellowed from the study. 'Be with you in a few minutes. Just need to get this report finished for next week. Your Mother is in the sitting room watching some slushy movie or something.'

'Nice to see you too dad,' Rachel whispered under her breath and went into the sitting room where her mother was engrossed in her movie.

'Hi Mum,'

'Hello darling, interesting bit in the film; soon ends; speak then,' and she turned briefly to blow Rachel a kiss.

'OK. Is 'Becca in?' But her enquiry about her sister got no response so Rachel left the room and went upstairs to her room.

Rachel took off her travelling clothes and stood in front

of the full-length mirror in her room. She was pleased with what she saw.

'Not bad my girl, all those aerobics classes with Cathy did pay off in the end after all – no pain; no gain,' she quickly dressed in a casual sweater and tracksuit trousers and went back downstairs for the Colonel's version of the Spanish Inquisition.

CHAPTER 21

The following few days Mel went around in a daze. Her head was a maze of thoughts, ideas, fears and regrets. She didn't know who she was anymore, or what she wanted to be or do. She thought about Iain, but this only made her more confused. She went to see Gill to talk to her friend even though she knew Gill was still wrapped up in her own problems and had actually called in sick as soon as they had arrived back home from the holiday. She had wrestled with her conscience at letting the hospital down but couldn't think how she could deal with other people's trauma when she couldn't even process her own.

'I've been thinking about it, and I think I blame my mum for my weight problem,' said Mel.
'How can you say that? Your mum's always tried so hard to be there for you,' Gill was shocked at Mel's accusation.
'I don't think she did anything intentionally and I know she had a hard time after Dad left. I suppose food was the easiest thing to turn to,' said Mel upset that Gill should think she was ungrateful for all the sacrifices her mother had made for her.

'She was just doing what any mother would do,' said Gill. 'Just think about it – even now when we have more food in this country than we can eat, we still give chocolates or fruit or wine as gifts to say thank you or to say get well, to say congratulations or just to say anything at all.'

'I know. Hell, all this talk about eating is making me hungry.' Mel said convinced she'd heard her tummy rumble. But that empty feeling, Mel realised, was not due to a lack of food, but more to a gap in her life – a gap she'd tried to fill with food for years. Now, however, she knew that it never would. But would Iain help her any better? That was something she didn't know but desperately needed to find out.

'You're regressing,' said Gill looking Mel straight in the eye.

'I'm just thinking. My outlook on life is changing and I'm scared and a bit confused. I think I just feel a bit betrayed, that's all.'

'Who by?'

'By my mum,' Mel said, 'I know it sounds awful, but I've been thinking about my attitude to food. I think she sort of...well, manipulated me a bit.'

'How?' said Gill confused.

'I think she tried to make me dependent on her, you know, like killing me with kindness type of thing. If I was fat, I was less likely to find someone and leave her. So, she made me dependent on her. Whenever I felt sad, she gave me food; whenever I felt tired or cold, she gave me food; whenever I had a bad day in school or work, she gave me food. She even gave me food whether I had a bad day or not.'

'That was because that was all she could give you. You were poor remember?'

'Yeah, but all I really wanted was to feel wanted.' Mel's words cut the air like a knife. The stillness that followed was deafening.

'I always wanted you, Mel. You were my best friend. You still are,' said Gill.

'Thanks Gill. I know you care, and I do appreciate it. But don't parents really screw up your life?'

'That's a fact.'

'Anyway, I'm going to do it this time. I've found out where the nearest Slimming World Group is and I'm going on Tuesday come hell or high water.'

'Good for you! I wish I could just go to a class and solve my problems.'

'You could – it's called group therapy. Have you been to see the doctor yet?'

'No.'

'Gill, you promised you'd go as soon as we got back.'

'I know, but…'

'But nothing, I'll plague you until you do.'

'You'll have to join the queue with all the other things plaguing me in my life.' Gill looked away and her eyes started to fill with tears. She knew then that she was her own worst enemy and that Mel was her best hope of getting over all this, together with Maureen, her mum, but she couldn't dream of telling her what was wrong. This made her feel even more miserable than she was already and she knew that she had to do something but not just yet. *Maybe tomorrow when I feel I bit better,* she thought, *maybe tomorrow.*

CHAPTER 22

The following Tuesday evening at 6pm precisely, Mel took a deep breath and entered the hall. It had changed a great deal from what she remembered as a child. She had attended Sunday school at this church for over ten years from a sweet innocent five-year-old until at the age of fifteen when she had decided that religion was boring and there were much better things to do on a Sunday morning like sleep late or hang around with her friends. It seemed strange now coming back when she needed help once more, this time help of a different kind, emotional not spiritual, but perhaps they were more similar than she cared to acknowledge.

The hall still had bare floorboards, but it had had a lick of paint and there were now curtains at the windows and posters on the walls. These posters seemed to be a vain attempt to pass on the good news about life ever after to the non-believers who used the room for purely recreational purposes. Mel couldn't help thinking that the people who ran the Church were perhaps flogging a dead horse in this endeavour, but she did give them top marks for trying.

'Welcome,' said a well-built woman in her mid-forties

who had approached Mel, almost as if she could smell fresh prey. 'There are no strangers here, only friends you haven't met yet.'

Mel thought that this must be part of the diet as it was making her feel like throwing up there and then. 'Hi,' said Mel rather more timidly than she would have liked, but she thought this woman was scary in the extreme and seemed to be almost hyperactive in her mannerisms. Mel couldn't decide if it was genuine enthusiasm or a severe nervous disorder.

'I'm Betty. And you are?'

Mel could see that this whole experience was going to be painful, but necessary after her ordered little existence had been shattered by the holiday. Her first act of adapting to her new existence was coming to this slimming club. She hated the idea and a little voice inside her kept saying *'give it a few weeks and you'll be back to your old ways,'* but this time her attitude was different because this time, it was because she wanted to lose the weight. She wanted to get rid of her protective coat, in a word, she wanted to live.

Mel took a deep breath before she replied, 'I'm Mel and I'm fat and I want to be thin.' She had said this a little too loudly and all the other occupants of the room suddenly stopped their idle chatter and turned to stare at her. Mel felt ten years old again. She felt as she had felt at her first ballet lesson. She felt as she had felt at her first day in secondary school. She felt as she had felt on her first day at work. In short, she needed a bar of chocolate like her life depended in it.

'Good. It's nice to see such a positive attitude. I'll go through the plan with you and then we can weigh you and you can meet some of the other members.' Betty went through the plan and it surprised Mel how much she could eat and apparently still lose weight. She listened to the others recant their week and how Betty seemed to be able to control even the most pessimistic member into continuing to try, even though they'd put weight again that week and were close to giving up. Mel pondered that Betty's job was a mix of salesperson for the plan and Mother confessor for the pathetic. She did both well, and Mel decided to continue coming at least for a few weeks to see how it went. On the way home Mel stopped off at Lidl to get a few essentials such as wholewheat breakfast cereal, semi skimmed milk, fat free yoghurts and a few low-fat hot chocolate drinks just in case.

CHAPTER 23

The streets of London always mesmerised Iain as he strode confidently along Piccadilly towards Hyde Park. The balmy air of the summer evening was heady, and this added to his excitement of this occasion. He had chosen to go for the short walk along Piccadilly after visiting his favourite tailor, Henry Poole & Co in Saville Row then had cut through the Burlington Arcade, which he thought had become far too tourist-orientated for his liking. He had stayed chatting for far too long at Poole's but had managed to be measured for a new suit, a tedious task but so essential if you wanted to look your best, and to order some bespoke shirts into the bargain. Travelling as he did, seemed to put a strain on his clothes even more than his large physique managed to do but he loved good clothes and made sure that he only bought the best. Only the best of everything was good enough for him.

He had arranged a meeting over dinner with a small group of potential investors for a shopping centre development in Madrid he was putting together, and he had had to move heaven and earth to get them to agree to see him. He knew that only the Ritz would tempt them enough to attend. The development was going to be a state-of-the-art structure, and he was very excited about the whole project, but he still had to get some final financial backing in place so that the deal could be finalised.

As he reached the hotel he hesitated and wondered if he should have brought along some female company to help soften up the investors. Rich men always appreciate a good-looking woman to share dinner with and he usually arranged for one of his assistants to accompany him. Lucia was one of his favourites for the job as she was always very professional and so charming to his guests. The arrangement always worked well, and he was a little annoyed that she'd been unable to come to London with him this time as she was away in the States finishing the paperwork for another deal he had just tied up.

I'm either getting too good at this job or I'm working too hard, he thought as he climbed the steps of the hotel and taking a deep breath, he entered the hotel lobby and headed for the cocktail lounge to find his dinner companions.

The meeting went well, and they all dined on the best that the hotel was able to offer, which was very fine indeed. After several hours of drinking, talking and most of all eating they shook hands on a deal and Iain was able to retire to his room at the hotel, a happy man.

He stripped off and dived in the shower. The hot water peeled over his skin like a woman's hands, and he relaxed for the first time in days. He thought of his villa on Majorca and wished he were there now. He loved the tranquility and beauty of the island and the easy-going nature of the local people whom he called friends. He thought back to the girl he had rescued from those lager-louts earlier in the summer and he smiled.

She was stunning, he thought, *being with her was a breath of fresh air. I felt warm and safe somehow when I was with her, but she was only there for two weeks and I don't need any ties, I don't know how to reply to her texts,* he sighed and rinsed the shampoo from his thick hair, *perhaps I should have arranged to meet her on this trip, she'd have turned heads in the restaurant for sure with that flowing red hair and those beautiful green eyes.'* Iain found that he was getting more than a little aroused at the thought of Mel which only confused him more. *Iain Ferguson - you're a bloody idiot. But let's face it, I'm too busy to have a meaningful relationship and Mel is too good for a mere fling. If I had her, I'd want her forever.*

Leaving the shower, he climbed between the crisp cotton sheets of the huge bed and fell asleep, a sleep of fitful excitement and confusion.

CHAPTER 24

Over the next few weeks, Mel worked hard to lose the weight and succeeded in dropping a stone in a month. She felt ecstatic but found that her mother was starting to sabotage her. Sarah had taken to buying chocolate bars, crisps and fizzy drinks for no apparent reason as if constantly catering for some imaginary children's party. Mel simply binned the offending articles when her mother wasn't looking. The fridge was stocked with salad and lean meats and every room in the house had a bowl of fresh fruit in it. It started to resemble a greengrocer's shop at times.

'Am I looking baggy since losing all this weight?' Mel asked Gill one day. 'Should I join a gym perhaps?'

'You could do, but just not the one 'he' works at please.'

'No worries, I heard from Cathy that Vince packed in his job there last week and he's working for the council now, on the bins. Perhaps he'll put himself in the rubbish lorry too, now that would be a good thought.' Mel laughed to herself at the thought of Vince in the back of a refuse lorry flailing around whilst being crushed by the compactors. 'I think I'll go and see Jon or Andy next week for an assessment. They're having a special offer at their club waiving the joining fee. I still can't resist a bargain, and we all have to be careful with the pennies after all.'

'I suppose,' Gill said not really interested in Mel's goings on. She still had problems of her own and sometimes she resented Mel her cheerfulness. Mel had noticed this in Gill but decided to ignore it and not to pander anymore to Gill's moroseness. Mel did feel sorry for her, but she thought it was best to let Gill work through her feelings for herself for a while. If she tried to push Gill, she knew she would only make things worse.

In any case Mel had enough worries of her own. She was particularly worried about the increase in her mother's drinking. She had even discussed it with her grandmother when she had met her lunch earlier that week.

'Why does she feel she has to drink? It's so unlike her,' Mel said.

'Your mother is using the drink to fill a gap in her life. It's probably only a phase but let me know if it gets worse.'

'What do you mean by gap, Gran?'

'Your mother has been a tightly strung bow for years. Her love for you is just about all she has to keep her together. She knows that you're a woman now and that you've got your own life to live. Forgive her Mel. She's coped as best she could all these years. If you ask me she needs a new man in her life. Any suggestions? She's a good-looking woman and any man who caught her would be a very lucky man indeed.'

'I can't imagine Mum with anyone other than Dad.'

'No, and neither can she, and that'll be her downfall.'

At the time, Mel had thought that her grandmother was being overly dramatic, but she had begun to see a change in her mum, and it did worry her. But not enough to actually say anything to her yet. That was not the way in her family. If you had a problem, you kept it to yourself. No one ever discussed anything important. Even when her father had left, there was no real discussion of how they would cope, or what had really happened between her mum and dad. No one ever asked Mel how she felt about it. When Mel had tried to talk to her Gran, she'd been told to keep her chin up and just get on with it. At ten years old, that isn't always as easy as it sounds, and Mel had only Gill to confide in. In part this was why Mel had begun to think that the break-up of her family had been her fault, so out of guilt, she'd eventually stopped even talking to Gill about it.

Mel arranged to join to the gym and to see Andy for a fitness assessment at the gym.

'Tell me the worst, I know, I'm a hopeless case but I have to try something.'

'Don't be so hard on yourself. You're still young and your body can still pull itself together. It'll need discipline, but let's assess what you want to achieve first,' said Andy sympathetically. He had seen much worse cases in his career as a fitness instructor, but he was still positive enough to help people if they genuinely wanted to help themselves. Andy was by far the most empathic of the two twins and he often took things too much to heart as a result.

'How are you and Rachel getting on?' Mel said wheezing like some asthmatic having an attack, as she underwent a session on the step machine. She sounded more like a woman of ninety than a twenty-five-year-old and she realised how much she'd abused her body over the years.

'Rachel's wonderful. I love being with her. She's so in control of everything.'

'And that doesn't bother you?'

'No, I think it's great. She organises everything and all I have to do is sit back and enjoy it, she's so good at thinking up great activities and things.'

This amazed Mel, who just considered Rachel to be a complete pain in the arse most of the time, but if Andy and her were happy, then Mel was happy about it too.

'What do your mum and dad think of her? Have they met her yet?'

'Oh yes. We all went for Sunday lunch the other week. I think Mum's pleased we've both found such nice girls. She was always worried what we'd end up with. She's very conservative in her tastes. Everything has to be just right, so Rachel and her got on like a house on fire.'

'I've seen Rachel like a house on fire before – and you're saying they both survived?'

'Very funny, Mel, yes, they both survived. How about you and Iain? Rachel says he hasn't managed to get over here yet. He must be so busy.'

'Yes, he is, but we do talk on the phone a few times, and there's WhatsApp and Zoom and stuff, so it's cool, I'm pretty busy too, I want to get myself in shape before he sees me in the flesh again anyway, I want him to be so amazed at how I look - so we've got our work cut out – OK?'

'OK, you're the Boss,' Andy stood to attention and saluted Mel.

'Steady on – I'm not Rachel you know.'

Mel went to the gym every day after work. She pushed herself as she had never pushed herself physically before. She almost became obsessed, but she eventually decided that three times a week was quite sufficient and losing 2-3 pounds a week on her diet was also quite ample. Her figure improved but more importantly than that her general health and fitness grew in leaps and bounds. She felt so full of life that she sometimes found it hard to stop and her boss even remarked on her improved productivity.

The downside to this was that she realized that she hated her job. It was boring and mundane, and she started looking on recruitment websites for alternatives.

'There must be something better than this dead-end existence,' she said, 'I could be anything or anyone. Like...next to Iain on a deserted beach...completely naked.'

'Now there's a thought to conjure with,' Rachel said when Mel revealed this idea to her and Cathy at their usual Saturday coffee meeting.

'Oh, please stop it! I know you and your thoughts, I'm trying to enjoy this Ryvita and Marmite without throwing up, thank you,' said Mel struggling to swallow her snack as it was.

'How's Gill?' said Cathy.

'She wasn't feeling too special today, so she said to say hi, but she won't be coming,' said Mel with a mouthful of crispbread.

'What are we going to do about her?' asked Cathy

'I don't know. I've tried so hard but feel she's resisting me every step of the way.' Mel said. 'She's hurting herself you know. She's got so many bruises and little cuts on her arms, she always has to wear long sleeves. I was around her house the other day and she rolled up her sleeves to wash her hands and I saw them. When she realised that I'd seen them, she quickly pushed her sleeves down to hide them.'

'I noticed that she keeps going off into trances. She seems to be somewhere else.' Cathy had observed this in Gill a few times in the last weeks.

'We all know where she is when that happens.' Mel said and the others nodded in agreement.

'She needs professional help.' Rachel said

'How are we going to make her do that? She's just as stubborn as ever.'

The women all sighed but Mel knew that she had to do something. She'd have to make Gill seek help. The only question was how?

Later that day Mel decided to confront Gill. She went around to her house and after the usual pleasantries with Gill's mum, she went up to Gill's room to talk.

'You missed a good morning. Are you feeling any

better?'

'So-so,' was Gill's reply. 'I just want to be alone sometimes. That's all. Nothing wrong with that is there?'

'Nothing at all, but not when it happens all the time. We're worried about you Gill. We all want to help but sometimes I feel you push us away. It's at times like this that you need your friends more than ever and we're all here for you.'

'I know, and thanks, but just leave me to myself. I'll get over this. I just have to work it out for myself, that's all.'

'No, you don't and that's what I'm saying.' Mel was feeling awkward but knew she had to press on for Gill's sake. 'I think that you'd find it easier if you talked to someone about this. Someone who knows about these sorts of things and can guide you and help you.'

'I don't need anyone's help, OK?'

'You do, stop being so stubborn, we all need help sometimes, even you…before you destroy yourself,' Mel leant over and caught hold of Gill's arm and pushed her sleeve up to expose her wounds, 'look at yourself! Look what you're doing to yourself. Stop it Gill, before it's too late.'

Gill pulled her arm free from Mel's grasp and quickly covered up her arm. She was embarrassed that Mel had exposed her secret like that. She just wanted to forget. Her pain helped her to forget, but she didn't want anyone to know. She wanted to deal with this alone; she wanted to make everything go away. How could she do that if everyone knew about her?

'Please think about it Gill. I'll come with you if I can get time off work. Have you told your Mum yet?'

'God no, I can't tell her, she wouldn't understand, she's too busy, I don't want to disturb her, she cares for so many people she's too busy for me. I can do this on my own.'

'No, you can't. If you won't tell her, I will.' Mel knew that this was an ultimatum, which could possibly end her friendship with Gill, but Gill's health and happiness were more important. Mel was prepared to risk losing Gill if it meant saving her. Gill looked up at Mel with horror on her face. She felt she was being betrayed and to make things worse, it was by her best friend. The pain cut through her as surely as if Mel had stuck a knife in her heart. Gill panicked. Her eyes darted around the room. How could she get out of this situation? There didn't seem to be any way and eventually the panic started off a chain-reaction inside her which ended in her releasing her tension in a flood of tears. She sat on her bed and sobbed. Her face became contorted under the emotion that she was trying to handle. She just wanted to die that very moment.

Mel sat motionless and looked away from Gill. Her pain was too much to bear. She thought about what she had said and worried that it might have been the last straw for Gill.

'I'm sorry, Gill, I shouldn't have said that, forget I said it.'

Gill was silent which unnerved and frightened Mel even more. Gill looked awful. Mel wanted the old Gill back, and would have done anything to make it happen, but she felt helpless as if she were a little girl surrounded by adults all quarrelling and being angry and she couldn't do anything about it.

Gill drew in a deep breath. She looked up at Mel and said calmly and softly, 'I'll think about it. I will tell Mum but in my own time. I hear what you say. Thank you, Mel, you're a true friend. Could you leave me now? I'm a bit tired, as I didn't sleep well last night. I think I'll lie down for a while. Could you tell Mum on the way out that I don't want to be disturbed? I'll get my tea later after she's gone to work. Thanks Mel. I'll see you soon, ring you tomorrow, OK?'

'OK, Gill. That's fine. I'll tell your mum you're going to have a sleep.' Mel rose and kissed her friend on the forehead and whispered 'I love you. Get better soon.'

CHAPTER 25

After Mel left, Gill turned to her mirror. She saw how awful she looked, so she went into the bathroom. She knew that her mother would be going out to work soon and she decided to have a long hot bath. She settled into the warm foamy water. It soothed her. She knew she had a lot of thinking to do.

'I'm off to work now Gill, you'll have to get yourself something for dinner, I didn't have time to prep anything, sorry,' Maureen slammed the door after her.

That was typical of Maureen. She was always so busy helping other people, that she sometimes forgot to help those nearest to her including herself, but Gill didn't mind. Her mum was a saint as far as she was concerned.

Gill sat in the bath until the water had gone cold. The house had become quiet, but she loved its silence, it seemed to soothe her. She felt uncomfortable, so she got out and dried herself in a big fluffy towel. It made her feel safe for a moment and she smiled.

In her room she closed the curtains to keep out the dreariness of the evening. It had started to rain, and it looked cold and damp outside. Gill didn't want to feel cold or damp, so she climbed into bed. The duvet felt warm, and she wrapped it tightly around herself. The warmth and fatigue let her slip into a deep sleep.

When she awoke the house was in darkness, cocooned in her feather tomb, she had dreamed of being free from all the pain she felt every day, the pain of not knowing who she was anymore, the confusion of needing help but not knowing how to ask for it. But she realised it was only a dream, and she started to cry. She felt angry, then she felt sad, she simply didn't know how to control her feelings anymore. Her face contorted as she let out another silent scream, one which no-one would ever hear. It drained her of all energy, and she found her despair overwhelming.

'I can't cope, I can't live after this, I'm too afraid to deal with this and too ashamed to ask for help. God help me!' Gill shouted out loud. Her words reverberated around the empty house and echoed back to her blandly and cold.

There's no one there to help me, who am I kidding, there's not even God, she thought. *If God did exist, then why did he allowed this to happen to me?* She reached into the top drawer of her bedside cabinet and took out two boxes of tablets. She carefully opened all the blisters and arranged the tablets in small rows on the top of her cabinet. She counted them, twice.

This should be enough, Mum would know better than me, but I can't ask her, can I? No, I can't ask anyone. I need a drink,' Gill reluctantly got out of bed and went downstairs to the sitting room. She opened the dresser door and took out a bottle of vodka and a large tumbler. She didn't bother to measure it, she just filled the glass. She took a swig and winced at the taste. She liked vodka and Coke but neat, *God that's disgusting,* she thought, *why the hell am I drinking it? Dutch courage, why else.* She refilled the tumbler and took it back upstairs and shut her bedroom door. The tears started to run down her cheeks, she was feeling so desperate that she didn't know what to do.

'I don't want to die,' she said out loud to herself as if by telling herself she would change her mind. 'I just don't want to live either.' She picked up a tablet and put it in her mouth and swallowed then took a sip of the vodka to wash it down. She repeated the process several more times, the taste of the vodka jarring on her body like the poison it was. She began to feel drowsy, her eyes were sore, and she found it hard to open them properly, but she didn't care anymore. *What's the point*, she thought, *of caring for myself when no one else does?* She knew in her heart that this was not true, but in her altered state of mind, she'd convinced herself that she was indeed all-alone.

She started to drift off into sleep again. She dreamt about a little girl whom she felt she'd known once. A little girl who had good friends but was always alone. A little girl who dreaded going home for fear of what would happen there. She saw the little girl, her big eyes filled with an emptiness that was eerie. The little girl held out her hand and beckoned to Gill to join her. But Gill was uneasy about the situation; it didn't feel right. Something was wrong, very wrong. Who was this little girl? Why did she want her to go with her and where? Then she heard a voice calling to her from behind. It was soft and familiar but so distant. Gill turned around and walked towards the voice, all the time looking over her shoulder at the little girl who was disappearing into the distance. The girl looked sad, her arms outstretched almost pleading silently with Gill to come back but Gill felt that the voice was her key.

'Gill darling, are you asleep? You don't look well. Wake up!' Maureen's voice was soft and gentle, but it hid her fear about what Gill had tried to do. 'Gill, wake up!'

Gill felt herself falling down a long passageway towards the voice until eventually she landed softly on her bed. She opened her eyes and tried to focus on where the voice was coming from.

'Hello darling, are you OK? I was worried about you. You seemed to be in such a deep sleep. Have you been drinking?' Maureen picked up the glass beside Gill's bed and smelled the contents. There wasn't a very strong odour, but she guessed it was vodka. 'What have you been doing Gill? I think we need to talk, don't you?'

Practical as ever, Maureen was under no illusion as to what Gill had tried to do. The remaining tablets were still lined up on her bedside cabinet. Maureen had seen enough in her years of caring for others to know the signs. 'I'll make some coffee. Can you get up? Do you feel sick? It would be good to be sick if you can. I'll get some salt water, that'll help. Everything will be just fine, my petal.'

Gill felt the despair of failure but also the exhilaration of life. She tried to move but it immediately made her feel nauseous, and she slumped down again. She didn't know what to say, she was embarrassed and yet relieved. 'Mum, I'm sorry.'

'Don't fret, petal, everything will be OK.'

Maureen left the room and Gill forced herself to get up. She sat on the edge of the bed. She didn't remember much but what she did remember caused her to draw in a deep breath. How stupid she'd been. Why had she felt she needed to do it? She remembered her conversation with Mel. She remembered how scared she was at the thought of going to talk to someone else about her experience. She was especially upset at the thought of telling her mother. She raised herself slowly off the bed and dashed to the bathroom and in an almighty effort she threw up all the poison she had ingested. Along with it came the grief she had bottled up inside her, and the despair and broken dreams she'd held back hoping they could somehow be mended.

Gill stepped into the shower and let the warm water flow over her damaged soul. Her body felt used and old, so old and tired, but she also felt a new hope somehow. She felt she could perhaps start to manage her thoughts, not control them, but at least bend them slightly to ease her pain.

She suddenly remembered the little girl in her dream and wondered who she was. Why had she been there and what did she signify? She felt she knew her face but could not place her. Perhaps she didn't really exist anywhere except in Gill's mind.

'Are you nearly ready, Gill? The coffees are poured.'

'Coming, Mum.' Gill dressed herself quickly. She already felt better just because she'd thrown up. No doubt she'd have the most awful headache later and her stomach was felt like a boxing match was taking place in it. She went downstairs and found her mother in the sitting room. They sat in silence for a while sipping the strong black coffee. It helped Gill feel alive as she felt the hot liquid slide down her throat.

'Shall we talk now?' Maureen said after a suitable pause. 'What happened on holiday?'

'I...well I got into an awkward spot with a man.' Gill slowly said, not knowing quite how to say the words she knew she had to admit. Maureen remained silent. She knew that she had to leave Gill to tell it in her own words and her own way.

'The man was someone we met on the first night. I thought he was nice. I then went for a stroll with him and...well he forced himself on me. I tried to make him back off, but he was a strong guy and...' Gill looked up at her mother and tears welled up in her eyes. 'He hurt me, Mum and I'd never done anything to hurt him. He was awful to me. I just want to forget it all, but I can't. I live it again and again everyday...'

'He raped you.' Maureen said in a matter-of-fact way. 'That's what we're talking about here isn't it? He forced you to submit to his will. It wasn't about sex, it was about him getting the better of you. That's what hurts the most. Being beaten. He won and you lost, and you didn't even know why. Injustice hurts especially when you can't fight back.' Her words were so clear and calm. It was as if she wasn't talking to her daughter but giving a lecture to an assembled class of trainee nurses. Maureen had seen this type of thing so many times in her life. She knew that she had to break through the sheer emotion of it to make Gill see that the problem was not a physical one but a mental one. Gill had had her dignity taken away from her. She had been a victim. That had been the thing which had hurt her the most. Like the indignity of slavery, like the indignity of a public humiliation, Gill had been subject to someone's will over her own and had lost. Maureen knew she had to make Gill see that it was not her fault and that she now had to build herself back up again.

'Who have you told this too?'

'Only Mel and Rachel and Cathy.'

'Not anyone else such as the police or doctors or counsellors?'

'No. I just couldn't bring myself to do that. I wanted to heal myself. I wanted to help myself. Isn't that the Keane way? Never ask for help, only give it.'

'Perhaps, but even a Keane needs help sometimes, let alone a McDermott like me or an O'Leary like your Gran. We all need help sometimes and this time, it's your turn. No use denying it. Only thing to do now is work out what help you need. Can we do that together?'

'I'd like that Mum,' Gill suddenly didn't feel alone anymore. She felt she was holding the hand of an angel flying up to heaven and peace again and that this was going to be so much easier now than trying to do it alone. 'What can we do?'

'We can get you to a doctor and then to some proper help. Too late for the police, though what good they'd have done. Is Mel being supportive?'

'Very, she told me that I had to get help, but I sent her away.'

'Never send away a good friend when you need her and never ignore her when you don't. That's the soundest advice I can give. Firstly, we'll make an appointment with the Doctor. Agreed?'

'Yes, Mum, sounds good.' Gill sighed and the heavy load she had been carrying for weeks suddenly lifted from her shoulders. Maureen sweet talked the receptionist and got Gill an appointment for the following evening, and Maureen managed to change her shifts so she could go with her.

The Doctor had treated Gill since she was a baby but took even this news in his stride.

'I'll refer you for counselling, but it would be quicker if you went private. The NHS can't cope with the numbers anymore,' he said calmly.

'I'll go private. I've wasted enough time already. I just want to get back to normal,' Gill said thankful that he was being practical and not judgmental as she had feared.

'Here's the number to ring for an appointment to get some tests done since no protection was used, best to be sure you're alright, Gill. The tests will take a few weeks to come through but as soon as they're ready they'll let you know. Most importantly of all, Gill, try not to worry.'

'I'll ring them tomorrow, I promise. Thank you, Doctor, for being so understanding.'

'Nothing to be understanding about. These things happen. They have done for millennia and not doubt will continue to do so. What we have to concentrate on, what you have to concentrate on, Gill, is putting all this behind you and get on with your life and remember we're all here to help.'

'I'll make sure she does, Doctor,' said Maureen and they left the surgery with lots of new information and new hope. 'I think you'll be fine, let's just sort all these things out one at a time. I'm starving. I'll order with that new-fangled Uber Eats thing your brother put on my phone, how about fish and chips?'

'Fish and chips sounds great.'

CHAPTER 26

Over the next few weeks, Gill managed to organise several positive things. She went for tests at the hospital later that week and contacted the private counselling organisation and arranged for an assessment interview, which went well, and she was booked in for a series of twelve sessions.

'I'm really scared of going to these therapy sessions,' she said to Mel over coffee. 'I don't know what to say.'

'They'll tell you all that. They know what they're doing. It'll be great and you always know your Mum and I are here to talk to as well,' said Mel reassuringly. 'Did they say what the counselling will be about?'

'They use the Cognitive Processing Therapy evidently.'

'Gosh! That sounds painful.'

'Actually, it is, I've got to relive the experience and write everything I remember down and then they challenge me to think about it differently. The woman who'll be my therapist said that the system really works but I'm still scared. I've relived the event in my mind over and over since that night. I keep asking myself questions – could I have acted differently? Could I have avoided it happening? Was I to blame?'

'No, you weren't, and you don't need her to tell you

that, I can.'

'Still, these things niggle in the back of your mind. I guess that's why I need therapy,' Gill smiled at Mel and Mel smiled back. The two girls knew that this wasn't going to be easy for Gill, but it was the only way she could ever hope to be free of what had happened.

Gill started therapy the following week. The sessions were hard to deal with at first, but then she learnt to trust her therapist and found that she looked forward to going. Gill was still not sleeping well though. Sleeping was too vulnerable a place and she avoided it as much as possible. If she awoke in the night, she had to get up and do something. But she was conscious that she mustn't wake anyone else in the house. Today was one of those nights and Gill resigned herself to yet another early morning and got out of bed, got dressed and went downstairs.

In the kitchen she sat at the breakfast bar and stared into space. *What am I going to do if the tests came back positive? The results are due soon*, she thought considering that this was the reason she had woken up so early. Until she knew the results, she still felt that her life was in suspended animation.

The door opened and in came Maureen.

'Not able to sleep, petal?'

'No. Best to get up when I wake up or it gives me a headache trying to get back off.' Gill replied. 'Don't you worry. Go back to bed. You need your sleep. You have to be up for work later.'

'Don't worry about me, I can live on the smallest amount of sleep, just like Margaret Thatcher.'

'Mum, you're nothing like Margaret Thatcher, thank God. You care about people'

'Too much sometimes. But I'm just like your Gran. She was the same, and no doubt her mother before her. Let's face it Gill, we're a family of carers.'

'But Gran lives her own life now. She doesn't do as

much for others as you do.'

'Maybe not now, but when she was your age she was always going around other people's houses caring for the sick, the elderly or those who were just downright melancholy. People used to call her Florence Nightingale. And I just grew up to be the same. I'd go with her on her visits when I was a little girl and see the care she took of these people, people that often got no help from anyone else not even the state. I knew I had to carry on as she'd done. But it's not always easy. You've got to take on some of these peoples' misery as well. It's infectious,' Maureen sighed and made a pot of tea.

'Tea - the elixir of life, how did we ever manage before they brought tea back for us to drink? I can't imagine life without my tea, can you pet?'

'No Mum, tea is everything and is always there when you need it, here's to tea; tea and sympathy,' she raised her mug in a gesture which Maureen copied, and the two women smiled at this ridiculous sentiment.

'I've got to go back to bed now if I'm going to do an early shift later. Take care, sweetheart, everything will be OK.' And she kissed her daughter on the top of the head. Gill remembered that she hadn't done that for years.

She's always too busy helping others to really have much time for me or my brothers but I know that she really loves us, Gill thought, *Dad isn't the affectionate type either. I can't remember seeing much of him when I was a child. He was always working away and when he was home it always seemed to end in rows. I wonder why he still works away now. I'm sure he could get a job with less travelling. Perhaps it's for the best. At least he and Mum don't argue anymore.*

Gill sighed as she thought of friends like Mel whose parents had divorced. She couldn't imagine that happening to her family. *What would Father James say?* Gill smiled at the outrageous thought of seeing their priest's face if her parents told him they were thinking of getting a divorce. *He would probably have a fit.* Gill felt a bit calmer and decided to go back to bed and at least try to sleep.

CHAPTER 27

By the Autumn, Rachel and Cathy had moved into a flat in a fashionable area close to the town centre. The flat was kept immaculately.

'I've got to hand it to you, Rachel. You may have lightened up a bit, but you still know how to run a tight regime. The washing up's done, the washing pile's under control and I can't see any dust for miles,' Mel said full of new respect for Rachel who had nevertheless lost a lot of her uptight characteristics since the holiday in the summer.

'Nice to see you haven't lost your sense of proportion though when it comes to being clean and tidy though,' said Gill. 'How are you coping with all this Cathy?'

'I manage,' she said somewhat preoccupied.

'Well, we must be going. Are you two seeing the boys this evening?'

'You bet,' said Cathy suddenly full of enthusiasm, 'and I can't wait. I think I love Jon more and more each day.'

'Steady on, girl, or you'll make us all embarrassed,' Mel said, 'how do you cope with living with a lovesick bird, Rachel?'

'I keep her under control, of course. Great to see you, we'll have to arrange a night out, just the four of us.'

'Maybe,' said Gill, 'but not just yet, you coming, Mel?'

'Right with you, see you two, don't get up to any mischief now,' Mel said, and Cathy blushed. This made Rachel and Mel laugh out loud, but Gill had already made her way down to the car.

'Is she alright, really?' said Rachel.

'She'll get there, she's still got a long way to go but she'll get there,' Mel said and followed Gill out of the flat.

'Just time to tidy up before the boys arrive,' said Rachel but Cath had already headed for the bathroom and was starting to get herself ready to see Jon. Rachel muttered to herself about the youth of today as if she was some fifty-year-old. She did enjoy sharing with Cathy though, even Cathy was anything but tidy. The freedom to be herself that she hadn't had at home, was worth the extra work of tidying up after Cathy. Rachel's father had 'inspected' the flat and had given his seal of approval much to Rachel's relief.

Rachel's family had been very supportive unlike Cathy's who hadn't fared so well. When her father had got home from work on the night she came back from Spain, he may have been tired, but he was also still angry that she had defied him, and he make it quite plain.

'You're an evil whore, Catherine Jones and I don't want you under my roof anymore. You've chosen Satan and may God strike you down where you stand,' but evidently God hadn't been listening to Jed Jones' rant as he hadn't struck her down which relieved Cathy greatly. She'd looked at her mother who hadn't told her that anything was wrong. Her look of innocence and accusation had cut into Martha like a knife. She'd been torn between warning her daughter and being obedient to her husband. The years of conditioning had won, and so she had acted as if everything was OK.

Cathy had run upstairs and grabbing as much stuff as she could put in her suitcase that she had only just started to unpack and had run from the house. She knew that there was no point in arguing with a bigot, there was no use trying to explain her point of view because if it was not exactly the same as his, then she was wrong, and he was right. She rang Rachel on her mobile and caught her before she'd gone to bed. Her friend hadn't hesitated in coming around straight away to collect her from the end of her road and had taken her back home with her.

Rachel's father may have been authoritarian, but he was nothing if not fair. He had no hesitation in allowing Cathy to stay and even offered to go back to the house with Cathy to get more of her things.

'We'd better leave it until he's out, I've got a key so we can get in whenever we need to,' Cathy had said in a surprisingly level-headed way. The following afternoon when her father and mother were at church, they had returned, and Cathy had salvaged as many of her things as she could. Jed had been on an angry binge after she had left the night before and had started to destroy Cathy's things, but Martha had insisted he calm down for his health's sake and come to bed where she had tried to soothe him and make him forget. She had done worse in the name of peace before. That night it would be no worse nor better.

The girls had eventually decided that even though life at Rachel's house was safe and pleasant enough, they needed their own space, and it was then that they had moved into their small flat. This was like being let out of prison for Cathy who had never known the freedom of not having to explain her every move before. She started staying up late and coming and going when she pleased until eventually Rachel had to take her in hand.

'If you don't calm down, you'll blow a fuse. Just because we live away from our parents doesn't mean we have to let ourselves go. We still have jobs to do and now we've got a flat to look after as well.' Rachel said.

'You're right, Rachel but this is all so new to me. I'm so happy. I feel like a new woman.'

'Any particular new woman?'

'Very funny. You know what I mean. I just want to experience life. I feel I've been pent up for so long. I now know what it must be like for those babies they wrap in swaddling. When they're finally allowed to kick about and use their arms it must be heaven, poor babies, I'd never do that to a baby of mine.'

'Nor me. I may believe in being organised, but I do respect the freedom of others, it's a pity not everyone does,' Rachel thought of Jed Jones and the tyranny with which he ruled, and she loathed him for making her friend unhappy. She would always have a place in her heart for Cathy and would always protect her the best she could. Cathy and she were still very close and had no inhibitions about having physical contact, but she knew that it was Jon that Cathy now loved and wanted so she knew that their bond could be no more than friendship, but they also had a deep understanding with each other which she hoped would last forever.

Later that evening after a great night out with the boys, the foursome headed back to the girls' flat for a coffee.

'Come over here,' Jon said and beckoned to Cathy whispering in her ear. The couple walked hand in hand towards Cathy's bedroom and didn't even look back. The newfound freedom that living in the flat had given Cathy was a perk she relished, and one which Jon approved of wholeheartedly.

Cathy snuggled up in his arms on the bed and looked for all the world like a China doll being held by her loving owner.

'I love you, Cathy, you're such a special person, I'm so glad we met, can we stay together for always?'

Cathy raised her head and tilted it slowly to one side. She felt there was something Jon was trying to say but she couldn't let herself believe it to be true.

'Are you asking me something, Jon?'

'I think I am. Will you marry me?'

'Yes. When?'

A broad smile started to spread across his face, and he lay there beaming like a Cheshire Cat. 'Whenever you like.'

'As soon as possible, I think, after all the baby will need a name.'

'Baby?' Jon sat up.

'Yes,' said Cathy. 'I was hoping you'd ask me soon, I couldn't keep my news to myself much longer and I didn't want to think you only asked me because I was expecting.'

'Cathy, I love you and this is just great news, when's it due?'

'End of March.'

'March? But that would mean that you became pregnant while we were in Majorca.'

'Yes. Our first time, it just proves we should be together, don't you think?'

'It proves we should have been more careful or rather I should have been, I'm sorry Cathy, what have I done to you?'

'Just made me the happiest woman in the whole world, that's all,' Cathy in her newfound carefree way, 'shall we ask Rachel to organise the wedding? She'd love that and she'd be so good at it too.' The couple started to laugh at the thought of how much Rachel would enjoy organising a wedding. It was a job she had been made for. Then they fell into a deep and peaceful sleep, the sleep of fulfilment and dreams.

When they awoke, Rachel was already up and preparing breakfast. Cathy shyly went up to her friend and putting her arms around her waist, whispered in her ear. 'Jon has asked me to marry him.'

'What? But he can't, no, I mean, well, you haven't known him long enough. You're so young and …'

'Rachel, I thought you'd be pleased,' Cathy recoiled, 'you knew I was pregnant, this makes everything wonderful, he asked me before I told him, I thought you wanted the best for me, I thought you loved me,' and she ran sobbing from the kitchen into the bathroom and slammed the door.

'I do love you,' Rachel said softly to herself, 'but I wanted to look after you, I wanted us to always be together …'

'What's wrong with Cathy?' said Jon, 'did I just hear her crying? What happened, Rachel?'

'I'm sorry, Jon. She told me your good news, but it took me so by surprise I think I said the wrong thing. I'm sorry,' she grabbed her bag and left the flat. She needed time alone to come to terms with her feelings. She ran along the path, which led from the apartment block and finally came to a stop near the lake in the park.

Why do I feel so irrational? she thought, *I know Cathy loves Jon, it was a foregone conclusion that they'd end up together.*

'But I'm so possessive, I must stop it, Jon and her, they're just so great together, but I want Cathy to be with me too,' Rachel sighed as she held onto the railing in front of her like a drowning man.

'Then you'd better decide what it is you really want.' Andy was stood behind her. He had followed her out of the flat when Jon had explained what had happened. 'I love you too, Rachel, but I can see you love Cathy, Jon and I aren't blind or stupid, you know, we knew there was something going on, but you'll have to choose in the end. Having your cake and eating it isn't really an option, not when we're married.'

'When we're married?' Rachel spun round to face him.

'Yes, when we're married. You don't think that I'm going to let someone as gorgeous as you go, do you?'

'What? I don't know.'

'Good. Then let's get some breakfast if Jon hasn't burnt everything by now,' he took her hand, 'we can talk about all this later, but now food first.'

'Andy, I think we've got to talk about this now. I enjoy being with you, but I don't know what I want right now, it maybe you but it may not, I just don't know.'

'What do you mean 'you don't know'? What is there to know? I love you, we're good together, we were made for each other.'

'It's not you, it's me, I don't know if I want to be with a man or…'

'A woman?'

'Yes. I like sex with you, but I like sex with women too.'

'What women? I thought it was only a thing with Cathy.'

'Well, yes so far it is but Cathy's getting married so who knows?'

'And you were going to tell me this when? Thanks Rachel, you're really a prize bitch, you know that?' Andy stormed off back to the flat to collect his things.

'Where's Rachel? Is she OK?' said Jon.

'How the hell should I know? She's probably in the arms of some dyke already, I'm going, see you later.'

Rachel came back to the flat when she'd seen that Andy had left. She avoided speaking to Jon and Cathy and locked herself in her room.

'I'll find out what happened, perhaps it's best you go now, I'll call you later,' Cathy was concerned for her friend but also disappointed that her fantastic news had seemed to spoil the day.

'I love you, Catherine Jones,' said Jon

'Catherine Owens, please,' she kissed him and went to find out what was going on with Rachel.

CHAPTER 28

It had been pouring with rain all Tuesday and by the evening Mel was in two minds about going to slimming group. When she got there though, she noticed that the group was unusually large. She thought how she could be doing better things but knew she had to stay. She secretly enjoyed hearing the excuses of the others who made out it wasn't their fault that they hadn't lost weight that week. *If it isn't your fault then whose is it?* thought Mel.

'OK, Ladies, good evening, how are we all tonight?' Betty chirped up as enthusiastic as ever and the class went quiet. The hush was a bit unnerving. 'Where is everyone, Carol?' she said to her helper on the pay desk. 'They must have all gone home.'

The class laughed a hesitant and self-conscious laugh which really said we don't want to be here, but we can't leave now because everyone will see us and talk about us behind our backs. The insecurity of being fat was writ large on this gathering.

'I'll try that again, shall I?' Betty tried to sound cheerful but had had an awful day and really wanted to be at home in a deep hot bath with a bottle of Chardonnay she had chilling nicely in the fridge. She liked her job but hated having to traipse out in the pouring rain trying to persuade people, who'd made it their life's work being fat, that coming to this slimming group was the best way to find the new them (or rather the old one who had got lost in all the folds of blubber). 'Good evening, everybody,' she said even louder.

'Good evening, Betty,' the reply echoed off the walls of the hall and sounded more pathetic than usual.

'That's better,' said Betty with a big beaming smile on her face. 'This evening I'll talk about cooking. I've noticed that some of you have brought in some packets for the boxes to show us and I see that there are some surprising additions. She held up a packet for ready-made soup. 'I didn't expect to see this in here. Not very good really is it. Making soup is easy, we don't need this, we can make our own and save our allowances, why they could amount to at least a large glass of wine.'

Mel was puzzled. 'I thought we could spend our allowances on what we liked or are you saying we have to spend all our time in the kitchen so we can get sloshed after?'

'No, that's not what I'm saying. Of course you can…'

'That's OK then, I thought I might have misread the book that's all,' Mel interjected.

Everyone in the class stared at Mel wondering how she could talk to Betty like that. *My God, to these people Betty's like a God,* she thought, *and probably just as powerful, she's got the power to humiliate you if you step out of line just in the tone of her voice, no humiliation the ads said, yeah right, well that's a load of bollocks, we're all humiliated just being here.* Mel was feeling particularly negative that evening and knew that Betty was really a good soul, trying against the odds to change people who deep down didn't really want to change.

'So, let's see how we've all done this week,' said Betty ignoring Mel's comment. Mel thought how annoying Betty's little expressions and mannerisms were. *Why do I come here?* Mel thought, *because I've got the will power of a gnat, good answer, girl. I can't argue with that.*

Betty continued to announce the loses and fudge over the gains of every member of the group and then ask them how they felt about this week's results. This always took what seemed to be an eternity, but it did give Mel a chance to study the others in the group. There were about twenty who regularly stayed and almost that number again who just came to weigh and then hurried off to their lives elsewhere. Mel couldn't understand why people paid good money each week just to be weighed. It would have been cheaper to buy an expensive set of scales and ask a friend to keep a record of their weight changes. Perhaps that was the point though – many of these people either didn't have a good enough friend to do that for them or more likely they didn't want anyone they knew to know what they actually weighed. Here at least you could have anonymity. You could even give a false name if you wanted. Mel smiled at this thought and began to imagine what she could have called herself. *How about Donna Kebab or Cherie Trifle...or maybe Flora Spread and let's not forget the blokes, now then...how about Rock Cake...or there's Will Power or I know what I'd call myself, Ivor Belly, that's the one.'* She chuckled to herself until she became aware that everyone was looking at her.

Betty had turned towards her and was saying 'and Mel, she's had a slight gain this week but still has an overall loss of 2 stone 8lbs.' Rapturous applause rose from the others especially those who had also gained. They felt better in themselves that they were not the only ones who had let the side down. 'So, what do you think caused that?' asked Betty.

Mel thought for a few seconds pushing all the truth answers from her mind such as perhaps it was those cream cakes she had scoffed with Gill when she was feeling down or the chocolate bar she had eaten before she had had to see her boss to explain why her targets had not been met that month. No, she would lie as usual. No one was really interested, least of all Betty. Mel knew that. When she had

had a bad day a few weeks ago and had taken Betty's offer of 'I'm always at the end of a phone, just call me to chat' Betty had made it perfectly clear that Eastenders was far more important than saving Mel's mortal soul from the packet of chocolate biscuits on the table in front of her. Mel had never rung again not even when she found herself wandering trancelike into the Chinese Take-away or being magnetically drawn into McDonalds. She had nearly given up at that point, but as she had paid in advance for a course of sessions to get the discount, she felt obliged to at least try and get her money's worth. 'I guess it's just my time of the month or something – you know, water retention and all that.' Mel knew this was guaranteed to make the other members cringe in embarrassment especially the few men who were brave enough to stay each week.

Betty sighed. She knew this was only an excuse, but she had to play along with it. 'Ah well never mind. Sure to come off next week, don't you think? Now Class what can Mel do to help this situation?' Mel thought that the only thing to help not get periods and water retention would be a hysterectomy but considered that this was a little extreme just to avoid a few pounds weight gain for a few days every month.

'She could drink more water.' Marge offered as a solution. It had never made sense to Mel how drinking more could make you retain less but the logic was there somewhere she was sure of it.

'Avoid fizzy drinks.' Pete said much to everyone's complete surprise as he rarely spoke even when it was his turn to make up excuses for gaining weight after every weekend the rugby had happened to have been on.

'Very good ideas, well done group.' Betty said in such a way as to sound genuine but somehow also patronising all at the same time. This Mel decided was a gift she must cultivate herself. It could be so useful in all sorts of instances especially when talking to her boss.

'Well, have I spoken to everyone?' and without waiting for a reply, Betty ended the session on her usual note. 'Onwards and downwards – I want to see less of all of you next week,' Betty shouted in her usual chirpy self, thinking to herself *thank god that's over for another week, now to get home and open that bottle of wine and get that bar of chocolate out of the freezer.*

Mel left the hall chatting idly to some of the other members. Polite small talk between people who wanted friends but just didn't know what to say or how to say the things they did manage to think of. The fear of being ignored was a very powerful thing - almost as powerful as being made to look stupid or rejected by the crowd. Quickly they all drifted away into the night, back to their homes, their bran crackers or their hidden chocolate bars, back to an eternal fight between wanting and needing. Wanting food but needing love, acceptance, control. It was easier to stuff a Mars bar in your mouth than risk facing up to their real problems.

So, what are my real problems? she thought as she walked home, *I haven't heard from Iain for days, I message him, but it always took him ages to reply, I hate waiting, and look what has happened, takeaways, chocolate, cake, why do I bother? I really need to speak to him, to see him again, but he's a busy person, and anyway, I want to have reached my goal and look fabulous before I see him again,'* she kept reminding herself of this, *I want to stun him so much that he whisks me off to his villa and makes love to me all night.* Then she realised, she'd arrived home.

She secretly dreaded going inside. Her mother had become almost obsessed with making her eat rubbish food. Mel had started by pretending she liked the little treats her mother bought for her but eventually they had had several rows about it. Mel knew her mother loved her, but she had to see that keeping Mel fat wasn't the best thing for Mel. *Why can't she see that?* Mel had asked herself over and over again. *It's as if she's trying to kill me with kindness. Why can't she just understand that I'll still love her whether I'm thin or fat.*

The light was on in the hall and Mel could see the flicker of the TV through the sitting room curtains. Mel's mother, Sarah, was watching a documentary about wildlife endangered in some obscure part of the world and didn't look up when Mel entered the room. The room had an eerie feel as the only light was from the TV that dimmed and brightened at random intervals according to the programme. Sarah appeared mesmerised, not really listening nor understanding but intently looking at the screen. Eventually she turned her head slowly towards Mel who was still stood in the doorway.

'Did you have a nice evening, darling? You missed a good programme on global warming earlier. Have you eaten yet?'

'No, I haven't eaten but I'll get myself something in a minute. The class was OK tonight, but I've put on two pounds.'

Sarah's eyes lit up, but she soon became mesmerised by the TV again.

Mel wandered into the kitchen and realised that the fridge was again filled with unhealthy fat laden snacks.

I'll have to get away for a while. I can't cope with this anymore. Why won't she just leave me be the person I want to be? Mel salvaged something moderately healthy to eat and went up to her room to surf the internet for a suitable location to retreat to, the sooner the better she thought to herself.

Mel found a reasonably priced health resort not too far away and booked for a week when her Spanish class would be on its half term break. She loved her Spanish class. It made her feel like she was back on Majorca with Iain, and she was determined to impress him when they next met. Whenever that would be.

'A health resort? Wow, how posh, whatever made you book in there?' said Gill.

'I need to get away. Mum's driving me mad buying all that crap food and drinking all the time. It's dragging me down. I've got to get away to keep my sanity,' said Mel. 'Talking of sanity, how's your counselling sessions going?'

'They're going well. I should be graduating as a full-blown psychopathic loony any day now,' Gill pulled a daft face at Mel.

'Good to hear it, are you coping better now? You seem better.'

'Yes, I am, I feel more like my old self, I can see that it wasn't my fault, I think that was the worst bit, I blamed myself, I kept thinking that I could've avoided it happening somehow but at the end of the day, it was Vince's problem, and he tried to make it mine. Well, he's not going to succeed.'

'Well done, Gill. We're all very proud of you. Shall we go out tonight? How about the cinema and then a Pizza?'

'Pizza? Is part of your diet?'

'No, you're right, how about a McDonalds salad instead?'

'It's a deal, start as you mean to go on and it'll set you up for the Fat Farm.'

'Yeah, lettuce coming out of my ears, I can't wait.'

CHAPTER 29

After settling herself into her room at the health resort, she went to see Sven her trainer for the week. He was so typical of what you would consider a health instructor – tall, muscular, fit, bronzed and to cap it all Swedish – that she got worried, *I've been set up, she thought* and looked around her half expecting Ant & Dec to appear from behind a pot plant or something. But nobody appeared and Mel felt faintly disappointed.

Mel prepared herself to be lectured on her wayward lifestyle choices by Sven but to her surprise he was very understanding and suggested they have a spot of lunch together so they could talk over her plan.

Lunch was not as capacious as Mel would have liked but was strangely filling. 'Who would've thought that salad could fill you up so much?' she said.

"Ah, that is the secret,' said Sven with just a hint of a Scandinavian accent which Mel thought was very sexy. 'We need to discover that what we thought was boring and bland is in fact exciting and surprising, we are learning already, let us look around the facilities and then we can go through ideas for the week. Does that sound OK?'

'It sounds great,' Mel was a little stunned at the

friendliness but also the lack of blame and retribution, which she had expected. She also thought it odd that he always spoke about 'we' as if the King was speaking about himself. She looked around a few times thinking there were others joining them.

The plan, which Sven had devised, seemed fair and surprisingly interesting to Mel. She reminded herself that she was here to make progress with her transformation and not to rebel and cheat and that she had to keep her inner gremlins at bay to make sure that they didn't sabotage her efforts. *They're experts at doing that,* she mused as she started on her program, *but not this time.* After the first, day she even looked forward to her meals which were simple but as the ingredients were so fresh and organic, their taste was out of this world. Once she had lost her craving for rubbish food, she found the thought of eating a McDonalds actually turned her stomach.

Her pampering schedule with a bit traumatic at first but she soon relaxed herself about showing so much flesh to a comparative stranger.

This massage is so good, why haven't I done this before? Mel though, drifting off into deep relaxation as Sven worked his magic on her tense and tired body.

'I could get used to this,' she said out loud.

'And why not?' came the reply from a fellow inmate in the cubicle next to her, I love coming here, I try to come at least three times a year but often business makes that hard, I'm Elizabeth Madison by the way."

'Melissa Wright, pleased to meet you. Have you been to any other resorts then? How does this compare?'

'Far better, my dear, some of these types of places are run and staffed by amateurs, they don't know the first thing about how the mind works or the body for that matter, two lettuce leaves doesn't count as healthy food to me or anyone else except the odd rabbit, and pain is not obligatory if you want to get back into or keep yourself in shape, the holistic approach gets the best results, not torture and deprivation.'

'I must say I am pleasantly surprised at how good it is here, I haven't felt the need to cheat once yet,' Melissa said proudly.

'No point, my dear, especially at the prices they charge but you only get what you pay for. Ah, that's better,' Elizabeth sighed as her masseur ended her session. 'Off for a snooze now, I think and then get ready for dinner, I'm famished, only kidding, see you later, Melissa. Enjoy your stay.'

'I will, be sure of it.'

This encounter summed up the whole week. Relaxing, pampering, country walks, eating and more pampering. Sheer bliss. *I can't understand why didn't I ever do this before?* Mel mused, *because you were too lazy, too mean and feeling too sorry for yourself,* her inner gremlin replied. *You're right*, Mel answered but knew this was not going to be the case anymore.

The week was over all too quickly and after having received the results of her efforts, she said a fond farewell to Sven, to whom she had become very attached, and headed home feeling like a new woman. Her head was clear, her body supple and toned and her mind at ease for the first time since she didn't know when.

Melissa arrived in Birchen Grove and walked into the house. She started to be uneasy about the atmosphere as soon as she entered. The house was cold. It felt unloved and unwanted as if the life had slipped away from it. The walls seemed to bear down on Mel as she walked slowly towards the sitting room door. The bright clean sumptuousness in the health resort was in stark contrast to her home. The dirty wallpaper was old and peeling in the corners. Everywhere needed a good 'lick of paint' as her grandmother would have said, some love and attention would have been good for a start. But neither her nor her mother had had any inclination to improve the house. It was just a place to sleep and keep their things. It wasn't a home, it hadn't been since her dad had left.

The feeling of heaviness however was stronger today than ever and she was afraid to enter further in case she should stumble upon an old childhood memory, as painful and raw as if it was only yesterday that it had happened. Her health break had changed her, but now she felt just the same as always and in some ways worse. The dread that overcame her as she entered the sitting room was making her sweat. She felt the drips of moisture running down her neck, cold and irritating. But the room was empty.

Mum's not in, time to get unpacked and sorted out, oh and I need a cup of tea like my life depends on it, she thought and went into the kitchen but her uneasiness returned and she panicked as she went to fill the kettle, her hand began to tremble and froze until the water poured over the lip of the kettle and poured over her hand. The coldness of the water brought her back to life and she dropped the kettle and looked up to the ceiling. Something was wrong, terribly wrong. She spun around and walked as if weightless through the hall and up the stairs. She grasped the banister as if to keep her feet firmly on the ground. The last few steps towards the bedroom door in front of her were like a marathon. Her hand found the handle and as she twisted it open the coldness of the metal seemed to burn her skin leaving her handprint for all eternity branded into it.

The room she entered was dim, the curtains drawn shut, the half-light making eerie shadows around the room. Mel walked carefully over to the bed. The form under the bedclothes was small and oddly shaped, like an untidily made bed or pile of old clothes. It was motionless. Mel reached out to touch the duvet cover, hovering over the shape like an eagle assessing its next prey. Her fingers stretched out as if her hand was pulling her back, but she knew she had to know. As her fingers submerged themselves in the softness of the duvet, she felt the hardness beneath. She clasped the wadding and pulled slowly at the material. Her mother lay curled up as if sleeping a deep and hard sleep.

'Mum!' Mel whispered. But the shape did not respond. 'Mum! I'm home. I'm home, Mum. Are you asleep?'

The silence deafened her, Mel grasped the duvet even harder until her fingers dug into each other and she felt the pain of her nails on her own flesh. She fell forwards onto the bed and enveloped the shape. It was hard and so cold. *This can't be Mum, but it looks like her,* Mel lay there for what seemed forever suspended in disbelief. 'Mummy! Please get up, I want to show you something, I had such a nice time at the health resort, I want you to know all about it, Mummy, please wake up, I need you to know.' Mel stared at the corpse and refused to believe what had happened. The tears began to trickle down her cheeks. They stung her skin as the saltiness ran down into her mouth. She tasted the warmth and swallowed instinctively like a baby's first taste of milk. 'I met some nice people whilst I was away, Mummy, you would like them...' Mel started to unfreeze like melting ice. The reality dripped into her consciousness, and she felt her emotions start to decay and rot. She noticed for the first time the strange smell in the room - an odour of despair and surrender.

Mel reached for the phone by the bed and dialed a number. 'Gill? I think I need your help. Mum's not well...not well at all...in fact, I think we need to get someone to check her over as soon as possible. Can you come round?

'I'm just ready for a shower but will be there in say half an hour? Is that OK?'

'Um...no, not really, I think...she's dead...' Mel dropped the phone and slid to the floor weeping uncontrollably.

The insistent sound of the doorbell awoke Mel from her despair with a start. She pulled herself away from the bed and went slowly downstairs. She could see the outline of

Gill at the front door, and someone was with her, Mel let them in, Gill had brought her mother Maureen, who always knew what to do in any situation. Gill took Mel into the sitting room and Maureen went upstairs.

Gill put her arms around her and Mel felt safe and loved. She snuggled into her embrace and held tightly to the only person who really understood her. Mel took a deep breath and looked up at Gill with questions pouring from her eyes.

'No worries, Mel. We'll sort it all out.'

'I should have been here, shouldn't I?'

'You can't know that, these things happen, they just happen, if it was meant to be, then it was meant to be, and there's no use worrying about what-ifs. Your mum was a lovely woman who had had a hard life, this may be what God wanted for her. It was her time, Mel, it was her time to move on.' Gill for all her practicality was also very philosophical. 'Some things are out of our control, Mel, we all have control of our fate but even the strongest person should remember that some things are just too big and too strong for us to control. This is one of them. Remember the prayer we learned as children:

God grant us the serenity
to accept the things we cannot change...'

Mel joined in and the two women chanted together....

'*The courage to change the things we can*
and the wisdom to know the difference, Amen'.

'I love having you as a friend, Gill.' Mel sobbed.

'That's good, because I love being your friend, let's have some tea.'

Maureen entered the kitchen as Gill and Mel were making tea. She had that practical look on her face and Mel knew that whatever had to be done would be done properly and efficiently.

'It looks as if your Mum took too many sleeping tablets by mistake. Easily done when you've had trouble getting to sleep. It makes you forgetful and then you take some more when the first lot don't work fast enough. I've seen it happen before. She'd have passed away in her sleep, Mel, she looks peaceful enough, I'll ring the doctor, we'll need his confirmation so we can arrange for the body to be moved. Who's the family undertaker, Mel? Can you remember?'

'Mum always kept information like that in the sideboard. I think we had a family plot in the cemetery, but I don't know any more than that, but she always said she wanted to be cremated....' Mel stared down at her teacup. She couldn't believe she was being so calm but then what else was there to be?

Maureen rang the doctor who arrived shortly, and she showed him up to the bedroom to confirm the death. He had been the family doctor for many years and knew both Mel and her mother well, so rare these days of large practices and locum doctors. 'She was always so composed,' he said, 'how long has she been drinking, though?'

'She used to have a drink or two in the evening to help her sleep.' Mel said. 'I can't say really how much she drank, I have been away for a week so I don't know what she may have done, is that what killed her?'

'It's the combination of drink and the pills that does it, I did explain that she shouldn't drink alcohol when taking these tablets, but lack of proper sleep can make you forgetful, that's the only explanation, had she seemed depressed about anything recently?'

'She seemed fine when I left, but I know she was becoming more inwards over the last few months since I got back from holiday, I never thought she would do something like this, I wish I had never gone away,' Mel broke down and cried.

'One thing you can be sure of Mel, she would have felt no pain. I'll have to call the police. They have to be informed on the coroner's behalf in these matters. You'll then be able to arrange for the undertaker to take the body to the mortuary. It will be a routine matter, they won't take long, there will have to be a postmortem, I'm afraid, I assume you have no objections to that.'

'No, none if it's necessary then fine.'

The police arrived shortly afterwards and after taking statements and examining the bedroom, they conferred with the doctor and confirmed that a postmortem was going to be necessary. Maureen asked if it was OK for her to arrange the room so that Mel could say goodbye to her mother. The policeman saw no reason why she couldn't.

The doctor handed Maureen the death certificate and left. Maureen went upstairs and shortly after came back down.

'Do you want to say goodbye to her, Mel? Let's go see her together.' Maureen helped Mel to her feet. They went into the bedroom where Maureen had opened the curtains and the window and somehow transformed the room from the scene of death into a bright and inviting space where light danced around the room and seemed to perform a tribute for Mel's mum. Mel considered this and smiled.

'Mum would have liked to have seen those lights dancing, she loved colour and movement, I think she was so disappointed that I could never dance well.' She walked over to the bed. Maureen had arranged the covers nicely and Mel's mum did indeed look happy in a still and silent way. She had everything she wanted, well almost everything – Mel standing by her, light dancing around her and sleep, yes sleep and the peace that she craved the most.

'I think the shock upset me more than anything,' Mel said, 'I never expected it, you don't do you, you always think parents are going to be there forever. I know they aren't, but you still kid yourself they will be.'

'I know it's hard, Mel, but it's just the natural order of things, I always pray I'll never have to bury any of my kids.' Maureen said, 'I'll deserve my rest long before they do.'

Mel moved towards the bedside cabinet. Laying on it

was her mum's journal. She had kept it since she was a girl, but no one had ever been allowed to read it. It was her private friend, her confidante, the place she always put her innermost thoughts and fears. Mel picked it up and felt her mother's presence very strongly. She opened it to the last entry and started to read out loud the words her mother had written.

'I can't sleep anymore. I just feel so alone. I wish Mel were here. I have got some tablets from the doctors this week. They should help but so far, they haven't. I will take some more just in case I need more to get me off to sleep...

...I still haven't drifted off and I feel so tired so very tired. I am so tired all the time. Why is that? What makes people tired, really tired I mean? I think I will have some more tablets. They must do some good or the doctor wouldn't have given them to me. I feel so alone. Where is Mel? I love her so much. I need her so much. I wish she were here now.' Oh Maureen.'

'Shush! It simply showed how much she loved you. Don't read more into it than there is. She loved you. It was only natural that she wanted you to be with her. It was not your fault. None of this is. Let's not spoil the moment. Come on, let's leave her now. Her soul has gone to God already. She is happy with him. Do you remember that quote we put on my father's wreath at his funeral when you and Gill were children?'

'Yes, I do. It was something about living in your heart, wasn't it? It was so beautiful. What was it? I'd like it for mum's funeral as well.'

'It was by Thomas Campbell: *'To live in hearts we leave behind is not to die.'* I think it is so apt for those we love, don't you? I thought it's such a lovely gesture' Maureen said smiling, 'It would be wonderful for your mum too Mel. Sarah was a kind and gentle woman about whom I never heard a bad word. She will be missed, not just by you, she was a light that shone in a storm, Mel, a mother to be proud of.'

'Thank you, Maureen, I appreciate that thought.'

After the undertaker had been contacted and copious amounts of tea drunk, Maureen decided what to do next.

'I think I'll call our Graham and ask him to come over and wait for the undertaker. Mel can't stay here. Gill, can you help Mel get a few things together. We'll order a takeaway for our house, my shout, Indian or Chinese, girls?'

'I'd like Chinese, how about you, Mel?'

'Chinese sounds great.'

'Ooh, and Mum, as this will technically be a sleep-over, does that mean we can stay up late and eat chocolate and sweets in bed?' Gill said.

'Only if you're good and you brush your teeth really well afterwards,' Maureen said.

'Great, I'll order the food now and save time, I'm starving.'

Mel smiled. *These people are definitely mad*, she thought, *but I love them dearly.* She looked up towards the bedroom and sighed. *Mum's in heaven now*, she thought, *but she'll live on in my heart forever, after all, that's true immortality.*

CHAPTER 30

After the food arrived and the second bottle had been opened, the women sat down around the coffee table in the sitting room and tucked into their feast.

'Gill, open a bottle of that wine from the cabinet, not sure if red is exactly appropriate for Chinese but who cares, I like it.'

'Red sounds great, Maureen,' Mel started to cheer up a bit and the food did smell really good.

When they had demolished most of the food and nearly polished off a second bottle of wine, they were all feeling very relaxed.

'You know, you never really grow up until your mother dies.' Maureen suddenly commented. 'She's the one tie to your childhood that holds you in its grip, the umbilical may have been cut but the cord remains.'

'Is that right Mum?' Gill had never thought of herself as being grown up or still a child. The concept of this transition suddenly unnerved her. 'I'd have thought it was life's experiences which made you grow up.'

'They do, but there's always that link to the past through your mother. She was with you when you were just a couple of cells dividing for all you were worth, it was she who was with you at the very moment of birth and even today when so many women go out to work and leave their children with strangers, it's still a mother who is the best person who can really make the pain go away when they fall, when their tummy feels sick or their teeth want to come through. There's always a place in our hearts for Mum. My mum still treats me like a child and I'm fifty-three years old. It infuriates me sometimes and at other times, I find it very endearing. Life's a funny old thing sometimes.'

'I can't think of life as funny anymore, Maureen. I don't think I ever did,' Mel said reaching for another spring roll.

'You should, my dear, you're young and beautiful, life should be fun for both Gill and you, I know it may not seem it ever can be at the moment but think what Sarah would have wanted for you. She doted on you, you were her whole life, and she was very proud of you – she used to tell me all the time. She'd sit in my kitchen having a cup of tea and tell me all about the things you'd said or done, her whole conversation ran around you. Live with that knowledge that you were loved....'

'And still are,' Gill interjected.

'Very apt point, Gill.'

Mel's first night without her mother being just there was peaceful enough. In many ways her own grief was one of feeling abandoned by her but in the back of Mel's mind she kept saying that her mum was finally free. No longer did she have the responsibilities which had been thrust on her by her husband's abandonment and rejection. She was now free to be the woman she should always have been - soft, kind, frail and loving – eternally a girl in a woman's form.

Mel's grandmother called around the next day after Maureen had phoned her to tell her the sad news. Mel's paternal grandmother was an even more practical and matter of fact woman than Maureen.

'So, when's the funeral? Do you want any help with organising it, Mel?'

'I don't know yet. The funeral directors will liaise with the hospital, I think. The coroner's got to be involved evidently and then there's a postmortem because they have to find out if was the tablets or the drink that killed her...'

'Drink? I'm only surprised that she didn't turn to it sooner what with the life she had to put up with, still, could have been worse, your dad could have stayed around and made all your lives a misery with his selfishness.'

'Why do you say that, Gran? I thought, well I always hoped, that he'd come back, and we could be a happy family again.'

'Happy family? Mel, my darling, I love you more than I have ever loved anyone else, but please, men like your father and his father before him never make happy families. They're weak and easily led by a pair of long legs and a pretty face. He'd never have stayed much longer even if Bridget hadn't caught his eye and dragged him off. Oh, how I wanted to smack that bitch more than once. But in the end...well...less said the better,' Mel's Gran rubbed her hands together in obvious anger but went silent.

Mel was a little confused about her grandmother's comments. *I always thought Gran loved her son but there's more to this than I know. What did she mean by less said the better? How can I ask her?* Mel's Gran saw the confused look on her granddaughter's face and knew that she shouldn't have said those things about her son.

'Oh, I'm sorry, I can't explain things now, my dear. But I think you should consider going to visit your father when all this funeral business has been finished. It's about time you knew for yourself. You need to know, Mel. Take my word. Text me when you're ready and I'll give you all his details. We can talk again soon. Let me know the funeral arrangements. I must be off, Bridge Club beckons, and you can't be late – bad form you know.'

The whirlwind that was Mrs. Wright senior departed leaving only a faint amount of chaos in her wake.

'Has she gone?' Gill and Maureen peeked through from the kitchen. 'I never know if I should be more friendly with her or not, she's such a tyrant at times, the local Women's Institute are scared stiff of her. But give her fair due, she's always been very good to your mum,' Maureen said.

'And to me, especially after Dad left,' Mel was very fond of her Gran, 'she could've just left us alone after he left, but she always made a point of visiting and helping out wherever she could, she even helped me to get through university. She was so embarrassed when Dad said he couldn't afford to help even though he was loaded. I owe her a lot.'

'Well, you are her flesh and blood even if her son didn't want to be part of that. What did she say altogether then?' Maureen was everything if not nosy.

'She says I should go and see my dad, she says I must do so after the funeral or when everything's sorted. I don't know, it still hurts too much and with mum dying I feel so vulnerable…'

'Leave it until you're stronger, Mel, then have another word with her about it. She may be right, she does know him better than you do after all,' Gill was getting back on form and was becoming more like her mum each day where common sense and practicality were concerned. Her ordeal in Spain seemed to be behind her but Mel sometimes noticed a vacant look in her eyes and knew that she was either having a flashback or a moment of self-crisis. The counselling sessions seemed to have helped but there was still something haunting her. Mel wished she could help but she needed all her strength just to survive herself right now.

Several days later, they managed to get the coroner to

release the body for burial. The cause of death was noted as death by misadventure caused by ingestion of sleeping tablets mixed with alcohol. The funeral was set for the following Friday. Mel was dreading the funeral, as it would open the wounds she had worked so hard to close and heal over the last week.

'Why don't you ask Iain if he can come over for the funeral?' said Gill.

'I'm not sure if I want him to see me in this state.'

'But it's a good excuse to contact him again.'

'I've been messaging him regularly, he sometimes replies, but I don't know, I'm not sure if he's even interested in me.'

'I think he is really, but he's shy, that's all. Go on ring him up.'

'OK. I'll ring him up – but only because you bullied me to.'

'Whatever the reason, just do it and let me know what he says.' Gill left Mel to make her phone call. Mel dreaded doing it but knew that Gill was right. She did want Iain to be there right now. She needed him but she was so scared that he would say no. She sat down in her living room and dialed his number. It seemed to take ages for an answer but when she heard his voice she just melted into the phone.

'Hello, it's me. Mel. How are you?'

'I'm fine. How are you?' said Iain.

'I'm fine too. Well, no, actually I'm not. My mother died a few days ago. The funeral's next week. I was wondering if you could spare the time to come over for a while. I'd really like to see you again...'

'I'm really busy at the moment. I'm in the States at the moment and won't be back for two weeks. Sorry but I won't be able to make it.'

'Oh!, that's OK.'

'Well maybe later? Great to hear from you again. I'll give you a call when I get back to Europe, maybe. I have to go, I've got a call waiting that I just have to take. Take care Mel. Sorry to hear about your mother.' The phone went dead. Mel went dead inside as well. She sat for ages numbed by the conversation. She didn't know what to do or say. She just wanted to stop breathing and join her mother. Mel wasn't sure if she had just been brushed off or if he was genuinely busy. When she told Gill, Gill made light of it as usual.

'No worries, he was probably just busy like he said. You said he's always flying off here there and everywhere, he's an important man remember. We'll cope. Maybe you were right – now is not a good time to see him again anyway. Best to get the funeral over and everything sorted first, it'll be OK – trust me.'

Mel smiled. It was the one constant in her life – she always trusted Gill.

The next day Gill was proved right. A huge bouquet of flowers arrived for Mel from Iain.

'See he does care – I told you,' Gill said just a little smugly.

'I know, but it would have been nice to have seen him as well.'

When Gill got home from Mel's, her mother had just arrived home from work. Maureen was shattered, her shift at the nursing home at been particularly difficult. One of the residents, who had been ill for a week, took a turn for the worse and had died in Maureen's arms. His family had been told about his condition but had not arrived to be with him, she didn't know if it was from choice or necessity. Maureen was used to this. It happened all too often.

Gill seemed edgy and even though she was exhausted, Maureen had to ask her what was up. 'What's on your mind Gill?'

'I've had the results of my tests, and I've got an infection. Oh Mum, I'm so scared, I feel I've been given a second kick in the teeth, I should've had my tests earlier and then I could have started treatment earlier and...'

'Stop worrying. What infection is it?' Gill showed her mother the letter from the hospital. Maureen read it carefully and then looked up at Gill.

'Well, it's not as bad as it sounds, at least it's not AIDS or HIV so we'll just have to sort it out. Remember, it's not your fault and you're not the one who had the infection in the first place, it was him. Let's see...they suggest you go and see your doctor immediately. There we are then, have you rung him?'

'No.'

'Why not?'

'I'm too embarrassed. I feel dirty all over again, I thought I'd just got the smell of him out of my mind and now I feel like my skin is crawling with his filth...'

'Then even more important to get this sorted and get on with your life. Stop torturing yourself Gill. Be thankful for the good things and stop seeing only negatives. You're getting on my nerves a bit you know,' Maureen knew she should not have said that, but she was so tired both physically and emotionally that she just hadn't been able to stop herself. 'I'm sorry, pet! I'm just so tired and we lost a resident today and he had no one to cry for him. Can we please try to get these things in perspective? I love you. You are more important to me than anyone else, but I also care about my residents. They need me too. Sometimes I just can't be all things to everyone, and it splits me apart.'

'Sorry Mum. I know I've been over-reacting sometimes, I know you love me, and I know that I'm lucky in so many ways. Remembering the good things not just the bad ones is difficult, but I do understand I have to. What would Dad have said if he were here? LMF? – Low Moral Fibre!' and both Gill and her Mum laughed.

'What the hell does he know about moral fibre, low or otherwise? He never took responsibility for anything or anyone in his life. Bloody hypocrite.' Maureen didn't mince her words when it came to talking about her husband in front of Gill anymore. She had done when the children were young, but she felt they had a right to know whom they were dealing with. 'But he was always full of helpful nonsense in a crisis – you could certainly count on him for that.'

'Mum, you are the worst and the best,' Gill looked with admiration at the small woman who was a storehouse of energy and help, a source of inspiration. 'If I could be half the woman, you are, I would be great indeed.'

'If you were half the woman I am, love, no one would notice you – you'd be too tiny' The two women hugged each other, and Gill got her phone to book an appointment with the doctor for as soon as possible. Gill knew that life had to go on and she knew she had naval gazed for long enough. At least her problems could be healed and solved with a dose of penicillin. She thought about her friends and hoped that their problems were so easily solved too. She thought of Mel and her decision to visit her dad. *I don't think I could do that, not after all these years and the way he'd just up and left. Mel must have much higher moral fibre than I thought*

CHAPTER 31

'This place hasn't changed much,' said Gill as Mel and she entered the nightclub where they'd chosen to meet in order to celebrate Cathy's hen night together. 'All the same old faces. I bet the drink prices have gone up though.'

'You sound like me.' said Mel. 'I thought I was the tight one. Trying to take my place now, is it? I see – competition.'

'No, Mel, how could I possibly compete with you?'

'True – just remember that. Come on, let's have some fun.' The girls walked over to where Rachel and Cathy were stood. Though it wasn't even midnight yet, the place was getting busy, and it was a struggle to pass through the crowd in places which accentuated the steamy feel the club had always had. Hot bodies and rising passions.

'This is an ideal place to find someone to tease,' thought Gill but then winced at the thought. That was before. Now she looked more like a nun out for the evening. She was wearing a polo-neck top with three-quarter length sleeves and a pair of baggy black trousers. She still had a certain something about her and several heads turned as they crossed the room.

In the crowd, one head turned more in disbelief than

admiration. He had a wry smile even and he saw his chance to cause trouble, which was and always had been, his middle name. Vince stayed in the shadows and observed his prey. *She looks different somehow,* he thought, *not the tart I picked up in that bar in Majorca, she looks like a frightened rabbit caught in the headlights.* He smiled to himself. *Serves her right, the whore! She bloody well led me on and then played the scared virgin, huh, but I showed her alright.'* He chuckled as he remembered the way he'd forced himself on her, the smell of fear and the look of a broken spirit. *I done that, good evenings work if I do say so himself, and here she is joining in the fun, well we'll soon see about that.* He smiled.

'What's with the smile, mate? Seen anything interesting,' said Steve coming back from the bar with another round. 'Looks dead here talent wise tonight. Shall we go to the Nags Head and try for a lock-in instead?'

'Mate, you never see the obvious, do you? Always missing the opportunities for some fun, forget the drink, I smell a shag.'

'Where? Tell me! Don't say it's those two dogs over there by the toilets, please, or I'll know you've finally flipped.'

'No, stupid, look over there.' He pointed in the direction of Gill and the others who were still oblivious to their presence.

'Oh, not those again. I thought you said she wasn't that good and wouldn't be bothering with her again and as for the others, well the only descent one, I've heard, is up the duff and getting married to one of the Thompson Twins from the Club. Vince, you lose the plot sometimes, I worry about you, really, I do.'

He noticed, however, that Mel was with them as well but somehow, he thought she seemed to have changed. He then realised she'd lost a great deal of weight. 'Perhaps things aren't that bad after all, I didn't notice the fat bird had got her act together.' Steve was beginning to see the interest Vince had in the group. 'So do we make a hit on them or what?'

'Hold your horses! I don't want to shag 'em, I want some info from 'em,' Vince said. 'We'll wait a bit but keep your eye on 'em. Now where's my bloody drink?'

'So, when are we going to make our move? If you wait much longer, they'll have gone home,' Steve was getting fed up with being messed around by Vince. 'I'm starving anyway, fancy a curry? That new place done the end of the High Street don't know us yet, so we could try there, but this time try not to throw up all over the place. You were fucking gross last week, mate, even for you.'

'You go on and order me something, I'll catch you up.' Vince had noticed the group of girls were moving towards the door and he knew his chance might be soon.

Gill, Mel and the others had had a great night out oblivious to their secret stalker. Gill had danced with Mel a few times but had shunned any advances from men. The booze hadn't flowed like it used to. Gill was fearful of losing control and Mel was so into her weight lose that she didn't want to blow it. Cathy now five months pregnant so was confined to drinking lemonade all evening and now was starting to feel sick as a result.

'I think I'll have to get home to bed,' she said. Rachel had had enough too, so they all decided to leave the club. Rachel went to find a quiet spot to call an Uber while Gill and Cathy went to the toilets.

'Hello, Mel! Long time no see, I wanted to ask a favour.'

'Vince!' Mel's calm voice pierced his ear with its coolness. 'What do you want?'

'Well…this isn't easy for me, but I wanted to speak to Gill, explain my behaviour and all that,' Vince put on a sheepish voice which didn't fool Mel for a minute.

Mel breathed a deep sigh. She could not believe he was talking to her and worse that he was asking to see Gill. She hated everything about Vince but somehow, she did feel that talking to Vince would be helpful to Gill.

Mel found Rachel and the others soon joined them.

'I don't think that would be a good idea,' Rachel and Cathy agreed. 'He's a complete bastard. He doesn't deserve to be forgiven, more like shot if I had my way,' Rachel said.

'Where is he now?' Cathy realised that he must have been in the club for some time, looking at them, perhaps looking at her and she felt scared.

'Don't worry, he's gone outside and said for Gill to meet him around the corner in the car park at the back of the supermarket, I think he's on his own, I didn't see any of his usual mates around at least.'

Gill stood completely still, and Mel put her arm around her. The colour had drained from her face, only her lipstick and her eye shadow remained, and it made her appear like a Halloween ghoul. 'You don't have to do it, Gill,' Mel said.

'We can go and sort him out for you,' Rachel said. 'I would take great pleasure in doing that...'

'No, I think it would be good for me to confront him, if I run away, then he's won, and I'll be his victim forever. I don't want to do this, but I must, you do understand don't you?' Gill turned to her friends and Rachel and Mel nodded. They knew she was right but were amazed that she was being so brave about it.

'We're coming with you, no arguments,' Mel knew she would be speaking for Rachel as well.

'Absolutely,' confirmed Rachel. 'Cathy, I don't think you should come, stay here by the doormen, we won't be long.'

The coldness of the November night air caught them unawares. They wished they'd brought thicker coats. They walked the short distance to the car park. It was dimly lit. They looked around cautiously in case it was a trick on Vince's part, and he did have friends with him. They saw a shadowy figure coming towards them out of the gloom. Gill knew at once that it was Vince. Mel caught hold of Gill's hand and squeezed it. Gill was petrified but knew she had some of the best friends a girl could ever want with her at that moment. Her mind flooded back to Majorca, and she started to relive the trauma she'd gone through, she could hear his voice and smell his breath, she could feel his rough hands on her body and the pain they inflicted. As Vince got nearer to the girls, she fought to forget that summer night and concentrated hard on staying in the present.

Vince had come alone. He still hadn't wanted to discuss the events on holiday with even his best mate Steve whom he'd known each since they were kids but there were some things a man never discussed with his mates. The events in his childhood had been one of those forbidden subjects and the Buggery Twins was definitely another.

'Hello,' said Vince trying to be his usual jovial self. Gill just stared at him and gestured for him to get on with it, to say whatever he had come to say. *I'm not going to play the victim,* she recited in her head the mantra she'd learned in therapy, *playing the victim is always a choice, never a given.*

'I wanted to talk to you to tell you how I feel about…well…what happened in Majorca. I know now that I shouldn't have done it. I've become a changed person especially since your revenge.' Vince pleading was very convincing. 'After my experience with your friends, I think I've finally realised the error of my ways.'

'My friends?' Gill was confused. *Had Mel and Rachel done something without telling her?* she thought.

'Yeah, the girl from Madrid, the Spanish police and …not to mention the Buggery Twins' Vince shuddered as he remembered them.

'The Buggery Twins?' Gill was even more perplexed and turned towards Mel for an explanation. Vince noticed this reaction and realised that Gill didn't know anything about what had happened to him. He kept up the charade though and continued.

'I know I hurt you but understand that this is hard

enough just to have asked you to see me, I know you must hate my guts, but I really am a changed man now.' Vince was playing his part with real zeal now. 'How did you know that it would take an experience with those men to make me see the error of my ways?'

Mel could see that Gill was confused. She stepped forward and announced proudly, 'I organised that event and I'm glad you enjoyed it. You deserved it, you scum...'

'Mel, that's enough. I think Vince has obviously learnt his lesson.' Gill was actually feeling sorry for Vince. *Perhaps it was me after all that caused him to behave like he did, perhaps I did lead him on, he seems so sorry...oh God! What am I doing? He's got inside my head, no, this isn't happening, this is wrong,* Gill started to panic, and her breathing became shallow and fast, she had no idea what to do.

'Anyway, I've got to go now' Vince said oblivious to the reaction he was causing in Gill, 'I think I've learnt enough, so long slag, see you around,' he blew her a kiss and walked off.

Gill brought herself back under control. 'Not if I fucking see you first, loser!' Gill said and a resounding 'here! here!' was heard from her friends who stood behind her. Gill turned to them to indicate that she could handle this, and they went quiet. She followed Vince. 'I pity you, Vince Thorn, I pity all men like you, you're sad, pathetic excuses for humanity.' Gill paced around Vince in an unnerving way, though she was shaking inside, and her stomach was churning with fear and confusion. But she knew that this sorry piece of nothing had to be her prey now and on her terms.

'Remember this, scumbag, what we've arranged once we can arrange again - at any time.' She stopped pacing and looked Vince directly in the eye. She didn't flinch and it unnerved him that she had become so aggressive, he was not used to aggressive women, he felt a little intimidated, he felt like a little boy being told off by a very large teacher, he didn't like how he felt, and he hated Gill even more for making him feel like it, he hated all these women.

'I just wanted...'

'I don't care what you want. You and your wants are irrelevant, nothing matters any more but what I want, is that clear?' Gill raised her voice almost to a scream and the echo around the empty car park was deafening. 'Now piss off back to the cesspit you came from and do the world a favour, drop dead!'

Gill turned and headed back towards the car park exit. After a few steps, she turned and said in a calm voice which reverberated like a huge bell, more than if she had screamed it, the words ringing in Vince's ears, 'and by the way, you aren't any good at sex either, a ten-year-old would be better than you.'

Gill turned and breathed a huge sigh, a sigh of relief. She felt good but the stress was beginning to show, and her eyes had begun to well up with tears. The others followed her and stood close to Gill.

'He can't see me like this, take me home Mel.'

The three women walked back to the club, collected Cathy and got into the waiting taxi.

'You were fantastic, Gill, but I still say we should have smashed his stupid face in,' Rachel said in her usual direct manner.

'Can we stop somewhere? I need to compose myself before I get home.'

'Good idea, in fact, let's go somewhere to talk and perhaps have a drink or something to eat.' Mel said enthusiastically. 'Eating always helps me.'

'Mel, you'll make me as fat as a pig at this rate,' Rachel said.

'No chance – salad and diet Coke, where's the harm in that?' She smiled and the girls started to laugh. All of them knew that six months ago Mel would have heaved at the thought of eating salad. What she would have ordered every time was a plate of something really fattening with chips on the side and pudding to follow washed down with a milk shake.

The women decided to tell the driver to take them to an all-night diner where they ordered as healthily as possible but decided that dessert was obligatory and should hold as many calories as physically possible.

'What?' said Mel with a mouthful of chocolate cake. 'I know, I'm on a diet, but if you can't enjoy yourself once in a while, what's the point?' The chocolate, from the 'Death by Chocolate' pudding she was eating, dribbled down her chin and the others laughed.

'Good to see you haven't changed that much after all, Mel,' Rachel said. 'We loved you just the way you were.'

'But I didn't, this is the first blow out I've had since I don't know when. I deserve it, and no, it doesn't mean I'll go back to my old ways, those days are behind me, honestly' she looked at her friends who were staring at her in incredulity.

'Never mind about that anyway,' said Gill, 'what I want to know about is the Buggery Twins.'

'Yeah,' said Rachel. 'What on earth was he on about?'

Mel put her spoon down reluctantly and draw in a big breath. 'Where do I begin? After you told me about what had happened with Vince, I felt so helpless. I wanted to help. I know you said you didn't want anyone else to know until you'd come to terms with it yourself, but I had to talk to someone. So, I told Iain, and I asked his advice. He came up with the idea. He knows all sorts of people and he knows that behaviour like Vince's is bad news for the local area...

'OK. So, you told him and what did he say to do?' Rachel was anxious to know what was behind Vince's odd remarks.

'He said Vince needed to see things from a different perspective. He said that if Vince could realise that he was punishing others for something which was probably in his past, he was really punishing himself and then he might be able to alter his own behaviour.' Mel took a sip from her

Diet Coke, 'It was long shot, call it shock tactics if you like, but I just had to do something.' Mel waited for a reaction, but none came so she continued.

'Anyway, he arranged the whole thing. All I had to do was point out Vince to this girl Iain knew from Madrid, no one would know her locally so she couldn't be traced if Vince complained, she lured him away from the others and then some friends of Iain's took over. They'd borrowed some uniforms belonging to the Policia Municipal and had arranged with a local real estate chap to use some old police station that was on the market for conversion to a holiday home or something.

'They then arranged for two really nasty guys whom I suppose are the Buggery Twins to 'show Vince the error of his ways.' They'd been told that Vince was a child molester and as they hated men like that, they enjoyed doing whatever it was they did to him. Your guess is as good as mine, but I think their name explains a lot, don't you?'

Gill and Rachel were lost for words and looked at each other in amazement. Then they started to smile, and this escalated into shrieks of laughter so loud that Mel thought they were going to be thrown out of the diner.

'No wonder he was nervous,' said Gill. 'I thought he was hallucinating.'

'I just thought he was on drugs,' said Rachel.

'No, afraid not. He was just plain scared.' Mel said and the laughter started all over again. Tears ran down Gills face and she thought about all the other tears which had run down her face over the last few months and how much better this type of tears was.

'I was going to say that he might have shit himself but then I suppose that didn't happen for a good few days,' Gill found she could laugh at the situation. She was finally letting go of her experience and moving on. She was so glad that Mel had persuaded her to meet with Vince, much against her initial thoughts and also that Mel had gone behind her back and told Iain.

'I must remember to thank him for helping me,' Gill said, 'In fact I have to remember to thank a lot of people for helping me. This is going to become a new habit to learn.'

CHAPTER 32

Vince sat down on a barrier at the back of the car park. He couldn't believe how Mel had got the better of him. He seethed with anger and lashed out at a nearby parked car with his foot.

'Frustrated are we, Vince?' A girl barely sixteen was walking towards him out of the darkness adjusting her short skirt as she walked. Despite the cold November night, she had bare legs and a flimsy blouse which clung to her breasts, her nipples showed through, erect from the cold. Her dark skin shone in the light from the overhead security lighting and as she got close to Vince she smiled. Vince heard a noise at the other end of the car park and a man's footsteps hurried off into the darkness.

'What do you want, slag. Bit late for a kid like you to be out, isn't it? Oh, but then this is when you do your best business – when no one can see you properly!'

'You didn't seem to mind how I look in the past, Vince,' the girl said stoking Vince's shoulder. 'So, the girls you picked up didn't want you then, if I heard properly. Never mind. How about a quick one? I'll do you a good price – just for old times, eh?'

'Just because I was the first one up you all those years

ago doesn't mean I'm interested in going there again. You're a right slag, Hayley, you know that? But then like mother like daughter. How is the old slapper? Still pulling or gone so saggy no one interested anymore?'

'She's still doing OK. She's got her regulars and her Giro so she's OK. How about you, Vince? Down on the old love stakes? Let me make you feel better. Just a quick one. We can do it right here and I won't charge you much – a special rate for old time's sake.'

Vince looked Hayley up and down. He remembered forcing himself on when she was only thirteen. She was nice and tight then, but she'd been on the game for a couple of years now, so God knows what she'd be like now. But he was feeling tense and a shag, even with her, wasn't such a bad idea.

'OK. How much?'

'For you - ten quid.'

'Daylight robbery, but OK, get your knickers off and bend over. I don't want to look at your ugly mug.'

Hayley slipping off her underwear turned around and leant against the barrier. Vince didn't take long and wiped himself in her skirt when he had finished.

'Thanks, Hayley, you're not so bad. See you around.'

'What about the ten quid?'

'I'll have to owe you.'

'Bastard!' she said as she flew her fist in his direction. Vince caught hold of her arm and twisted it back until she cried in pain.

'Rich coming from you, I knew who my father was, any ideas about yours?' He pushed her back again the barrier and she winced as the cold hard steel hit her back. Vince swaggered away towards the Indian restaurant to meet Steve as Hayley hurled a tirade of abuse at him. Despite his shag, he was still seething with anger. 'So, the cow had her revenge on me, or rather that fat bitch friend of hers,' Vince muttered to himself, 'probably jealous because I chose her friend instead of her. Jealous cow! Well, we'll see who has the last laugh. If they want lessons, I'll teach them a few they won't forget.' Vince arrived at the restaurant.

'I ordered you a Vindaloo and Pilau rice,' said Steve. 'I thought you were never coming.'

'I'm here now, got any beers in? I need a drink,' Vince said. He had found out what he wanted to know and now had some thinking to do, and he definitely needed a few beers to help him do it.

CHAPTER 33

'You look beautiful,' Rachel said to Cathy as she finished putting on her dress and veil. 'You look like a fairy princess. I love you.'

'I love you too and I love Jon so much too, I'm so happy, Rachel, and I couldn't have done any of this if it wasn't for you, you will always be in my heart, you know that don't you?' Cathy said looking at Rachel and feeling a little awkward about their relationship. 'You do understand that we must be over now? Now that I'm going to be married, it wouldn't be fair to Jon otherwise.'

'I don't really understand, but I do accept it. You'll always be very special to me, Cathy. After all we were both virgins really, weren't we?'

'Me more than you, I'll always remember our first time together, it was very special to me and remember the look on the girls' faces when we told them, that was priceless.' Rachel stepped forward and hugged Cathy.

'You take care, and if you ever feel...well you know...I'm always here for you no matter what or who else is in my life,' Rachel felt herself welling up with emotion. 'But enough of this sentimental clap trap.'

'Come on, let's see the bride then,' Mel and Gill were in

the sitting room waiting for Rachel and Cathy. They'd sensed that the two of them needed some time alone. Mel and Gill had often thought how Cathy was going to marry a man and still have Rachel as her lesbian lover but then what did they know how such things worked.

When they saw Cathy, they were stunned. 'You have always been so beautiful, Cathy,' said Gill, 'but today you have excelled yourself. Jon is a very lucky man.'

'I'll second that,' said Rachel admiring the bride who would never be hers.

'Now Rachel, less of that ogling the bride or you'll have your hand in her knickers before we can turn around,' said Gill.

'Gill! What a thing to say,' said Mel astonished at Gill's remark.

'Very true though,' said Rachel, 'I would have,' and she winked at Cathy who blushed at the thought. 'Anyway, the car's waiting outside and they're bound to get booked if we keep them much longer.'

The four women soon arrived at the church. Rachel held Cathy's hand as they walked down the aisle. Cathy's family or rather her father had told her they would have nothing to do with the wedding and as no-one knew how to get in touch with Cathy's brother Luke, Rachel had agreed to give Cathy away. It was only appropriate after all for that was what she was in fact doing.

They had chosen a small local Anglican Church near their flat for the ceremony, the vicar there had been happy to hold the service for them after hearing about Cathy and the problems with her father. The church was a wonderful choice. It was intimate and held the guests as if in an embrace rather than rattling around as they would have been in a large church. The old stonework added to the atmosphere and the rich wooden pews and ornate fret work gave an old-world feel befitting such a romantic union. It was as if King Arthur and his Queen themselves were about to be joined in married bliss.

Jon turned as the music started and saw his bride float towards him. He squeezed Andy's arm. His angel had come down from heaven. His perfect woman – kind, caring, soft and innocent. The church was packed with mainly friends but also the relatives of Jon. It was all decked out with white flowers and ribbons. Rachel had thought this appropriate for her virgin lover, even though Cathy was nearly 6 months pregnant.

The organ sounded in the background and a harpist sat patiently in the corner waiting for her cue to start her repertoire.

'This is a beautiful wedding,' said Mel to Gill. 'We shall have to have Rachel organise our weddings one day, don't you think?'

'Who else? It's a given,' said Gill enjoying the occasion which did bring back her childhood hope of finding her Prince Charming and having a fairy tale wedding like Cathy's.

The Vicar began the service and after singing an upbeat hymn (chosen by Rachel) they settled down to the ceremony.

'Dearly beloved, we are gathered here today…'

At the back of the church, a lone figure sat right in the corner out of sight of everyone. She had a nervous eye on the door and an adoring eye on her daughter. Cathy's mum, Martha, had decided that for once in her life she would do the right thing not the one her husband had told her to do. She had defied him and was attending her only daughter's wedding. She had managed to buy a new dress by scrimping on the housekeeping for months, ever since Cathy had told them about her wedding plans. She had seen a lovely lilac outfit in a shop in town run by two ladies who loved clothes and ran their business more for their own amusement than for huge profits. She had asked if they would keep the outfit in the shop saying it was to be a surprise for her husband on their anniversary. The ladies had readily agreed and had pressed the outfit beautifully ready for the big day.

She also bought a pair of lilac shoes which she knew she would never be able to wear again, and the ladies had said she could borrow a lilac handbag that matched the outfit as long as she didn't damage it. She looked wonderful but all the more for having a beaming smile of pride on her face as she saw her little girl looking like a princess. She had wished she had been allowed to have such a pretty dress for her own wedding but the Brethren in her church had never encouraged such frivolity.

The Vicar then enquired if anyone knew of any just reasons why these two people should not be joined in holy wedlock. Rachel thought *yes, I do because I know the bride loves me and I love the bride*, but she knew she would have to keep that thought to herself. Her friend's happiness was more important than her own.

Andy also thought he had a good reason and thought, 'I have a reason – this marriage will split up Jon and me. We'll never be the same again. I've lost my brother, my soulmate, my twin forever.' But he would keep that thought to himself as well. His brother's happiness was more important than his own.

'Yes, I have a reason.' A voice boomed around the church echoing off the carved stone walls and reverberating through the archways. 'I have the most important reason of all. This woman is not a virgin, she is a whore of the devil and should be dammed to Hell.' Cathy shook with fear, the same fear she had known all her life. He had turned up after all - not to celebrate her happiness but to ruin it. 'I am her father and as God is my witness, I forbid this marriage.'

'I see,' said the Vicar calmly. 'I think we should adjourn into the vestry and discuss this matter there.' He nodded to the organist who calmly began to play a soothing refrain as the congregation sat in amazement at this outburst. No one knew Cathy's dad. They stared at him in disbelief. How could a father say such things about his daughter? It was unbelievable.

The Vicar ushered Cathy, Jon and Mr. and Mrs. Owens, his parents, into the side room. Cathy's father followed as did Rachel even though she was not strictly family, she knew her place was beside Cathy to protect her. She knew Cathy's father and what a bully he was. From the back of the church appeared the lone figure. Dressed in lilac and looking bold but a little hesitant she walked up the aisle. Cathy's mother opened the door to the vestry and went in. She turned to Rachel and smiled. Rachel smiled back more in amazement than anything else but also out of admiration for the courage this woman was showing just being there.

'By all that is good, what are you doing here woman? And what is that you have on?' Cathy's father was already in a rage and itching for a fight, but the sight of his wife was totally unexpected and put him a little off guard.

'I am here to see our daughter get married,' she replied calmly. She turned to the Vicar 'take no notice whatsoever what this man has to say. There is no impediment as to why these two young and beautiful people should not be married and live a long and happy life together.'

Both Cathy and her father were lost for words but for different reasons. Cathy found her voice first and rushed to her mother, hugged her and whispered in her ear. 'Thank you, Mum. I know how hard that must have been for you to do this. We are both very grateful.'

'Not so fast, my girl,' her father recovered his composure and was determined that everyone should listen to him. 'I have said that this woman is not fit to be married in a church, though God knows this place is hardly worthy of such a name. She is a whore and a fornicator. I forbid this wedding to take place.'

The Vicar rose to his full height, which was impressively more than that of Jed Jones, and taking a deep breath, he tried not to be emotional in the face of such an insult on his church. 'I can only stop this wedding if there are justifiable grounds under the law. Your opinions do not count, sir, unless they materially affect the ability of these two people to marry. I have spoken to both of them at length and have not seen any such justifications. Your accusations are invalid…'

'And totally untrue,' Jon interjected. 'Cathy is the purest most perfect person I have ever met. She is goodness and light and is head and shoulders above you and your bigoted attitude and bullying ways. I will not tolerate you talking about my wife in such a manner. Be careful what you say, sir.'

'Calm down, son,' said Clive Owens, Jon's father. 'I am sure we can sort out this misunderstanding.'

'There is no misunderstanding, these two people cannot marry,' said Cathy's father angrily.

'Yes, they can,' said Martha, 'and with my blessing. I brought Cathy into this world, and I agree there is no purer a girl on God's earth, her purity is in her heart where it truly counts, so be quiet, Jed and go on home. I'll be home later, and I'll cook you your favourite tea. Vicar, please go on with the ceremony. These two young people have too much love for each other to be kept waiting any longer.'

'I agree, the vicar said, 'I believe that there are no reasons why this couple should not marry and therefore I will continue with the ceremony. Any person or persons who object on personal grounds may leave my church.' The Vicar opened the vestry door and looked at Jed who stared in disbelief but left peacefully. He had never been contradicted before and especially not by his wife. He vowed never to acknowledge the marriage nor speak to his daughter again and as for his wife, he would deal with her later.

The rest of the ceremony went by uneventfully. The couple got over the ordeal quickly being completely caught up in their love for each other. Everyone at the wedding could see how much in love they were. Even Andy had to concede that his brother did look very happy and perhaps it was more envy than anything else that was making Andy feel sad inside. The reception was held at a local five-star hotel, which Rachel had negotiated a very good deal with. It helped that she was their accountant.

Cathy noticed her mother sat alone observing the dancing. 'Come and join in, Mum.'

'Oh no, I couldn't, but you go on, it's too late for me but you join in life and have fun, lots and lots of it, I'll have to be going soon, I've got to get your dad's tea, he'll be waiting.'

'Let him wait, just for once, Mum, I don't want you to go, I'm scared what he might do to you, please stay, you can use my room at the flat. Please Mum, I saw the look in his eyes, he's going to hurt you, I know it,' Cathy was filled with fear for her mother's safety even though as far as she knew he had never hit her mother, but he could be really cruel in other ways. It filled Cathy with dread. 'I am so proud of you today, Mum, I never thought you had it in you to stand up to Dad.'

'Sometimes you just have to do what you have to do. Duty is more than just duty to your husband, I have come to realise that duty to your children is just as important if not more so. God gave you and your brother to me to care for and protect. I feel I've let you both down so much, I wanted to make up for it today, I owed you that much. Don't worry about me Cathy, darling, I'll be alright, God will look after me,' she kissed her daughter and hugged her softly. Cathy decided to get Jon to try to persuade her mother to stay at her flat that night but when she came back Martha had gone, the chair she had been sat on was empty and for a moment so was Cathy's heart.

'Cathy, come and cut the cake, we're all starving,' Mel

caught hold of Cathy's hand and squeezed it. 'Rachel will take care of your mother if she needs help. Be sure of it. And so will we all. She was very brave coming today. Did it make your day?'

'Yes, it did. More than you can know,' said Cathy, glad that she had such good friends. 'Now where's that cake, I'm starving too. Good thing Rachel made me choose a dress with room for eating in it. She's so sensible,' Cathy headed towards the cake stand with Jon in tow, looking into each other's eyes with a love which everyone knew was going to last forever.

'Yes, Rachel is sensible - sensible enough for all of us – thank goodness,' said Mel quietly and clapped as the happy couple cut the cake that everyone was dying to eat. *This partying is such hungry work,* she thought.

Andy observed the happy couple. He didn't really feel like partying, but he could see his mother looking at him with a concerned look on her face. *Oh no, if I don't join in more, she'll suspect something. She always seems to know what I'm thinking. Better put on my happy face,* thought Andy and he flashed a wide smile at his mother who relaxed. Andy danced with several girls and finally caught up with Rachel when the slow section started.

'It's a good wedding. Well done for organising it so well, Rachel. You really are so good at this. Perhaps you could organise my life sometime,' said Andy as they danced close together.

'It was a good exercise but not too difficult. When you know someone as well as I know Cathy I simply knew what she and Jon would want. The rest was simply organisation and timing,' she said.

'Speaking of timing, is now a good time to bring up the question of you and me? I know you are still confused about…well…sex and all that, but couldn't we explore together. I wouldn't cramp your style or anything, I just so much want to be with you. I think we might have something going together and I'm prepared to wait until you get sorted out in your mind. I don't mind sharing you with a woman. Another man and I might have a problem with that, but not a woman.'

'Why not a woman, Andy? Don't you think it's as serious if it's only two women together? Or do you think another woman couldn't compete with you in bed?' said Rachel somewhat defensively.

'I do take your sexuality and preferences seriously, I just want to be a part of your life, we're good together, aren't we?'

'Of course we're good together, that goes without saying,'

'I like you, I like being with you, I miss 'us', is that so bad?'

'No, I'm flattered, and I liked being with you too, it's just I feel I need something, and I don't know what it is yet. Perhaps it's you and perhaps not, I don't think it's fair to string you along, I need to explore my options, do a bit of reconnaissance if you like and find the lay of the land so to speak,' said Rachel feeling that this conversation was not helping Andy, only prolonging the inevitable. 'We were an item but now…well…we're having a break if you like. Please understand it isn't because there is anything wrong with you, it's me, I need space, and I need some time. Please respect that.'

'I do. But this is hard. I'm sorry I bothered you especially today, it's all the romance of a wedding, it makes people make fools of themselves,' Andy said thinking he had probably blown it with Rachel forever.

The music stopped and the couple drifted off the dance floor. Rachel excused herself to the toilets and Andy decided that he needed some fresh air. He stepped out into the gardens only to bump into several couples trying to catch an intimate moment together on the terraces. This didn't help him, so he decided to call it a day and left the hotel. He needed a walk. He needed to think.

Cathy was the first to notice that Andy had left the

wedding. 'Did you see him go? Did he say where he was going?' she asked Rachel.

'No, he didn't. We danced and then I went to the toilets. I haven't seen him since, but I wasn't looking for him either. Cathy, Andy and I are over. I like him but I'm still searching not like you. I envy you and Jon, you're so beautiful together, I know you're going to be so happily married and have lots of babies. I insist on that.' Rachel kissed Cathy on the lips, 'I need to go home to change for the evening do, I forgot to bring the right shoes, can you believe it, see you later.'

'Thanks for everything Rachel, I'll always love you, you know that and so does Jon. You'll be welcome any time,' said Cathy getting all emotional. 'Could you do me one last favour though? Could you call by Mum's house for me and see if she's OK? Dad will be out this evening at his Elders meeting so it's a good time to call. Let me know later if she's OK.'

'Of course I will. Now don't worry.'

'Jon and I are just going up to our room to change now...'

'Yeah, if you think I'm going to believe that's all you'll be doing, think again. Don't be late getting back down or I'll tell everyone why.'

Cathy giggled and went to join Jon at the lift. She hoped he had the same thing in mind as she did.

CHAPTER 34

Andy wandered around for what seemed ages, it was getting dark before he suddenly stopped and decided he was thirsty. There was a kiosk in a nearby carpark serving hot drinks to cold people. A hot cup of tea was what his mother would have suggested at moments like this, so he decided to take her advice.

Andy was beginning to think that Rachel was probably a lost cause, another casualty of women's sexual independence. He found her bisexuality intriguing but also confusing. *How can a woman prefer another woman to a man? What can they do that I can't and more?* he thought.

'What can I get you, love? You look a bit down, you need cheering up.' The woman behind the counter spoke with a chirpy London accent. He ordered without making eye contact, he didn't feel like interacting with anyone just at that moment.

'I'll have a cup of tea.' he said.

'Coming right up. Sugar?' said the woman behind the counter.

'No thanks.'

'What about something to really warm you up?' he was startled when he heard a soft voice, 'it's a cold night, best spend it with someone warm and friendly, what d'you say?'

The woman behind the counter was at the other end of the van busying herself with his tea and was paying no attention to him at all. He looked round and found that the voice had come from a girl stood by his side looking straight at him, piercing him with her big dark eyes, her coffee-coloured skin was smooth and blemish free, she wore only a little make up, but he couldn't work out exactly how old she was. Andy couldn't take his eyes off her. He knew exactly what she was offering, and it shocked him, but he was also intrigued. The girl was a little plump but not fat, just well rounded. He could see she had long well shaped legs and ample breasts. Her mini skirt was no more than a wide belt, and he became fixated with her body. Andy started to think about Rachel. At that moment he felt alone and deserted. This made him feel like reaching out to someone, anyone.

'Want anything else?' the woman behind the counter asked.

'Perhaps,' he replied. The woman looked from Andy to the girl.

'Stop hitting on my customers, Hayley, now bugger off!' she flicked some cold water over the girl.

'Bugger off yourself, Vera. It's a free country.'

'Nothings free with you, now clear off or I'll call the police.'

'Coming?' Hayley said before turning away from the van and walking into the street. Andy paid for his tea but left it on the counter and walked after her.

'It'll cost you of course,' she said not bothering to look at Andy as he came up next to her. 'That's life after all.' She leaned over the railings of an old house and looked sideways at him. He could see right down her blouse. She was wearing a push up red bra, lacy and revealing. She licked her lips and then laughed out loud. 'Not in the market, eh? Sorry mate, thought you looked like you needed company.'

He stood close to the railings to avoid her seeing the effect he was having on her, but she was a professional and had already sussed him out.

'Where can we go?' he heard himself say to her.

'My flat's close by, it's warm at least, nothing grand but it does me, it's got a bed, a bottle and a bathroom, what more does a girl need?' The girl's openness was refreshing after the falseness of the girls Andy had been dating whilst trying to get to terms with his relationship with Rachel. They played games with him but not the sort he wanted to play. They just tried to mess with his emotions. This girl just wanted to mess with his body.

In ten minutes, they'd reached her flat. It had a stale old smell.

God, this place hasn't been cleaned in years, thought Andy, *but let's be fair, it's not much worse the average student flat Jon and I stayed in, only somehow it seems sad. At least students have a chance to move on but this place, if you end up living here, you're here for life or worse.*

Tabloid newspapers were strewn on the floor along with the remains of several takeaway meals. The carpet had seen better days and now was a strange brown colour which no doubt bore no resemblance to the original. The settee was sagging and looked as tired as the occupants it supported during their afternoon escapes into the world of sad soaps and even sadder reality TV programmes. Andy almost expected someone who had been a contestant from a 'get me out of here' series to appear from one of the rooms at any moment.

'Come in here,' the girl beckoned to him. He willingly obliged. The sitting room was too depressing a place to stay in for long and he hoped for better things in her room. He was disappointed. The same sad carpet lay on the floor and ashtrays full of various remains of escapism lay about the room. The bed was only a worn-out mattress on the floor and her few cheap clothes lay in heaps in the corners of the room. At the window were drapes which passed for curtains but ones which he knew his mother would have never allowed in her home, his home. He wondered what he was doing in such an environment. He knew only too well why.

'I've forgotten your name, sorry,' he said

'Hayley' she replied not asking him what his was. It didn't matter what his name was. 'Come and sit down, take the weight off your crotch.'

Andy smiled. He liked her for her directness. He sat down on the mattress as the girl took her shoes off her high shoes. Even though it was the middle of winter, she wasn't wearing any tights, and her legs had a faint mottled blue tinge to them. Sitting down beside him she put her hand on his leg. She could feel the strength of his well-toned muscles and she raised her eyebrows.

'You're in good shape, I bet you work out, don't you?'

'I'm a fitness instructor.'

'Wow!' she said. 'So, I suppose you don't smoke or do drugs or anything then?'

'No, it's not good for you,' he said and immediately realised the hypocrisy of his statement. When you lived in a world like this, something not being good for you was the least of your worries.

'Lots of things aren't good for you,' she said, 'but it doesn't mean you can't try them. You might even enjoy it, you never know,' and she opened a small box near the bed. 'Do you mind if I do? It helps me relax.'

'What's in the box?' he said enquiringly.

'Good stuff. I got it from a mate of mine down the pub last night. Go on, it'll do you good.' She opened a packet she had taken from the box and started to roll a joint with the deftness borne from countless practice and offered it to Andy.

'Not just yet, thanks,' he said not wanting to seem a complete dork in front of her. His first reaction had been to get up and run like hell, but he was mesmerised by this young girl.

'How old are you?' he asked her.

'Old enough,' she said defensively, conscious that she was probably just old enough to shag but not yet old enough to vote. She lit her joint and breathed in its acrid smoke deeply and slowly. The expelled smoke then rolled around the room and came to rest on all the surfaces it met, like a blanket of tranquility. Andy stifled a cough. 'Why don't you make yourself more comfortable before we start, eh?'

'Yes, but can we talk a little first, perhaps, I think talking is good, don't you?' Andy knew immediately how lame that sounded.

'It's OK if you've got something to say,' Hayley shrugged her shoulders, 'what the heck, shall we talk about you paying me, that'd be a good start.'

'Paying you? Oh, yes, how much?' Andy was so intoxicated by her and the smoke that was filling the room that the full meaning of what she had said didn't register for a minute. He then felt embarrassed and confused. He had never had to pay a woman to have sex with him before but somehow, he didn't seem to think it was going to be such a bad idea after all. No strings and as much sex, of whatever kind he wanted and all it would cost him was money. No emotions, no commitment, no crap.

'What would you like? I don't come cheap you know. I can ask £20 a time.'

Andy held back a smile when she said this. She thought that £20 was asking a lot of money to be defiled by complete strangers. Andy was intrigued. 'How much for a whole night?' he didn't want to be constrained by time, he was in no hurry to leave.

Hayley looked up at the ceiling and thought carefully. *He seems a nice guy and he looks clean, if I play this right, he could be a regular, but shit, no one's ever asked for an all-nighter, what the hell do I say?* She twisted up her face trying to look thoughtful.

'£50 quid – cash,' she hoped she hadn't priced herself out of such a good catch.

'OK!' Andy agreed more surprisingly to himself than to her. 'Now can we talk?'
'We can do anything you like but let's get more comfortable first, shall we?' She took the money, put it away in a drawer by her bed and turned towards him undoing her blouse. Her nipples showed through the course lace of her bra, and she fondled her breasts seductively. She then unzipped her short skirt and let it fall to the floor, kicking it across the room to land in the already growing mountain of discarded clothes. She ran her hands over her stomach where there was a tattoo depicting a snake disappeared down the front of her black lace thong. She pushed him back and straddled him, he felt her deftly undress him and as he lay there on the lumpy mattress, she went about her business as efficiently as Rachel doing a client's accounts. No nook or cranny went unexplored, and Andy felt his body rise and climax in ways he had never experienced before. The illicitness of the situation heightened his pleasure and even though he knew it was wrong to be doing these things with this girl, this only made him want her more. Eventually exhausted he fell into a deep sleep.

CHAPTER 35

Rachel drove home from the wedding reception to get changed ready for the evening do and then went around to Martha to check on her. The house was in darkness. She knocked the door but no answer. She was just about to leave when the door opened. It was Martha.

'Oh, Rachel, what a surprise, I didn't hear the door at first, I was in the kitchen getting Jed his dinner, he hasn't come home yet, I do hope he's OK. How is the party going? It was so fine, you did such a good job organising it all. I meant to say thank you earlier.'

'I love organising, it was fun for me, exhausting but fun. Cathy asked me to call around to make sure you're OK. Mr. Jones did seem very upset this morning.'

'He'll be OK, he just gets in a tizz sometimes but he's a good man deep down.' Martha tried to convince both herself and Rachel. She had faith in her husband. It was impossible not to have and remain sane, after all she had given the best years of her life to that man. She had to believe in him; she simply had to.

'Well if there's anything you need including a bed for the night, just let me know, here's my card with all my numbers on it, keep it safe and call me any time.' Rachel left Martha standing at the door. She looked worried but Rachel knew that it was not her business to pry into the relationship between a husband and wife. She hurried to get back to the party. There was still so much to make sure was organised properly and without her being there, God knows what might happen.

Martha shut the door slowly. She was worried but not unduly. She was sure Jed would see sense and come around to Cathy and Jon being married. They were such a good couple, they were made for each other. Martha was sure God had meant it to be.

She continued to busy herself in the kitchen preparing her husband's favourite dinner – battered fish and home-made chips with mushy peas. She had to admit she liked the meal herself as well, but as no one ever asked her for her opinion on anything, so she rarely gave it.

After the outburst earlier Jed Jones had left the church in a foul mood and had gone in search of his usual solace but had found none available to him. He then decided to go to his chapel. As a warden he had a key, and he sat down and prayed for guidance. But for once this didn't seem to help him. He needed more. He needed to talk to someone who would understand. His whole world seemed to be falling in around him like the walls of Jericho, and he was scared, he'd never had to justify his actions to anyone except his father and he certainly had never had to justify himself to a woman.

Jed Jones arrived home soon after Rachel had left, and Martha hoped he hadn't seen her leave. He sat down at the dinner table and waited for his food. He never announced his arrival. His wife was supposed to anticipate his every need, and if she didn't then he was justified in teaching her a lesson on the poor quality of her wifely duties. This was something he had had to do frequently in the early years of their marriage, but he thought that he had cured her of slovenliness and self-interest by now. That was until today. His ego still smarted from her disagreement with him in public over his daughter Cathy.

He sat at the table and waited until Martha came into the room with his dinner. It was served on a plate that had been part of their dinner service they had had as a wedding present from the Brethren. Several pieces had been broken over the years and each had resulted in a lecture on frugality, thrift and respect for belongings from Jed to the whole family.

Martha placed the meal in front of her husband. He did not acknowledge her or thank her but simply said grace and started eating. She sat down and poured him a cup of tea and one for herself. She did not feel like eating just yet. She would have something when he went out to his Elders meeting later.

He finished his meal in silence. She cleared away his plate.

'I've made your favourite pudding,' she said from the kitchen, 'rhubarb crumble with custard. I got the rhubarb yesterday from the market. Mrs. Flanders was in with her garden produce. Her rhubarb is by far the best there is. And her strawberries looked really tasty, but I didn't get any of them as they were a bit expensive. I do so love strawberries straight from the garden...'

Jed listened to her prattle, and it made him even more incensed. *Here she is offering her opinion on a frivolous topic such as strawberries,* he thought as he got up from the table, *while all the time that boy is defiling my Cathy. I brought my daughter up to be pure, I'd hoped she'd have married one of the Brethren, that would have been a good marriage. But instead, she went and defied me allowing a heathen to touch her and plant his seed in her and now Martha's supporting all this.*

Martha was still preparing the dessert. *What a wonderful day,* she thought, *it was so good to see Cathy happy and I was so brave wasn't I, saying all those things,* she smiled, *it doesn't seem to have annoyed Jed too much, thank goodness, so perhaps he'll come round to it eventually, perhaps then we can be a happy family with Luke back too of course, I do so miss him.*

Martha hadn't noticed Jed come into the kitchen. She didn't feel the knife at first either as it pierced the flesh between her ribs, but she suddenly felt a little sick and then the pain started to grow, she leant forward over the kitchen worktop and noticed that blood was beginning to drip from her mouth. She tried to speak but the knife, which had now broken into her lung had filled it with blood, and she found she couldn't say anything. She spluttered as blood flew around the kitchen. She noticed that some of it had splattered onto the lilac handbag which she had borrowed from the dress shop and her final thought was that now they would make her pay for it but then she was always the one who ended up paying for everything anyway.

Jed Jones watched as his wife slumped to the floor. He watched as the look of surprise on her face changed to one of serene contentment. He stood watching for a few minutes and then took the knife and washed it under the tap and put it back in the knife rack. He turned and left the room, went upstairs and changed his clothes that he had noticed were splattered with blood. He threw them into the laundry basket. *She can wash them later,* he thought and got ready to attend his Elders meeting, *everything will be OK again now, I've brought order back to my home, this was God's will.*

CHAPTER 36

When Andy woke up Hayley was sat beside him with a creased satin dressing gown on. She was rolling herself another joint and offered Andy one.

'No thanks. I'm not a smoker. I did say it's not good for you, you know,' he said trying to make light of a situation he was not comfortable with.

'Neither am I, but you still had me, several times if I remember right, you're a real animal when you get going, I'll have to mention you in my memoirs,' she laughed at the absurdity of anyone wanting to read about her life.

'Only if you write good things about me,' Andy said.

'Of course.'

He looked at her. It bothered him that he found her attractive. It bothered him that he had had sex with her, but he found he wanted her again. This bothered him most of all.

Andy looked at his watch. It was gone 3am. 'I'd better go. Don't want to keep you up,' he said and went to get up. Hayley pulled him back down.

'Don't go yet, stay and talk, you like talking, don't you? Anyway, I thought you paid for all night, you can't have your money back.'

'I don't want my money back.'

'You supposed to be somewhere else then? I wouldn't want to keep you from the little lady,' she laughed and looked playfully at him.

'No, I haven't got anywhere to be and no one to see either, my last girlfriend decided she liked girls better, a bit of a blow to the old ego really.'

'Well, I hope I put you right there then. She must be a fool to let you go for some hairy muff, I've tried it with girls, it's a fallacy that all pros are really lesos and that we don't enjoy sex with men, I wouldn't be doing this job if I didn't like a good poking, now would I?'

Andy smiled. 'No, I can't say you strike me as a woman who would shag for a living and not enjoy it, you certainly made me enjoy it, I'd like us to do this again sometime.'

'So do I,' Hayley said and then thought to herself *if I play this right, he could become a regular which makes for easy money.* She smiled at him and said 'I'm starving. Fancy going for breakfast?'

'OK. I'm a bit hungry too, besides I don't think I shall be able to keep my hands off you much longer if we stay here.'

Hayley smiled. It wasn't often that she heard that. It wasn't often that anyone said anything at all. They usually just got dressed and left.

She took him to an all-night café where she seemed to know everyone and ordered two specials and took two huge mugs of tea over to the table where Andy had sat down.

'Did you pay already for breakfast?' he asked.

'No, Stan knows me. You can pay on the way out.'

'Not quite the Ritz,' he said, 'but I bet the portions are bigger.' They laughed and chatted easily. He found he liked this girl and her sordid world. It made him feel he belonged but of course he didn't. He stood out like a sore thumb especially as he was still wearing his suit from the wedding, a bit crumpled now but still way out of place.

Other diners had noticed his clothes and accent and wondered who Hayley had got involved with now, they were used to her always trying to latch onto 'Toffs' in the vain hope of getting out of the hell she called life, but they knew it always ended with them dumping her when they had used her enough. She belonged here with them. They were sad for her that she couldn't see that, but she was young, she'd learn soon enough.

After the meal, they went back to Hayley's flat. Her flat mate Karen had got home a little before them.

'Where've you been?' she said.

'Out for breakfast,' said Hayley. 'Did you get any milk in on your way home? Where've you been anyway?'

'I had that stag night in Hendon to do, could have done with your help, there were six of 'em. God, I ache all over, I'm having a bath.' Karen said and then noticed Andy. 'Well, hello! Who've we got here then?'

Andy stared at Karen. He was taken aback at her striking resemblance to Cathy, it was uncanny except that she was probably a few years younger than Cathy.

'This is...oh, I don't know your name,' Hayley said realising that out of habit she hadn't bothered to ask him.

'Hello, I'm Andy. Pleased to meet you,' and he put out his hand automatically to shake Karen's hand. The gesture only made Karen laugh.

'Yeah, right! I'll see you two later, and no, I didn't get the milk, I forgot.' She headed for the bathroom, turning back to Hayley to said, 'Oh by the way if The Preacher calls by today tell him I'm out, I couldn't stand having him spouting on all that Bible talk – I'm too knackered.'

'He called by yesterday afternoon when you were out, he seemed to be in a right state and shouted at me as if it was my fault, he gives me the creeps, Karen, I don't know why you put up with him.'

'He's a regular and he pays well, but I know what you

mean, he creeps me out sometimes too.'

'Preacher?' said Andy as they went into Hayley's room.

'Yeah, one of Karen's regulars, he keeps spouting Bible verses and hell and damnation stuff to her whilst they're doing it, he gets off on it I think. The weirdest thing is, he calls her 'his little angel' and insists she calls him Daddy. He's a right pervert if you ask me.'

Andy laughed and thought how strange and sad the men these girls serviced must be. *And I'm one of them now,* he thought.

'Do you have a phone number so I can call you?' he said.

'Yeah sure,' Hayley was pleased that he was obviously keen enough to want to see her again. 'Best to phone first, you never know if I'll be free'. She gave him her mobile number and Andy left. He had to get home and change. He'd have to explain to his parents where he had been and why he had left the wedding early. He hailed a taxi on the high street. *I can't believe I did what I did last night,* he thought, *I must have been out of my mind. But she's so beautiful and she makes me feel so horny, I've got to see that woman again, well, girl really but old enough, definitely old enough,* he tried to convince himself.

CHAPTER 37

'I'm going to see Cathy's mum later so I must be getting on,' said Rachel to Mel as they finished their lunch. 'I hope she's OK. I've rung several times, but I can't get a reply. Cathy was so worried about her before she went on the honeymoon. I feel somehow responsible if anything has happened to her.'

'I'm sure she's OK. She's very busy that's all, running after that husband of hers most of the time. I feel so sorry for her. I'm glad Cathy found the courage to break free from that man. He's poison – I don't care if he is a so-called Christian – there's more to being a Christian than just saying your prayers all the time and reading the bible. That's what I find so hypocritical about all this religion stuff.'

'Ooh, we are on our soap box today,' said Rachel, 'anything else we need to get off our chest?'

'No, I think that'll do for now, but you never know about tomorrow – something is bound to get on my nerves and off I'll go.' The two girls laughed at Mel's propensity to fly off the handle over things that irritated her. They remembered back to the day they had gone shopping before their holiday to Majorca.

'At least you can't be worried about wearing flimsy clothes anymore, Mel,' Rachel said, 'I can't get over the way you've transformed yourself since we got back. Do you remember how we all said it was going to do us the world of good to go on that holiday? Well, it sure seems to have in your case.'

'Thank you, Rachel. I think Cathy has come out of it best of all though.'

'I hope so,' said Rachel thoughtfully, 'but I must get back to the office if I'm going to get off early to see Martha. I hope she's OK – I really do. I can always remember her at the wedding. She was magnificent the way she stood up for Cathy. I was so proud of her.'

'We all were, I don't think Cathy could believe her eyes when Martha went into that vestibule.'

Rachel had two meetings booked that afternoon and then hoped to get off by 4pm. She managed to do just that and by 4.10pm she was speeding along in her new red sports convertible she had bought when she had been promoted to Assistant Director the previous month.

As she pulled up outside the Jones' house, her car looked very much out of place. The run-down former council estate was more used to seeing clapped out old bangers or cars whose ownership was very cloudy parked in the street. The shiny new Mercedes was so conspicuous, Rachel almost felt like tucking it under her arm as she went to walk down the path to the front door. Most of the houses in the street had been sold to their tenants back in the 1980s but not the Jones', Jed Jones didn't believe in getting into debt and neither had his father who had been a tenant there before him.

Rachel knocked the door and waited. It was getting dark even though it wasn't even five o'clock. The winter dreariness only added to Rachel's unease about being there. She knocked again only harder. Still no answer so she debated whether to leave a note for Martha or not. *If*

Mr. Jones finds it and reads it, he might get upset and then that would only make things worse for Martha. I'll call later in the week, she thought and left the dismal environment trying to leave behind the sense of unease as well.

Rachel called by several times more over the next few days without success until in the end she felt she had to see Mel.

'I'm worried, Mel. She can't be out all the time. I've called at all sorts of times and days. It doesn't make sense. What can we do?'

'What do you mean 'do'?' said Mel, perplexed that Rachel should be so concerned. 'I can't see what we can do. When Cathy gets back, we can go with her to see her mother if you like. She's still got a key, hasn't she?'

'Yes, but still, I feel responsible. I'll go one more time in case it's just bad timing that means I've kept missing her, will you come too? I hate going there by myself, the whole area gives me the creeps.'

Mel agreed to go with Rachel that evening.

As they approached the house, they could see a light on in the front room.

'This looks promising,' Mel said.

Rachel knocked the door and eventually the door opened a crack and Jed Jones peered out. He stared at the girls.

'Yes? What do you want? I'm watching tele.'

'We were wondering if Mrs. Jones was in.' said Rachel hesitantly.

'No. She's out at a sisters meeting. I'll say you called.' And he shut the door.

'There, see? she's OK. He said she was out,' said Mel trying to ease the situation.

'No. Something's wrong, I can feel it, let's go, I need to check something out.'

Rachel sped along the city roads until she came to the

chapel that Cathy's family attended. The building was in darkness. She and Mel got out of the car and Rachel went to read the notice board.

'There, see? I told you, the Chapel's sisterhood meets on Thursdays, today is Wednesday, Martha isn't at any meeting, he lied.'

'But why? Why would he lie about where his wife was?'

'Because something has happened to her, she's left him, I bet, couldn't take it any longer.'

'Then where did she go and why didn't she tell you or come to see you? She knew you would help her, and God knows if she did leave him she'd need all the help she could get,' Mel said.

'True, but we need help, I can't work this one out by myself. Let's go see my dad, he'll know exactly what to do.'

'Your dad? That's a bit OTT, isn't it? This isn't a military operation we're in the middle of.'

'No, it could be something much worse,' Rachel said, and Mel couldn't help but laugh.

'Oh, come one, Rachel, you do overreact sometimes.'

'I could be wrong, but if I'm not?'

They arrived at Rachel's home. Her father, Colonel Ben Davis, was in his study as usual finishing yet another report this time about a training course which he wanted to get on his commanding officer's desk by 09.00 hours.

'Dad, we need your help, we have to plan a reconnaissance mission.' A light in her father's eyes lit up and he went into full Marines mode. Mel was swept along by two fanatical experts and even though she still doubted the validity of what they were doing, she was mesmerised with their efficiency and how well-oiled a machine Rachel and her father were. She had always hated Rachel for being so efficient but somehow this time it seemed like poetry in motion. Mel thought of all those times Rachel had seemed just plain annoying when she tried, usually in vain, to organise the girls. Mel felt a little guilty about how she had often shouted at Rachel for behaving like that when all she was trying to do in fact was to be helpful. Like now in fact. She was concerned about Cathy's mother, and nothing was going to stop her finding out if she was safe.

'We'll start with surveillance,' said The Colonel, 'that way we can assess if Martha is still OK and also the movements of Jed.'

'Can we start right away? I know something's wrong,' Rachel champing at the bit to get started.

'Only when we have planned the ops down to the last detail. Mel - when are you free to stake out the premises?'

Mel jumped when she realised, she would be involved in this. She'd hoped she could just stand back and watch.

'Um, well, I could keep watch any evening except Tuesday when its slimming club and Friday when I have my Spanish lesson. I've got to be in work from 9am till 5pm as well.'

'I can get time off if necessary but it's busy at the moment with a big new account we've just landed. Dad, can you do some shifts for us?'

'I'm sure I can come up with something, but I can't promise until I've had a chance to work out my schedule in more detail. Let's work on what we know first to see when we need to watch the house.'

'Mr. Jones works shifts so he could be out during the day or the night. If we can work out his shift pattern, then we can find out when he'll be away from the house. Martha doesn't go out to work. But then I think she hasn't been going out at all lately. I think he's keeping her locked up in the house, probably on starvation rations. Oh, I hate him, I really do...'

'Steady, Lieutenant, don't let your emotions rule the op. Keep a calm head at all times.'

'I know, I'm sorry Dad but I'm scared he's done something to her.'

'Rachel, he wouldn't do anything serious. I expect he's knocked her about a bit and she's too ashamed to go out until the bruises fade,' Mel tried to calm Rachel down.

'OK, we'll work on the premise that she's in the house but that she needs liberating in some way either from him or from her own fears,' Rachel regained control over her emotions once again. She knew she mustn't jeopardise the op.

CHAPTER 38

The surveillance of Jed's movements showed that he was working afternoons that week, so the 'liberation' was set for Wednesday evening. The Colonel had somehow got hold of some night vision specs for the girls to use and a set of walkie-talkies, Mel thought it best not to ask how. At six o'clock it was already getting dark as Rachel went up to the front door and knocked hard. She knocked again when there was no answer she went around to the back of the house where Mel and the Colonel were waiting. A dog barked as Rachel and Mel climbed over the rear fence that backed onto playing fields. Colonel Davis went back around to the front of the house and stayed in the car because he felt it was inappropriate for him to break into a civilian house and also he could keep watch for the girls better there.

'I don't want to do this, Rachel. Can we go home, please?'

'Stop being a wimp, Mel. We're doing this for Cathy, remember? Her mother needs us, now let's get into the house as fast as possible.' Mel was surprised at the speed which Rachel picked the lock to the back door and wondered if she had done this sort of thing before.

'What a pathetic lock,' Rachel said, 'it's an insult to put a lock like this on a door at all, he may as well have simply left it open.'

They walked into the scullery and using their night vision sights they could see clearly which way to go. They passed a scene of domestic squalor with pots and pans lying in the sink unwashed and food debris all over the kitchen table. The smell of sour milk and rotting food filled the room and Mel was glad to move into the living room to get away from it. The living room didn't fare much better with newspapers strewn over the floor and half-finished mugs of tea congealing on the coffee table.

'We'll try upstairs,' Rachel said quietly, 'it's more likely that he's keeping her upstairs in one of the bedrooms.'

'Shouldn't we call out in case we frighten her by barging in on her? I don't want her dying of fright on us.'

'No, she may hide herself with shame if we announce ourselves. Come on.' They climbed the narrow stairs to the first floor. The small landing had several doors leading from it and Rachel tried one only to find the toilet and then the bathroom next door to it. She turned to the next door and finding the door wouldn't open easily she put her force behind it and pushed hard. The door eventually gave and opened slowly. The smell from inside the room was worse than in the kitchen and Mel felt herself retching.

'Smells bad,' Rachel said.

'No kidding,' Mel was trying her hardest not to throw up. 'What the hell is in here that can smell so bad? He must have a dead dog in here or something.'

'No. Not a dead dog. Oh Christ, Mel, I didn't want to be right, but this is even worse than I thought.' Rachel had opened a wardrobe door that had been slightly ajar and saw the shape of a woman curled up on the floor of the cupboard. Hanging overhead was a lilac dress and thrown onto the body was a pair of lilac shoes and a small lilac handbag splattered with blood.

'Don't touch anything,' Rachel said with an authority which made Mel jump. 'Don't look in here either, we've got to leave, we've got to get out of here now,' and she pushed past Mel and down the stairs. Mel didn't know what to do. She stepped forward to see inside the wardrobe and gasped at the sight. She wanted to reach out and touch the body but remembered Rachel's words just as she leant forward towards the corpse. 'She must be dead, that's what the smell is, isn't it?' she said but Rachel was too far away by now to hear her. Just hearing herself say the words, helped Mel come to terms with the sight her eyes couldn't believe. She stepped away and shut the wardrobe door. She also carefully shut the bedroom door behind her and hurried downstairs to join Rachel who was already out of the house and pacing up and down in the playing fields wringing her hands and muttering under her breath.

'Rachel, are you OK?' said Mel, 'what should we do now?'

'I don't know, fetch Dad from around the front, I need to talk to him.'

Mel went and told the Colonel what they had found.

'You didn't touch anything?'

'No, Dad. We wore gloves the whole time and we didn't disturb the body. I knew there was something wrong. Why didn't I do something earlier? I might have prevented this, I could have done something, Dad, I let her die, I want to kill him.'

'Lieutenant!'

Rachel stopped and stood very still for several seconds before breaking down into tears and rushing into her father's arms. Ben Davis was taken by surprise at this display of emotion by his daughter and it embarrassed Mel to watch so she turned away. *I bet Rachel's never done that before in her life,* thought Mel, *she must be so upset, I can't imagine her ever needing anyone's protection. I think I could do with a hug too* and she joined in the group hug.

'Yes, well,' Colonel Davis said, 'we must go to the police, but we can't tell them you went into the house. We will just say that you're concerned about the welfare of

Mrs. Jones and think that something has happened to her. I'll come with you in case they try to fob you off. We must make them interested enough to go into the house.' Both girls nodded their ascent to the plan which seemed to be the only thing that made sense at that moment.

The desk sergeant at the police station was sympathetic but Mel could tell he didn't really take the Colonel's rendition of his daughters concerns totally seriously.

'Sergeant, I'm concerned too, I know Mrs. Jones well,' Mel said, 'and I know that there's something wrong. Are you going to ignore us? If she's hurt or ill or worse, then on your head be it.' She looked straight at the police officer, unmoving in her gaze until she had stared him down. He felt uncomfortable and decided the best thing to do was to get the matter off his desk and onto someone else's.

'I'll tell the Detective Inspector of your thoughts. Please take a seat over there and I'll be back shortly.'

The man disappeared into the labyrinth of corridors and offices in the police station. They sat for what seemed ages. Mel went and got Rachel a cup of coffee out of a machine in the waiting area.

'Here, drink this. It'll either help or finish you off completely.'

Rachel drank the hot liquid unable to distinguish if it was tea or coffee or even hot chocolate but not caring which. The hot sweetness helped her compose herself. She wanted to tell the police about the body but knew it would only mean heaps of trouble for Mel, her dad and herself. She kept quiet and waited. *Martha won't mind waiting a few hours longer,* she thought, *she waited her whole life to stand up to Jed Jones and now she can rest in peace.'*

'Please come this way,' the sergeant called to them. He led them down one of the anonymous corridors into a small room. Sat at a desk was a woman in plain clothes. She was in her mid-thirties with a very serious expression on her face.

'Sit down, please. My name is Detective Sergeant Williams, and I'd like to ask a few questions about your allegations concerning Mrs. Martha Jones…'

'They're not allegations,' interrupted Rachel. 'Something awful has happened to her and you have to do something.'

'We will do what is necessary to find out the whereabouts of Mrs. Jones. Firstly, I need to know why you think her husband has something to do with her disappearance?'

'He hates being contradicted, he's a bully, he bullied Cathy for years and poor Mrs. Jones has had to put up with him for all her married life, I'm sure he's killed her. He's a nasty piece of work.'

'What proof have you got that he has done any harm to Mrs. Jones?'

'Well…he threatened her at the wedding,' Rachel was grasping at straws, but she had to make this woman believe her fears. 'He lied about where she was the other day when we called to see Martha. He said she was at a sisterhood meeting, and she wasn't. Please go and look in their house. I know you'll find something. Please hurry.'

DC Williams looked at Rachel and tried to understand what it was about her and her two companions that somehow didn't ring true. She was sure that they were hiding something.

'I'm not going to action anything until I'm sure you're telling me everything you know. Do you want to add anything to your statements?'

Mel looked at Rachel who looked at her father.

'I believe that the girls have told you everything. I'm sorry if they haven't convinced you about this matter. I think they've told you enough. But if you insist on ignoring us for whatever reason you have, then we may as well leave.'

Rachel and Mel were silent more out of shock than anything else. They could not believe he was apparently giving up.

'I'll just have to have a word with the Chief Constable when I see him next at the Club. We won't waste anymore of your time, Madam.' He rose to leave and the girls duly followed. Rachel had never heard her father obviously name drop before. She was very impressed.

'I didn't know you knew the Chief Constable,' said Rachel as they left the building.

'I don't but she doesn't know that does she?' The Colonel smiled.

'Nice one Dad,' Rachel beamed with pride. She always knew her father was good at his job, but it seemed he had hidden talents as well.

'No problem, Lieutenant, just safeguarding the mission, that's all, I'm sure they'll send someone around to check on Martha now.'

The police car drew up outside the Jones' council house. It looked dark and sorrowful in the winter night air. It looked as if it was bracing itself for the onslaught of something awful, but it almost seemed to welcome it as if it would clean it of the horrible truth it had had to keep since the day of the wedding. PC Harper got out of his patrol car and shivered as a cold wind blew up from nowhere. He had been having a quiet shift patrolling the streets for any misdemeanours until he had been told to check this house to find out if the allegations from Mel and Rachel had any substance.

'Good evening, Sir. Are you Mr. Jed Jones?' asked PC Harper.

'Yes. Why do you want to know?' Jed said confused as to why the police should want to talk to him.

'I'd like to speak to your wife Mrs. Martha Jones. Is she in?'

'Yes, but she's busy making my tea. Why do you want to see her for? Jed looked annoyed. He had just finished his shift and wanted to eat his supper.

'May I come in, Mr. Jones?'

'Why?'

'Can I please come in and talk to you and your wife?' said Constable Harper calmly. There was nothing threatening about his voice or gesture and it would have been difficult for Jed to refuse him.

Jed Jones studied the Constable's face. He didn't see why he had to let him in, but he also couldn't think of any reason why he shouldn't. He stepped back from the door and went into the living room. Constable Harper entered the small hallway and gasped as he smelt the all too familiar smell of death. He kept his eyes on Jed who led him into the sitting room. PC Harper knew that the situation had quickly escalated, and he also knew that he was now in a very vulnerable position.

'Can you get Mrs. Jones, please.'

Jed looked at him and then turned and went into the kitchen. PC Harper immediately but discreetly called for back-up as Jed re-entered the room.

'She's not there. I could have sworn she was making my tea. I don't know where she is.'

'No problem, Mr. Jones. Perhaps she has just popped down the shop for something. Shall we just wait for a while until she gets back. I'm sure she won't be long. No one wants to be out in this weather. It's getting really cold, don't you think so?'

'Yes,' said Jed absentmindedly. He could have sworn Martha was in the kitchen but there was no one there. Where could she have gone, he wondered oblivious to the fact that within minutes there were two police cars pulling up outside. DS Williams strode forcefully down the garden path and knocked loudly on the front door.

'Shall I just go and see who that is for you, Mr. Jones,' said PC Harper being very careful not to turn his back on the man as he went into the hallway and opened the front door. They briefly conferred and the two officers went into the sitting room where Jed Jones was sitting down reading a newspaper.

'This is Detective Sergeant Williams, Mr. Jones. She'd like to have a look around your house. You won't mind, will you?' said PC Harper as friendly as he could.

Jed Jones nodded. He had nothing to hide after all and it might make them leave quicker so he could get on with his supper. DS Williams went out to the hall and told her constable to start looking upstairs.

'In here!' the voice of the constable came from the spare bedroom upstairs. DS Williams went upstairs and after a short while came down.

'Mr. Jones, is that the body of your wife upstairs?'

'Body? She's at a church member's house helping with a sick person. That's what she does. Helps others. That's God's way. We all have to help and spread the word of God.' Jed Jones said as if in autopilot.

'But you told me she was cooking your tea, Mr. Jones,' said PC Harper.

'Yes, cooking my tea. That's right. She's cooking my tea.'

The Detective instructed the constable to call the necessary back up. The constable was only too glad to get out of the house and its terrible smell.

'Mr. Jed Jones, can you please come with me to the station.' DS Williams said, 'We would like to ask you a few questions about your wife.'

'Can I get changed first,' he asked and went to go upstairs. He wanted to put on his Sunday best outfit as he thought that it was the most appropriate for a meeting in a police station. 'Where did that woman put my clean shirt?' he asked himself. 'I can never get her to do anything properly, I'll have to make do with my second-best shirt I suppose.'

'I'm afraid it won't be possible for you to change your clothes, Mr. Jones. Please come as you are. I am arresting you on suspicion of murdering your wife Mrs. Martha Jones. You have the right to remain....' But Jed Jones didn't hear the rest of the Detective's speech. He was confused. Why hadn't Martha ironed his best shirt? What had she been doing these past few weeks? Nothing was getting done anymore. He would have to have words with her about her slovenliness. It was getting just too bad.

Upstairs in the Jones' house lay the body of Martha Jones. The look on her face was still one of serenity just as it had been when she had drawn her final blood drenched breath that fateful day of the wedding. The day which had been the happiest day of her life but also her last.

The phone rang and The Colonel answered it. He listened very carefully. 'Thank you for telling us about Mr. Jones, Detective,' he said.

'I will need full statements, but they can wait until tomorrow. Thank you for being persistent,' said DS Williams, 'I did have trouble believing you at first. We get people coming in just trying to cause trouble for neighbours and people they don't like, so that in the end you just don't know who to believe.'

'No problem, Sergeant, we'll be in at 11.00 hours. Good night.'

Colonel Davis turned to Rachel and Mel who were still in a state of shock after the evening's happenings.

'It *was* her, wasn't it?' said Mel.

'Yes,' he said. 'I hope he didn't make her suffer. I think she'd suffered enough already, don't you?'

'God rest your soul, Martha. May you find peace at last, you deserve it,' Rachel said.

'Do you think he did it?' said Mel.

'Of course he did it,' said Rachel. 'Think about how strange he's been acting. Saying she's out somewhere when all along she was dead upstairs stuffed in a cupboard, the man's a psycho.'

'Who's going to tell Cathy? They're due back the day after tomorrow. What a home coming,' Mel thought back to the homecoming she had when she had found her own mother dead. 'At least she's got Jon…'

'And us,' Rachel said. 'She's got us too.'

'Of course, we're all here to help. I know how much she means to you.'

The Colonel drove Mel home, the night vision glasses safely stowed away in the boot along with the lock picking instruments, gloves and dark clothing. He'd put them back in his basement locker later.

CHAPTER 39

Cathy and Jon returned two days and Rachel and Mel were there to welcome them.

'I hope you had a great time. We've missed you so much.' They hugged each other but Cathy could sense that something was wrong.

'It's Mum, isn't it? He's done something to her, hasn't he?'

Mel and Rachel looked at each other. Rachel led Cathy into the sitting room and sat her down.

'I'm afraid he has, I'm so sorry Cathy, I tried to look out for her but this all happened after she left the wedding, and we didn't find out until two days ago.'

'What has he done?'

'Cathy, she's dead.'

Cathy sat in a fixed stare at Rachel.

'It's not true, say it's not true.' Cathy broke down and started to cry. The tears fell fast and full down her cheeks. Jon arrived with their bags from the taxi and looked at Cathy.

'What's the matter?'

Mel explained the situation whilst Rachel tried to console Cathy. Cathy just stared ahead with no flicker of understanding in her eyes. Her world had fallen apart just as it was beginning to make sense. She turned to Jon and her look pleaded with him to make it all better.

'I'm so sorry, darling, I don't know what to say.'

Cathy took a deep breath and much to everyone's amazement she stood up.

'I need a cup of tea. Anyone else want one?' she headed for kitchen. In autopilot she filled the kettle and got cups and tea bags. Jon followed her and watched as she mechanically prepared the tea. She seemed to be separate from the situation and Jon was at a loss as to what to do.

Mel came into the kitchen and nodded to Jon.

'Cathy, let's talk,' she said. The awful reality of losing her own mother flooded back into her mind and she held back an emotional surge that nearly choked her. 'We need to talk.'

Cathy turned around and realised the connection between the two of them and she moved over to Mel and put her arms around her. The two women held each other silently without moving. Words and movement would have destroyed the bond between at that moment. Jon sensed that he was not needed and left the room.

'Shall we go for a walk?' Mel said eventually.

'Good idea,' said Cathy softly. They put on their coats and went outside. The cold air on that November afternoon caught them and wrung the self-pity from them like a mangle. They walked arm in arm to the nearby park and found a bench on which to sit. The frost from the night before still clung to the wooden bench but it didn't seem to matter.

'It would be a cliché to say I know what you're going through,' said Mel.

'Yes, it would but I know it would be true. We're both orphans now. I could ask a thousand questions about what happened, about Dad, about everything that's gone on whilst we've been away but somehow it doesn't matter.

Nothing matters.'

'Everything matters, Cathy. They matter, our mums. And our dads. Life matters, but there's nothing which will change what's happened. That's the really numbing thing. Death is so final and there was always more to say. I think that that is the really hurting bit. Not being able to say anything again.'

'I shouldn't have gone away.'

'No, Cathy. You had to go away. It was right for you and Jon. He's your future and the baby. Nothing should change that. Martha wanted that. She did what she had to do and now you have to as well. I learnt that. Mum gave her life for me. She lived only for me and then she could see I was free, her mission was over, complete. I think about her and how she died and even though they put it down as misadventure, I think deep down that she meant it to happen.

'Martha knew what she was doing. And I think she knew what would happen to her. I saw her face, Cathy. She looked at peace. She knew her daughter was safe now and free. She knew you'd be OK. Believe me, mothers know these things.'

Cathy turned to Mel. 'She looked at peace? I'm glad. I loved her so much and I know she took a lot of the pain of living with Dad away from Luke and me. She was like a sponge for his venom. And now she can release it all back out. God will cleanse her. He'll protect her now like she protected me.'

'I'm sure he will,' said Mel. 'I'm getting cold now. Shall we head back. I'm sure Jon is worried.'

'Yes, but he needn't be. I'm with my friend. Friends are always there when you need them, don't you think?'

'Absolutely!' said Mel and they walked back to the flat with lighter hearts and richer understanding. The two women had shared a moment that would bind them together forever.

As Mel went home later, she could hear the words her grandmother had said on the day of her mother's funeral. *Perhaps she was right,* she thought, *I should go and see Dad and now's the right time, I need to put all my gremlins to bed once and for all, seeing Dad will bring me one step closer to being free, and God knows, that's what I want more than anything else in the world.*

CHAPTER 40

Mel drove along the tree lined street gazing at the houses along the way. They were all richly decorated ready for Christmas, and she wondered if the decorations were more for the pleasure of the occupants or to impress passers-by and just out-do the neighbours. Some of the houses were set back in their own grounds and she felt she had accidentally taken a wrong turn and ended up in some suburb of Beverly Hills. The size of the properties was overwhelming and put her own home to shame like some servants' quarters or woodcutter's cottage. Eventually there on the right was the house-name she had been looking for – Heavens-end.

What a naff name for a house, more appropriate to call it Heaven-send, Mel laughed to herself, *you're on good form today, old girl, but I'm going to need more than a sense of humour to get through this. God, this is going to be difficult,* she took a deep breath which calmed her nerves a little, *I wish Iain was here, why did he have to go to see his parents in Edinburgh? Why couldn't I have gone too? Oh, shut up! Concentrate on what we're doing, for God's sake.*

The polished wood front door to the house was huge, *why do they need a door that big? Who the hell is that tall anyway?*

Mel thought, *and I bet it's made of some endangered species too.* Her nerves were getting the better of her and her thoughts were rambling. She pressed the bell and waited. *Still time to run away,* she thought but then the door opened and there stood her father, Robert. He still had those deep blue eyes that had once looked at her with such love and affection. But he had aged and had seemingly shrunk. It was fifteen years since she had last seen him, but this seemed to be a man thirty not fifteen years older. The tall strong man she had known who would throw her up in the air and dance for hours with her was no longer there. A shadow had taken his place.

'Hello, Melissa. Do come in. Bridget is out Christmas shopping…'

'Oh good, it was you I came to see anyway, Dad.' Melissa said making it crystal clear that she didn't want anything to do with the woman who had torn her world apart.

They walked into a sitting room bathed in muted sunlight through soft delicate blinds. The décor of the room was straight out of a magazine, all beige and cream with matching and coordinating Christmas decorations festooned everywhere. Mel was sure she had seen the table lamp on the set of a make-over programme in the TV only the other week. It was a far cry from the faded browns and greens of their living room in Birchen Grove, but one thing which that room had always had which this one didn't, was a feeling of love and belonging. No one 'lived' in this room. It was only for show, for public examination. The people of this house either had no lives or 'lived' somewhere else.

'Would you like something to drink?'

'No, I'm fine.'

'I was sorry to hear about your mother, Mel. Please believe me when I say that. I did love her, but things change - people change, and….'

'Yes. Very true. People do change. I agree. That's

why I'm here now and not five or ten years ago.' Mel said. There was silence, an uneasy and prolonged silence. 'But I am here now, all grown up.' She had rehearsed this meeting a thousand times over the years, but now she was lost, like the little abandoned girl she felt she was, grasping at faint words and sentences. Mel composed herself. 'I am waiting for some answers, I guess. Answers to questions which have bugged me for years, but you weren't there to answer them, were you Dad?'

'I'm sorry....'

'Yes, sorry, but for what, Dad? I never could work that one out.' Mel got up and paced in front of the huge fireplace. 'It never made sense then and it doesn't now. Why Dad? Why? Why did you have to leave us and so abruptly and without even turning back to help us once?' Mel was precise in her speech and not emotional nor angry nor sad, just precise. Inside she was falling apart, melting under the heat of her feelings of hate, anger, loss, abandonment anything but preciseness.

'Mel, please, let's not argue. This is a great opportunity we have here to make up, to catch up on all the lost years and try again. I know it didn't make sense then and sometimes I don't know if it ever made sense to anyone, but it happened, and we can't change that.'

Mel looked at her father. A stranger sat opposite her, enveloped in his luxury chair, bound in cream leather. The man who had ruined her life and killed her mother as sure as if he had poisoned her himself. She just stared at him with empty eyes. Not knowing what to think anymore, not having the strength, if the truth be known, to feel anything. Her life had undergone such turmoil over the last few months, and she was still reeling along in its melt-water flood. She thought of Iain and how she longed to see him again. She thought of all the things that had happened to her and her friends, and she sighed. She thought of her mother, and she held back a tear, not daring to blink lest it escape and expose her inner turmoil.

'Where to begin? I suppose I'd like to know what's been happening to you over these years. I see you're still with Bridget.'

'Yes, Bridget and I are still married, we have a son who is fifteen next month, his name's Richard. Bridget dotes on him, spoils him a little perhaps.' Robert Wright hesitated a little as he spoke about the relationship between his wife and son. Somehow Mel got the impression that he was just an outsider in all of it, not the loved father and husband that he had been with Mel and her mum. 'We moved here just five years ago. It's very peaceful and the area is very sought after. Property values keep going up all the time, a good area always pays off. Where do you live now?'

'I'm selling the house in Birchen Grove now that Mum is dead, too many memories that I no longer need, I'll be sharing a rented flat with Gill Keane, it's close to the hospital where she works, and I can get the Tube to work easily. As I'm not sure where I'll be in six- or twelve-month time, there's no point buying. I don't want to get tied down. Must run in the family.' Mel bit her tongue at this cheap gibe, but her father seemed not to have caught the irony in her voice or perhaps had chosen to ignore it.

'My mother tries to keep me informed to a degree when I see her, but that isn't very often, I'm so busy with the business usually and Bridget likes to travel a lot, so we rarely have time to go visiting. Mother doesn't like coming to the house, it's out of her way a bit and you know how busy she is.'

That's odd, Mel thought, *she's always come around to see Mum and me at least once a week.* Mel thought of the treats she would always bring, just little things like chocolate for her or magazines for Sarah. Her father's words therefore spoke volumes. *Gran always was a woman who spoke her mind,* she thought, *no doubt she did it in front of Bridget once too often, that would account for the lack of visits, well, that and the fact that Gran always hated Bridget.* Mel glowed with pride for her feisty grandmother.

'Mum says you're doing well. Have you seen your Gran lately?' Robert tried to keep the conversation going but he was floundering. He had hoped in many ways never to have this conversation. Even though it was fifteen years since he walked out, he still wasn't ready to discuss things openly.

'I've seen Gran several times especially after Mum's death including at the funeral. She was always there when we needed her.' She flashed a glance at her father and held his gaze with an almost accusatory air until he looked away. She felt she had won that battle, but then didn't really recollect what the war was really about anymore. 'Why didn't you ever write or call?' Mel asked looking at the ground in front of her.

'I… found it difficult after I left, Mel. What with the divorce and Bridget wanting to make a clean break of things…. I suppose I should and could have, but I was in such turmoil, sometimes I didn't know if I was coming or going. Not much consolation, I know, but I can't put the clocks back. If I could, I would, Mel. Please believe me.'

'I don't know what to believe, Dad. I'm still very confused about the whole thing. It affected me very badly but it affected Mum even worse. We didn't deserve that. Was Bridget so much better than us?' Mel looked around the room. 'Seems she's helped you do alright anyway. Does she love you?'

'That's an unfair question, Mel, I can't answer questions like that. You and I have become strangers in effect. So much has happened over the last fifteen years. We are both different people.'

'Yes, I suppose we are but…'

A noise at the front of the house caused Mel to jump.

'Oh, that'll be Bridget. Are you sure you won't have a cup of tea or something?'

Mel replied that she was fine. W*hy is he so obsessed about me having some tea?* she thought, *will she tell him off if she sees I* *haven't had any refreshments? Wow! This isn't the man who used to live with us, Mum doted on him, he never had to lift a finger in our house.*

'Hello darling, did you enjoy the shopping? Melissa's come to see us.'

No, not us, Mel thought, *just you, Dad.* She observed Bridget, the legendary blonde who had ruined her mother's life and her own. The woman who stood before her was tall, elegant and slim, so slim. *Hmm, quite the skinny bitch, I see,* Mel thought, and hated her even more. She had long golden blonde hair, which fell around her shoulders and was arranged in a style that was far too young for her. Mel thought *that's the problem with women like her who retain their figures and then get stuck in a time warp with their hair and clothes, she just looks like mutton dressed as lamb.*

Bridget came across as a cool and calculating woman who always got what she wanted and was hell on steroids if she didn't. She'd obviously got Mel's father just where she'd wanted him, but then found out that he wasn't what she wanted after all, by then it was probably too late and social status held them both in a vice-like grip of upholding a respectable appearance no matter the emotional costs.

'How nice to meet you, Melissa.' Bridget managed to say between gritted teeth. 'I've heard so much about you from your father and your grandmother. I feel I know you already.'

'I doubt that.' Mel smiled, 'I've changed a great deal over the years and especially since my mother died. I doubt you know me at all.'

'Quite! But I hope that doesn't stop us getting to know one another now,' Bridget formed a faint smile, the sheer effort of this gesture made her face look like it was bringing on a seizure. 'Well, it was so nice to see you, do call again.' She gestured to her husband in the direction of the door. 'You'll have to excuse us now, we're expecting company for dinner and there is so much to do.'

'Don't let me keep you.' Mel found herself saying. 'Dad

and I were just reminiscing about old times, weren't we Dad?'

Robert physically cringed as he stood between the two women like a mouse trapped between two cats who were arguing over who owned it.

'Um...well...I thought I'd show Mel the garden. You've done so much to it since we moved in. You've worked wonders with that Landscaper you commissioned. We won't be long. What time are the guests arriving and who was it that's coming tonight? I'd forgotten we were having guests, my darling.'

Bridget face showed how annoyed she was that her husband almost giving away her ruse to get Melissa out of her house. There were no guests coming. That had only been a story to make Mel feel obliged to leave and she would remind Robert of that fact in no uncertain terms later.

'That'd be nice to see the gardens.' Melissa lied. *What a great idea, I need some fresh air, I seen and heard enough, all this has made me feel sick, there's too much to process, I need a Mars bar.*

She followed her father out into the garden ignoring the fact that Bridget was still in the room.

'I'm sorry about Bridget, but she's very wary of me meeting people from my former life. She gets nervous. She's very insecure about us at times. She's such a silly.'

'I'd have called it possessive, even manipulative,' Mel had learnt that mincing your words was a waste of time and she was determined that she was not going to do that now. 'Dad, you look miserable. She controls you, doesn't she?'

'Mel, how can you speak to me like that. I'm your father.'

'No, Dad, you were my father but now you're some else's husband. You don't have the right to tell me anything. It was you who abandoned me, let alone Mum, for that manipulating cow and let's face it, you've regretted it ever since. She's an A1 bitch, you know it, I know it and

Gran definitely knows it. It was her idea that I should come to see you after Mum died and now I know why. She knew that if I saw you and the bitch, I'd be able to get you out of my system once and for all. Gran's wonderful. She knows everything about life, and I only wish I'd listened more to her years ago. I pity you, Dad. I pity you!'

'Mel…'

'Don't interrupt me! I'll be going now. I've got a life to live, and you've stopped me from doing that for long enough. You had unfinished business back in Birchen Grove, but now I've finished it for you. Go back to your wife. Sorry I missed seeing Richard, but I guess he's a chip off the old block, so I doubt I'd have got on with him either, which is a shame. Goodbye.' Mel turned and started back to her car.

'Merry Christmas, Melissa,' Robert Wright said softly as his daughter walked down his long empty drive.

She could see her father still standing where she had left him as if caught like a frightened rabbit in the headlights of the juggernaut she had just driven through his life. She stood by her car collecting her composure. She looked down and saw the last of the autumn leaves skittling along the kerb, a large chestnut leaf landed by her feet, fluttering as if in the last death throws trying desperately to get way. She stared at it. Then lifting her foot, she stamped on it crushing it into a hundred pieces. When she lifted her foot, the wind scoped up the fragments and carried them off into oblivion. Mel was free now of the hold her dad had had over her, and she felt light enough to fly away too for the first time in her life.

CHAPTER 41

Andy found himself drawn more and more into Hayley sordid world. She wanted to escape from her squalor, but Andy became entranced by it.

'What's the suitcase for?' Hayley asked. It was three weeks after they had first met, and she had seen him almost every day during that time. 'You going on holiday? Anywhere nice? You won't forget the postcard and some duty-free fags.'

'No, I'm moving in,' said Andy. Hayley turned and stared at him.

'Oh really! Who said?' she asked.

'I did,' Andy grabbing her arm and pulling her close to him. 'I can't live without you, I've got to be here with you.'

'I thought we were going to move into your flat?' Hayley said. 'What do I need you for if I'm still stuck in this hell hole?'

'I like it here and I'll pay your share of the rent so why bleat on about moving. It's homely here.'

'Yeah right – as homely as a fucking pigsty. Is this how you lot live in suburbia with mummy and daddy then?' she said.

'No. Mum would have a fit if she ever came here, her house is immaculate – sterile even. This is so much more real.'

'Real my arse! It stinks here and I want out, get us a nice little flat, darling. I'd be *really* good to you,' and she started to undo his fly.

'Hayley, you are the baddest girl I know.'

'And that's why you love me, now show me how much.' Hayley forced herself to smile. Andy moving in wasn't exactly what she'd had in mind, but she could bide her time for a while at least, until he came up with the goods. He was her investment, but it seemed the payout was going to take a bit longer than she planned.

'Better get some food in then, if you're going to stay. We need milk, coffee, sugar and some bread and marg. Oh and better get some tinned ham, Karen likes that. You'll have to convince her it's a good idea for you to move in as well. Better get some cleaning stuff and some bog rolls too. And pick up 20 Benson and Hedges whilst you're at it. I'll put the kettle on.'

'Sure, I won't be long, perhaps we can party later,' Andy said.

'Yeah, whatever, now hurry up. I'm going for a dump,' she went into the bathroom and locked the door.

Andy didn't seem to notice that his wallet was always empty, he never noticed that Hayley often went out for hours on end, somehow, he was blind to it all, but he did know that if he was going to keep Hayley, he had to get some money. She was proving insatiable in more ways than one. He had become totally entranced by her. Her world intrigued him, and he didn't want to leave it. Cheap sex, cheap drugs and squalor was all around him. Andy was lost to his old world. He had found another one to drown himself in and he loved it.

CHAPTER 42

'Where's my gold cufflinks, darling? You know, the ones you gave me for our tenth anniversary,' said Clive Owens.

'I don't know love. I was looking for the rings that Grandma left me to wear this evening myself. I can't understand where everything is going lately. I'm beginning to think I've dreamt most of my jewellery up,' said his wife, Moira. 'I've put it down to being disoriented by losing both Jon and Andy at the same time.'

'What do you mean losing Andy?' said Clive.

'Well, he's never here and when he is, he seems distant. It's ever since Jon and Cathy got married. He's not coping well being separated from his twin. What do you think?'

'I hadn't really noticed, but now you mention it, well…he has somehow changed, but we have to let them live their own lives.'

'Yes,' said Moira, 'but we also have to guide them. I'm worried about the company he's keeping. Remember when we went around to his flat and found him with that girl. She was very unsavoury. And those clothes she had on. Anyone would think she was on the game.'

'Moira, what a thing to say about our son's girlfriend. It's nice to see him out with a girl again after Rachel. Splitting up with her really knocked him for six but he won't even talk about it. Even Jon's a bit cagey about talking about it. I don't think I understand young people anymore. Are we getting old, Moira? I just feel something's wrong. I feel I'm forgetting things or that things are genuinely going missing, I know where I've always kept things but lately, I can't find anything, I think I'm having too many senior moments,' Clive looked at his wife of thirty years and wondered.

'You know he's given up his flat now. And he's refused to tell us his new address,' Moira said, 'I'm worried about him, I feel like he's shutting us out of his life.'

'Nonsense, he'll come round eventually,'

Moira was not convinced but she was still preoccupied with her missing jewelry. 'Do you think we've been burgled, and we didn't notice? Perhaps they got in through an open window or we could have left the back door unlocked.'

'Don't be silly, Moira. Of course we haven't.'

'Then explain where all of grandmothers jewelry has gone.

'I can't.' Clive sighed. 'Life doesn't seem to make much sense at all lately. I'm worried more about our son than some jewelry, perhaps we should try to reach out to Andy.'

'That's an idea, we could ring him to see if he's coming to lunch on Christmas Day.'

'And he could bring his new girlfriend…'

'Clive, I don't think that's a good idea, even I have my limits to hospitality.'

'Moira, we've got to show willing, or we'll only push him further into her arms. It would only be for a few hours, and we need to invite Jon and Cathy as well. It would be a real family Christmas. That would be nice, wouldn't it?' Clive put his arms around Moira's waist and hugged her close. 'It'll be like old times.'

'Forgive me, but I can't remember too many girls like her coming around for Christmas lunch,'

'Moira,' Clive wasn't keen either but knew he had to make an effort.

'OK! But let's do it soon. That way I won't have too long to change my mind.'

'We'd love to come,' said Cathy. 'It would be so nice. Thank you for inviting us. Bye!'

Moira hung up the phone and sighed. If only all daughters-in-laws could be as lovely as Cathy, she thought. Now she had to tackle inviting Andy and his girlfriend. She dialed Andy's mobile and waited. A woman's voice answered. Moira was a little taken aback.

'Is Andy there? This is his mother.'

'God, I never thought you'd ring him here, I'll get him. Andy! It's you mum.' the voice shouted half into the phone and half across the room. Moira hoped that her hearing hadn't been permanently damaged, but she couldn't be sure.

'Yeah?' Andy said tersely. 'What do you want?'

'I...well your dad and I wondered if you were coming to lunch on Christmas Day? We'd love to see you and ... you can bring your new girlfriend. We're dying to meet her properly.'

'I'll see.'

'Well, do try darling. I'll do your favourite – roast beef and lots of Yorkshires. Please try to come.' Moira heard the phone go dead. She didn't know if she'd got through to her son or not but at least she'd tried. She felt the emotion of her conversation welling up in her eyes. She sniffed hard and turned to fill the kettle. *A nice cup of tea,* she thought. *Yes, that would be just the ticket, and perhaps a chocolate biscuit.* What she really felt like having was a stiff drink, but it was only 11am so she thought better of it. *What would the neighbours think?* she smiled to herself. *Oh, bugger what the neighbours think, my little boy's lost, I've lost him.* She broke down and cried.

When Christmas Day arrived, Moira looked at her watch and Clive paced up and down the sitting room.

'Calm down, Dad,' said Jon, 'He'll be here, he loves your

cooking, Mum.'

'We all do,' said Cathy. 'Thank you for inviting us.'

'It's a pleasure my dear,' said Clive. 'You are both welcome here anytime.'

'I don't think he's coming,' said Moira. 'I'll give him a quick ring and then we had better sit down to lunch or the food will be ruined.' She went into the kitchen. Clive ushered the others into the dining room and started to pour the wine.

'I'll just go and see if Moira needs any help,' he said.

'Oh, can I help too?' said Cathy.

'No, you sit there, you're doing too important a job making our first grandchild,' Clive went into the kitchen. He found his wife leaning over the sink, tears falling into the half full bowl of dirty water left in the sink. Their splashes were as silent as her grief. He put his arms around her and hugged her close.

'Is he coming?' said Clive.

'I asked him, and he laughed at me. He said he would rather die than set foot in our house again. He said it was like a prison. I then asked him if he'd seen the things we've been looking for. He went quiet. Then he hung up. He took them. I know it.'

'Moira, you can't know that for sure,' said Clive knowing that he had had the same conclusion as his wife. 'We'll find those things.'

'Yes, in some tacky pawn shop. My grandmother's jewellery. Clive, those things were all I had left of her. They meant the world to me. I'll never forgive him.'

Clive could not bring himself to plead for his son's innocence anymore. They served the lunch before telling Jon and Cathy the awful truth.

'Mum, I don't know what to say. I'll smack him from here to next week for hurting you,' said Jon.

'No. He's still your brother. He'll come around. It's that awful girl he's with. Nothing we can do now. Let's eat before it all goes cold. Anyone for extra Yorkshires?'

CHAPTER 43

The coldness of the February night made Mel shiver as she left the community college. The Spanish lesson this week had gone well. She felt very encouraged at her progress and longed to impress Ian with her new language skills.

'Buenos Noches!' called Derek, one of her fellow students.

'Buenos Noches!' replied Mel smiling at him.

'The lesson was good this evening, don't you think?' he said.

'Yes. I really enjoyed it, but I don't think I'll ever have to say, *where's the bull ring,* do you?' Mel looked at Derek. He was one of those men you just couldn't help liking. He was a lot older than Mel and was taking Spanish lessons as he was hoping to retire to Spain in a few years' time. He seemed to live each day with anticipation and his enthusiasm for life showed in his eyes. *I wish I could be as positive about everything as Derek is,* thought Mel. *He never seems to be unhappy about anything.*

'I suppose not,' he replied, 'but I'm sure to have some friend or other who visits and wants to see one. You never know when things will come in handy,' he said and turned to get into his car. 'Are you parked far away? Do you need an escort?'

'No, I'm fine' Mel went into independent woman mode about not needing a man's protection. She was touched though, that he would care enough to ask.

She walked around the back of the college to where she had parked her car. She had been late arriving that week because she had some work to finish before she could leave the office. She hated parking at the back as it was dark and scared her a bit. *All in the mind, Mel,* she tried to reassure herself and got her keys ready, so she didn't have to stop long in such an isolated place.

Because she had stopped to talk to Derek, most of the other cars had now gone and this made her feel worse. The walk back to her car gave her some time to think though about the lesson, the day and her life generally. She called it her therapy time. She was so caught up in the moment that she didn't notice a car was parked alongside hers. She didn't recognise it. As she walked between the two vehicles, she saw that the car next to her was not empty. She pretended not to have seen the man sat inside. Suddenly the door opened, and she was trapped between her own door and that of the car next to hers. Out of the car came a figure she immediately recognised. Mel looked up at his face. There was a smile on it, a wry smile, which spoke a thousand words and all of them ones Mel did not want to hear.

'Vince! What are you doing here?'

'I'd like a little chat, I think there are a few things we need to get out in the open.' Vince stood before her, too close for comfort and all she could think of the smell of his breath – acrid and stale. She could feel the hairs on the back of her neck rising along with her heart rate. 'Get in the car, Mel. Too cold to stand out here, don't you think. Let's go somewhere warm and cosy.'

Mel panicked and tried to get into her own car, but he was too quick and too strong for her. 'Now that isn't very polite. I did ask nicely, didn't I? Just like I asked your slapper friend Gill. She didn't seem to want to listen either. So, get in the car now,' he caught hold of Mel's arm in a vice like grip, she was no match for him as he bundled her into his car. Mel fell headlong across the front seat, and he pushed her over so he could sit down in the driver's seat. The engine started and the vehicle sped off spraying chippings in all directions, out of the car park heading for. the North Circular Road.

'I just need to sort out a few things with you, that's all, Vince smiled, 'I know a nice place where we can talk not far from here, a nice quiet place no one uses anymore.' He picked up speed and Mel thought that she didn't have any option but to see what he had to say. She was still confused as to why he had picked on her. Her mind was always so relaxed after her Spanish lesson that her mind just couldn't get into the right gear for the situation she was in.

They drove for about fifteen minutes before it dawned on Mel the potential danger she was in. *Why does he want to talk to me? How did he know I'd be coming out of the college? Where are on earth are we going?* Her thoughts flooded her mind with questions, but she had no answers. She tried to look around her subtly and tried to work where they were, but this was a part of North London she didn't know. *I must remember our route, it might be important.*

'Is it far to this place? I've got to get up for work in the morning and I don't want to be late getting to bed.'

'Oh, I don't think that will be a problem,' he answered keeping his eyes on the road as he sped along the dual carriageway. Vince took a sharp turning off to the left. He drove wildly, and Mel became even more frightened. The details of Gill's experience with Vince came flooding back to her and she started to breath heavily. She looked out of the window and tried to decide if it would be better to try to jump from the speeding car or stay put and wait for a better chance of escape later.

The car made several more turns into a labyrinth of industrial buildings, it was dark and gloomy, the lighting on was dim and the road deserted. Mel panicked and looked at Vince thinking she could perhaps cause him to crash and then she'd be able to escape. He glanced across at her and as if he had read her mind, he suddenly punched her in the face with the back of his fist. Her head ricocheted onto the headrest and the combination of the two blows rendered her unconscious.

Vince had reached his destination and dragged her out of the car. 'Christ what a lump,' he muttered under his breath, struggling a bit to drag her into the empty factory. He threw Mel into a corner and lit an oil lamp. The dim light from the lamp sent eerie shadows around the space which was filled with discarded equipment and machinery, tools and materials etc. He tied her hands and feet with some twine.

The movement caused Mel to stir and as she came to she saw Vince standing over her, his face was filled with hate. Mel pushed herself further into the corner and she studied his expression. His eyes were deep and dark and pierced her mind. His nostrils flared as he breathed deeply.

'You slag!' he said venomously and slapped her hard across the face. She just stared back unable to comprehend what was happening or why. She wanted to cry from the pain but fought hard to keep her composure. She thought of Gill, she thought of herself, and her fear paralysed her.

'I should kill you here and now for what you did to me,' Vince screamed at Mel. 'Do you know what those bastards in Spain did to me? And all because a jealous slag like you got upset over what happened to that whore of a friend of yours. She asked for what she got, and she enjoyed it.'

Mel started to shake with a combination of fear and anger. She wanted to hurt him for speaking about Gill like that, but she also feared what he was going to do to her.

'I ached for days because of you. DO YOU UNDERSTAND? I HATE YOU!' Vince lashed out at Mel and in his fury, he missed striking her again and hit his clenched fist on the side of a shovel hung up on the wall.

This only enraged him further and he started to kick Mel as she lay helpless on the floor. With each kick Mel winced and felt her body become more battered and bruised. She started to sob with pain and despair. Vince finished his frenzied attack and sat down on a crate nearby panting from the sheer exhaustion caused by his outrage. He spat in her direction and walked away. Mel saw the phlegm fall to the ground. It seemed to her to be full of years of violence as it oozed along the floor in a globule of hate. It mesmerized her, she stared at it becoming absorbed into it.

He looked across the room at her. 'What a pathetic sight you are,' he breathed angrily at her. 'I should teach you the lesson I taught your friend but that would be too good for the likes of you.' His anger was consuming him. He had hated her since he had found out that it was her who had set him up and he wanted to hurt her even more. He moved across to where she lay. She eyed him with the look of a frightened prey cornered and exhausted from the hunt. He touched her arm.

'You haven't had a man till you've had me,' he breathed in her ear.

'That's not what Gill said,' Mel heard herself say not knowing where the words had come from. With her newfound courage she continued. 'We were told how poor you were. *Nothing to write home about* was what Gill said. She said you stink as a lover and that was why she hadn't wanted to have sex with you. A girl can tell, you know, what a man's going to be like in bed and you were crap, and I bet you're still crap, so why bother? Go on then try if you like but it will only give me something to talk about to the girls.'

Vince stared in wild surprise at her response.

'I'm the one on control here not you. I make the accusations not you. You're my victim not the other way around.' He ripped at her clothes, but they weren't prepared to give up that easy. He looked at the wall to his side and saw a small saw hanging up. He reached for it and slashed at her clothes. The rusty edge if the saw cut through the materials but also through Mel's soft skin. Blood began to ooze from the wound and Vince stared in amazement at it, held as if in a spell released by the life force in it.

'Christ Almighty! What the fuck are you making me do?' Vince dropped the saw and backed off. 'I need some air.' He went out into the crisp winter night and breathed deeply. The coldness of the air filled his lungs. It caught his system by surprise, and he began to cough.

Mel could hear him from inside the building and desperately tried to think of what to do. The cut was starting to sting but her adrenaline levels were so high that she was able to blot it out of her consciousness. She looked around her through her disheveled hair that now hung limply over her face. She could make out that the factory was full of clutter, but at the same time, clutter which could be useful.

'Where the hell am I?' she said quietly to herself, 'and what sort of place is this?' She noticed the blood-stained saw nearby and she thought *if only I could get to it and cut these bindings, I could be free, yeah, but from what? Just the bindings but not the bloody building and not Vince.* The pain from her wound fought through and she winced. She rolled over and blood dripped onto the floor forming a deep red pool of despair.

I must do something, I must not be helpless. What would Rachel do? I wish to hell she were here now, I wish I'd listened more to her endless wittering about her survival weekends she spent with her dad. Oh God! How did I get in this mess? Mel's mind raced.

She pulled herself together and despite the pain of her injuries, she pulled herself up and dragged along the floor to the saw. She managed to get hold of it in her hands, but it was heavier than she had thought it would be, and she dropped it. The cold steel made a clanging noise as it hit the floor. Mel froze and looked towards the door.

Vince was too wrapped up in his own torment to hear clearly but thought he had heard something. He turned towards the door and hesitating only for a few seconds before bursting back into the factory. Mel had managed to maneuver herself and the saw back into the corner. She felt so clumsy, tears flowed down her cheeks as she realised that she would not be able to achieve her goal in time. Vince moved over to her and kicked her where she lay just for good measure. Mel held onto the saw as if her life depended on it.

'I'm going to teach you a lesson, I'm going to keep you here until you beg me to do you just to get free.' He turned the oil lamp out and left the shed. Mel heard the door being padlocked shut and then his car started and sped off into the night. She listened as the sound of its engine became fainter and fainter. She sighed and as she let her guard down for that split second her emotions unleashed themselves after what seemed an endless time and she started to cry uncontrollably. She wept the tears of the hopeless, she cried so hard that her tears seemed like silent screams in the blackness. There was so much emotion to get out, not just this evening but the last six months, her ordeal on holiday, nearly losing her best friend, actually losing her mother, seeing her father again and all this time not really knowing if Iain really cared or not. She wept for all these things as she had wanted to do when they happened but had used her self-control to bottle up her true feelings least the world should see them and mock her for them. Her head still throbbed but eventually she eventually fell asleep out of sheer exhaustion.

When Mel woke up, she could see a dim light poking its way through the dirty windows high up on the factory walls.

God, I'm cold, she shivered and realised she was still half naked after Vince's assault. *I must move*, she tried to get up, but she was so stiff from lying awkwardly all night and also from the beating she had had from Vince, that she just couldn't move a muscle.

'I must move,' she said in frustration. She stopped and

suddenly felt that Vince might be nearby and hear her. She listened but heard nothing. 'Get your act together Mel Wright and you need to bloody well get out of here now,' she screamed.

With an almighty effort, she managed to get onto her knees. The rough floor scraped at her skin, and she winced at the pains which were wrecking her whole body. Mel looked around and remembered the saw behind her and managed to position it so that she could rub the twine binding her hands. Eventually, after cutting herself several times on its rusty edge, she managed to free herself and collapsed into a heap and sobbed.

'No time to feel sorry for yourself, get moving,' she chastised herself. She undid the twine holding her ankles and rubbed them to ease the pain and tried to get onto her feet but had to hold onto a pile of wood stacked nearby. She staggered across the floor and found her handbag thrown on the floor.

'Shit! He's taken my phone and my purse the bastard, what can I do now? Where's the bloody door?' Mel was getting angry, she shook her head, 'what the hell's going on? This is London, this cannot be happening. I've got to get out of here, there must be someone outside.'

She found a door that looked like a fire door and pushed hard against it. It creaked but didn't budge. 'Open the stupid door!' she shouted and kicked it repeatedly. The creaking increased and the door gave way. Out of the building she shot and fell headlong into a large oily puddle.

'Great! What next? It'll no doubt rain soon,' she looked up to see dark ominous clouds moving in from the west. 'I don't believe this, this is a nightmare.' She then realised that she was still only half dressed, and she covered herself up the best she could with her torn clothes. It was bitterly cold, and she shivered with both cold and fear. 'I must get out of here.'

There were no signs of anyone having been around for

ages. The only tracks in the mud were from Vince's car. She started out of the yard surrounding the factory and walked up the dirt track hoping that she would get to a road and be able to hail a passing car. As she hobbling along the rutted track, she didn't hear the noise of the approaching car. She was too preoccupied with just keeping going that the car came around the bend and almost ran her down. She stopped and stared as the car door opened and out stepped Vince.

'Where do you think you're going then, bitch?' he came up to her. She felt her whole body wince even before he had touched her and felt helpless to fight him off. She was simply too cold and too battered to defend herself. She slumped to the ground and started sobbing.

'Get up, bitch. Back we go. I'm not finished with you yet, not by a long way.' He yanked at her arm and dragged her towards his car over the rough stones bundling her into the boot slamming the lid shut. In the dark she felt the warmth of tears run down her face, but no noise came from her. She was paralysed with fear and disappointment.

Not back to the shed, not there, not more of this, I want this to stop, it must stop. This isn't real, it can't be, she thought. The car bumped along the track and then stopped with a jolt. The boot lid opened and the light streaming in blinded Mel. An arm reached out and grasped her by the hair like a vice dragging her out of the car and through the mud into the building she had just left. He threw her into the corner again and kicked her hard on the thigh.

Mel attempted to get up and putting her hand out to steady herself, she felt something hard behind her. She picked up the object slowly and standing up she turned towards Vince who was pacing around in front of her muttering.

'I should kill you. I should. You bitch!' he turned towards Mel and saw her raise her hands above her head. 'What are you doing?' he screamed and lunged at her, 'I told you to lie there. You should do as you're told. All women should do as they're told...'

As if in slow motion, Mel's swing continued. As the shovel hit Vince on the head the momentum was such that it just kept going. The blow struck his skull and slid down to his shoulder as he buckled under its weight. She returned the swing and struck him again, this time on the arm with the same ferocity. He melted down onto the dusty floor. Blood began to flow from a wound in his shoulder like lava from an erupting volcano, picking up particles along its way and running through the debris like a hot molten river. The look of surprise on Vince's face was complete. He had never known a woman who had ever struck back.

'This isn't right,' he croaked, 'I'm the power. I'm the man. You should obey me.' His thoughts were a repeat of the way his father had spoken to his mother. He realised he had become his father. 'You're my victim... MY victim...' His thoughts trailed off. His eyes fixed on Mel, startled but strangely empty and sad before closing.

Mel dropped the shovel. It lay in the pool of blood. She had no real feelings at that moment except one of relief. Elation began to creep over her skin, covering her body and making her shiver. Her thoughts were garbled and unclear but there was one overwhelming theme to her thoughts as they cleared. *I'm free, Gill's free, we're all free.*

CHAPTER 44

Mel stepped away from the body. The blood trickled from his wounds as if evil was ebbing away leaving an empty worthless shell. She breathed deeply and pulled herself back to the situation before her. She stumbled to the doorway and holding its frame bent over double and tried to throw up. The culmination of fear and exertion had forced her stomach to retch in an effort expel the feelings it had, but there was nothing to throw up.

She turned towards Vince's car and went in search of her mobile phone. She found it on the floor by the front seat, but the battery was dead. She then noticed that he had left his keys in the ignition, she jumped into the car and drove off along the rough track spraying chippings everywhere. She got to the main road and let instinct decide which way to turn. She was eventually in familiar streets and found herself driving along the road where Rachel's flat was. She parked the car badly on the kerb and ran up to the front door and fumbled with the doorbells. Several people answered her and eventually she recognised Rachel's voice. 'Let me in, it's Mel. Rachel let me in.'

Rachel gasped at the sight of Mel. Her blood-stained

muddy clothes and matted hair made her look more like the missing link than one of her best friends.

'You've been attacked haven't you? Well, first things first, I'll take some pictures of the state you're in, then we'll get out of those clothes, and I'll clean those cuts for you. You look terrible.' Rachel helped Mel slowly undress. The pain from her beatings made it difficult to move easily and it took the two women ages to finish Mel's clean up.

'I've killed him.' Mel said. 'He kidnapped me and then I killed him, what should we do?'

'Hold on. Killed who?' said Rachel.

'Vince!'

'Vince? Jesus, Mel. What are you talking about? How?'

'With a shovel,' said Mel as if it was the most natural answer to Rachel's enquiry.

'A shovel? Where?'

'In a disused factory somewhere in North London, probably around Hendon, I don't know where exactly.'

Rachel boiled the kettle and made Mel a strong cup of tea to help her calm her nerves before thinking what to do next. She stared at Mel while pondering the situation. This was not the ordinary run of the mill situation, but she kept her cool as Mel knew she would.

'Are you sure he's dead?' she eventually said.

'Yes! There was blood and he didn't move. I hit him on the head – really hard.'

'I see,' Rachel had to think. 'Have you told anyone else?'

'No, I didn't know who to tell, I came to you cause you're always so calm in a crisis, I'm scared, Rachel. Help me!'

'Of course I'll help you, but we've got to be sure we're doing the right thing. Could you find the place again?'

'I might be able to, but I'm scared, he was so...' Mel took a deep breath to help her steady her nerves. 'Do we really have to go back? Can't we just call the police?'

'We will, but we'll need to be able to tell them where he is. If we can't, they'll think we're wasting their time, think Mel, where was it?'

Mel closed her eyes and tried to retrace her drive from that fateful place. 'I think I could drive back there but I can't explain where it is.'

'OK. I'll call the police and ask them to come here, then we'll all go together.'

The two women drove back to the industrial estate in Rachel's car followed by the policewoman who had been sent to deal with Rachel's call. As they drew up outside, Mel felt anxious and started to panic. Rachel came over and helped her get out of the car. They walked over to the door that Mel had made her escape through.

'You had better stay here. I'll go and look inside,' said the police constable, a little out of her depth in this kind of situation. Entering the building, she adjusted her eyes to the dim light and looked around, eventually coming back outside to the two waiting women.

'I can't see anything in there. Can you perhaps show me where all this took place?'

Mel and Rachel entered the factory. Mel looked across towards the spot she had spent the night, tied up and beaten and shuddered. Her wounds although dressed stabbed at her nervous system as her body remembered her ordeal at Vince's hands and boots. She looked over towards the place he had fallen, but his body was not there. The blood stains on the floor showed that something suspicious had happened but there was no sign of Vince. She spun around and stared at Rachel.

'He's gone, but he can't have, he was dead, I know he was.'

'Are you sure this is the exact spot he fell, Miss?' the policewoman asked her patiently. 'It is dark in here, could it have been somewhere else?'

'Well…it could have, but I'm sure it was here, there's his blood, for Christ's sake! He must be here.'

'Just stay calm, Miss. Sometimes you can get a little disorientated.'

'Over here, look there's blood stains leading across the floor, lots of blood,' said Rachel, 'and the trail leads outside through the other door. Come on!'

'Now Miss, leave this to me, please,' said the constable, a little worried in case either woman was harmed whilst in her protection, but of course neither woman took any notice as Rachel hurried towards the door followed more slowly by Mel.

Outside, the blood trail became less distinct as the gravel surface had soaked it away. Rachel's tracking ability was being put to the test, but she was in her element. She moved back and forth like a bloodhound on the scent.

'Here, he went this way,' and she pointed towards some scrub land which surrounded the factory. 'Come on, he can't have gone far,' and she sped off into the forest.

'Wait!' cried the constable in vain and she began to pursue Rachel whilst also trying to call for back up.

Mel was overcome by all this exertion and leant against a pile of large metal drainage pipes, trying to catch her breath. It took her ages before she had calmed down enough to breathe easily again. The others had disappeared into the scrubland, and she could hear Rachel shouting to the policewoman in the distance. *This would be almost comical if it wasn't so real,* thought Mel. Then she heard a sound behind her that made her hair stand on end.

'So, you thought...you could get the better of me again...did you, bitch?'

'Vince!' Mel said more quietly than she had wanted. 'But you're dead. I killed you.'

'Wrong again, bitch...I'm going to kill you...' he lurched forward. The sight of his blood-stained head and clothes was hideous and Mel tried to back away in both fear and repulsion. As she stumbled backwards she caused the stack of pipes to become dislodged and she could only watch as the pipes started to tumble forwards and reach Vince, weakened by his injuries. They thundered over him and on along the ground like stampeding cattle, totally oblivious to his presence. The dust they raised was choking and Mel coughed and wheezed as a cloud of particles enveloped her. She passed out from the shock and only came-to when Rachel spoke into her ear.

'Mel! Wake up! Are you OK?'

She noticed the constable bending over the body which lay about ten feet from her. It was motionless and lay crumpled in a heap on the floor. It looked like an old rag doll, forgotten and discarded. She turned her head away and started to cry.

'I want to go home.'

'We will, but you really need to go to the hospital first, Mel. You must be more badly hurt than I thought, I should've called a doctor before, I really hate myself for not seeing that sooner,' Rachel was very upset at not realising how badly hurt Mel was. 'I should never have gone off tracking and left you like I did, I should've stayed with you, I abandoned you to the enemy, what will Dad say when he hears about this? Please forgive me Mel.'

'Of course I do, you weren't to know, I thought I'd killed him, I never thought he could've dragged himself off and then must have doubled back to catch me here. We couldn't have known. No one could have imagined this would happen.'

The ambulance arrived and more police who set up the whole area as a scene of crime. The area was teaming with police forensic experts gathering evidence and trying to piece together the events that had led to such tragedy.

The real tragedy here, thought Rachel, *was that this all started from a good idea to go on holiday to the sun and have some fun and this is how it all ends.* Rachel got into her car and followed the ambulance to the hospital after calling Gill to see if she was on duty, Mel was going to need all her friends around her at a time like this.

CHAPTER 45

The circumstances surrounding Vince's death meant that a postmortem had to be carried out and after the police took statements from both Mel and Rachel, the Coroner called for an inquest. The ordeal was taxing for Mel who had to relive the harrowing events over again. The verdict of the coroner was that Vince's death had been accidental, but the girls knew that his death was anything but accidental. It had been brewing for whole of the twenty-nine years of his lousy life. No one seemed surprised at his death. None of his so-called friends attended the inquest, none of his relatives bothered to attend either. This summed up the worthlessness of his life and the irony that only those who hated him or never knew him were there.

'I've got to get away from this place,' said Mel, 'I'm exhausted by all this.'

'I agree,' Rachel said, 'you do need to get away. How about going to visit Iain, I'm sure he'll love to see you again, why not give him a ring, he can't be busy all the time.'

'I don't want to bother him, he does such important deals and stuff.'

'Nonsense, ring him now,' said Gill. 'Stop putting it off with feeble excuses, either you two are going to be an item or you're not.'

'You're right, as always, but I'm scared in case he doesn't really want to see me.'

'Well, I'd just ask him,' Cathy said. Everyone stared at her. This wasn't the Cathy they knew a year ago, but they loved her all the more for it.

'OK, I'll do it this evening, I promise,' Mel dreaded the thought that perhaps Iain wasn't interested at all but this not knowing was killing her, she knew she had to find out.

CHAPTER 46

Mel arrived at the villa and rang the bell. No one answered so she went around the veranda to the side of the house. The breeze wafted through her hair like the fingers of a lover, and she could smell the familiar citrus smells she had grown so used to in her few times she had been there. The scenery from the terrace was so comforting as she looked out over the bay and the intense blue of the sea.

'¿Puedo ayudarte? Can I help you?' the voice of a woman with a local accent called out from the doorway. Mel spun around and saw an attractive woman, her long black hair was tied back in the familiar fashion of the region which accentuated her fine bone structure and deep dark eyes.

'I'm looking for Iain Ferguson. Is he in?'

'No Senorita, he is not in. Can I help you or take a message?' The woman's English was good.

'I suppose so, do you know when he will be back?'

'Not until later this evening or maybe tomorrow. Who shall I say called?'

'Melissa Wright.'

At that moment a young girl of six or seven appeared from behind the woman. She was not as dark as the woman, but her features were just as fine, and Mel deduced that she must be her daughter. The girl looked at Mel and then at her mother.

'¿Que pasa, Mama?'

'Nada!' and she ushered the girl indoors.

'By the way,' said Mel, a little confused by the turn of events. 'Do you live here?'

'Yes, I live here.' The door closed and Mel started to think about the situation. *Who is this woman and who's that little girl and why are they in Iain's house, I've never seen either of them before when I was here, why didn't I ever meet her then?*

She turned and walked slowly back down the track to the town. She didn't notice the vibrant flowers or smell the sweet perfume as it filled the evening air. *I've made such an awful mistake, this woman and the child, they must have been away for the two weeks last summer, but there were no signs that anyone lived with him or perhaps I just didn't want to see them,* her mind was spinning with thoughts she didn't want, *why hadn't he said he was married? Well, that's a stupid bloody question, Melissa Wright, why do you think? It slipped his mind? He forgot? Oh, grow up, you've been had, just admit it. God, I'm so stupid.*

Mel reached the sea front and composed herself over a latte and a cake in a café. *I haven't come all this way for nothing, or have I? I need to find out, to hear it from him, to hear where I stand, he owes me that much.*

She booked into a hotel which seemed pleased of the custom out of season. The resort was virtually deserted. She settled into her room and then went out to get some fresh air, she needed to clear her head so she could think about what to do next. She sat on a bench overlooking the harbour. The marina and harbour were somehow different now, different boats perhaps, the boats moored during the summer were only for show she cynically thought and now the real fishing boats were back providing their owners a living over the winter months till the onslaught of tourists came flooding back to drown all semblance of real authenticity and reality.

She remembered how she had sat at this same bench on the first night she and the girls had been here last year. How lonely she had felt then and how that night had unfolded, for all of them, changes which they could never have perceived. She thought of their gains and losses. The loss of her mother who had given up her long struggle when she realised, she was no longer needed by Mel and therefore felt she was no longer needed by anyone. Gill's loss of her confidence and self-identity and her having to admit that she needed others as much as anyone else. Rachel's shackles of obedience and precision had been broken and she was free to be the woman who could just live for the sake of it not to some timetable or set of rules or orders. And Cathy who had awoken from a deep sleep like some lost princess and had eventually been the bravest of them all, standing up to her tyrannical father and blossoming into a strong and loving woman.

Mel smiled. The last eight months had been traumatic, to say the least, for all of them, but it had finally come good. They had all gained from their ordeals, painfully and emotionally purging themselves, making unpleasant decisions, taking the knock backs and loses. Each had found that by throwing off their shackles which childhood had tied them with they were able to be the women they had to be. All they had to do was dream enough.

'If you can dream it you can achieve it – dare to dream!'

Mel nodded at this quote she had said time and time again to herself over the years, persistent that even though she could dream, she would never achieve when it was only her who was holding herself back all along. And here she was to prove it.

'Sat alone on a bench at 8pm and not knowing what to do next,' Mel said out loud to herself.

'Then why alone?' a voice which she instantly recognised came out of the darkness and sat down beside her.

'You!' she said in a shocked voice. 'What the hell are

you doing here? Shouldn't you be at home with the lovely family? You've got a nerve talking to me.'

'What are you talking about? Rosa told me you had called. She was very impressed by your hair, by the way, she said she had never seen such a colour in her life.'

'Would you like a lock of it as a trophy then?'

'What for? And what trophy?'

'The trophy of leading me on and being married all the time, convenient that she was away those two weeks last summer, impeccable timing of me for sure.'

Iain remained silent and a look of perplexed concern came over his face. 'You think that Rosa is my wife? And I suppose that Sophie is my daughter. Wow, an instant family but sadly no, I'm a bachelor and always have been, I'm too choosy I'm afraid. They're my new housekeeper and her daughter, I thought I needed a few homely touches to the house and as I'm away so often I also needed someone to look after the place but thank you for the compliment. Rosa's a fine-looking woman and Sophie the sweetest girl you could ever meet. Her father worked for me but was tragically killed a few months ago, Rosa hasn't any family, so we agreed I'd employ her to look after me and I'd look after them in return. I'm disappointed that you thought less of me because of that. I'd always been as honest as I could with you but there were no strings between us. You never owned me you know. And life goes on even when you tourists go home. I thought I made that clear from the start. Besides, you never actually asked me if I was married, and I never took advantage of you in any improper way, did I?'

'Well, no…'

'Precisely.'

Mel felt so foolish that she had jumped to conclusions so easily. *All that pain for nothing,* she thought, *I'm such a prat.*

'I'm sorry. I should've trusted you. It was just that when you said I should book into a hotel and that you would meet me somewhere and then finding that woman and child at your villa, I just assumed. I'm sorry. Please forgive me.'

'Oh well if I must,' Iain smiled and looked at Mel. 'My, you have changed since last summer.'

'Yes, but for the better I hope,' she moved closer to him and looked straight at him, her soft green eyes full of mischief, 'I'm still the woman I was, I've just taken off my overcoat. I don't need it any longer. Hopefully, I've got you to keep me warm instead, I decided it was time to start living and I want to do that with you.'

'Hmm, that's an interesting proposition, I'll have to see the figures though,'

'I think that can be arranged,' she snuggled into his arms.

He looked down at her smiling face and knew that he'd been wrong to avoid committing himself to her all along. He also knew that he just had to kiss her.

The sensation of such a long-awaited kiss was so intense that both Iain and Mel swayed from side to side. Iain knew for sure that he had to keep this woman who had chipped away at his cool exterior from the first day they had met.

He remembered that first fateful night and that by pure chance, he had spotted those lager louts following Mel. He had followed the group to see what they intended to do. When Mel had turned into the ally way followed noisily by the boys, Iain had known that there was the potential for trouble. He knew that the street was a dead end and so couldn't fathom out why she had turned into it in the first place.

Listening to the boys shouting their abuse at Mel had incensed him and when they'd begun to touch her, he knew he had to act. It could've been folly as he was outnumbered but his mere size and presence at done the trick, and he felt a swell of pride in being able to help a 'damsel in distress.' Carrying Mel back to his villa had also been a risky thing to do, as he valued his privacy above all else.

Here he was nearly a year on, walking back to his villa with the woman who fascinated him since they had first met and had made him feel alive again. As soon as Rosa had told Iain that the young woman had called, he had changed. She had noticed that he went straight to shower and put on clean clothes. She also noticed that he had a spring in his step that she had not seen that often before – except perhaps when a big deal was coming together which always excited him.

'We will be going to see my friend in the next town tonight if that is OK with you Senor Iain. We will probably spend the night to save getting a taxi back in the dark. I shall prepare a supper for you before I leave.' Rosa had announced before Iain had left to find Mel.

'OK, Rosa,' he said. 'That'll be fine. See you tomorrow then,' and he had waltzed off down the track towards the town.

'Yes, OK,' Rosa had whispered after him. 'Go and find your beautiful young woman. You deserve happiness. Sophia and I will be fine, we will sort things out, no worries.' She had felt sad at the prospect of perhaps having to leave their new home. It had provided a haven from the world for herself but more importantly her daughter after her husband had died, but she had known all along that it was only temporary. She was sure that her friends in Soller would know somewhere for her to go if the time came.

All this Iain was oblivious to as he strolled along with Mel. He was feeling very proud and also happy, actually happy. All the deals in the world could not take the place of holding hands with someone you cared for and who obviously cared for you. They arrived at the villa to find it empty.

'Where's your friend?' Mel asked.

'She said she was going to see friends for the night. We don't keep tabs on each other. She just keeps the villa clean and tidy and cooks some meals for me when I'm here. She's a lot of sorting out to do herself, so I leave her to it. It suits us both that way. She said she'd make some supper. Shall I warm it up?'

'That'd be nice. I am a little peckish.' She was in fact famished as all the panic about Iain being married had drained her blood sugar which even the cake hadn't filled. She thought she would faint if she didn't get any food soon but had decided not to make too much of her appetite, not after her slip up on their first date. She remembered that evening in Juan's very well. Some of the things Iain had said had hurt very much, but she knew now that he was only being honest which was something she hadn't been much of with herself for years. He'd said things which she knew to be true but which her protective overcoat hid away from even herself.

Mel and Iain ate in silence both pondering on their relationship and where things would go next. They went into the sitting room after the meal and sipping the remains of the wine they'd had at dinner. Mel felt comfortable and at ease. She looked at Iain who was sorting out some music for them to listen to. Mel shivered a little caused by the chill on the air but also by her thoughts about Iain.

'Are you cold? I'll light the fire. It'll make it nice and cosy here for us. I feel we'll be up for a while. Let's face it Mel there's a lot to talk about don't you think?'

'Yes, there is.'

They settled down together on the settee, soft music floated around the room and the crackle of the logs on the fire made it a perfect romantic scene.

'Why did you come here to see me?'

'Because I wanted to. That's the long and the short of it. A lot has happened since we last saw each other, probably to both of us but I know especially to me. I've changed and not just physically either. I've grown and changed in so many ways but during all these changes there was one thing which kept haunting me. I realised that you had somehow affected me. I relived our moments together over and over. I thought that I was probably wasting my time, but I had to see if the magic I felt when I was with you was still there and…also if you …well if you'd changed your mind about tourists.'

'I still hate tourists. But then you aren't a tourist anymore, are you? I'll admit that you were on my mind often too. I'll also admit that this unnerved me. I've lived here for nearly six years now and I've vowed to myself that I wouldn't get involved with anyone. My business is very demanding. I have to travel often at a moment's notice. I also need to concentrate on my work…'

'Is that all there is to your life then…work?'

'No, I've got friends and hobbies…'

'Such as?'

'Well, I like music and walking and good wine and…'

'Yes, but who do you enjoy these things with?'

'I like my own company…'

'Why? Why not with others? What happened to you in the past to make you a loner?'

'I don't think I'm a loner, I've got a full life. I live well, I travel, I like nice things…'

'What about nice people? Do you like them as well?'

'What is this? A Spanish Inquisition? I don't think I like all these questions shot at me like this,' Iain got up and started to pace around the room. He felt under pressure and didn't like it. In business he was prepared for aggression but in his private life he liked peace and quiet. He was beginning to see why he hated people so much. They were a bloody nuisance.

'I'm only doing to you what you did to me that first night we went out,' Mel said. 'Not nice, is it? But do you know what? It really helped me. Not at the time – I just wanted to cry and run away, but later I thought about the things you said, and I knew you were right. It was then that I realised that I had to change or waste my entire life trying to be someone and something which was not me. I think you're the same and like it or not I have to say that to you because I... well, I love you.'

Mel knew that Iain was looking at her. What was he thinking she wondered. She didn't have long to wait to find out. Iain came over to her and bent down on his knees in front of her.

'I'm sorry,' said Iain. His hands reached out to Mel's, and they held hands and looked at each other. The moment was so intense that it was difficult to speak.

'I know you care, and I'm flattered that a woman as beautiful as you should do so, I know I'm a loner and I've become comfortable being so, I also know that I can't really go on being like it forever but knowing and doing are not the same thing. Change frightens the hell out of me sometimes, it's so much easier to stay the same. I'm astonished at the way you've transformed yourself, physically mainly but it seems you've also really changed inside, I didn't think improving on perfection was possible but evidently it is.' They smiled at each other, and this helped to release the tension. 'I don't know if I can change but I think I'd like to try.'

'Then you're in expert hands here, let me help you, I'd like that.' Mel slid from the settee and putting her arms around Iain she gently kissed him, the kiss was full of tenderness but also grew into passion as the couple crumpled onto the floor and melted into each other. Their bodies felt the warmth of love as the fire crackled in the hearth, its flames rising and flickering in the soft warm light

CHAPTER 47

'But we've got to go and help him,' Cathy pleaded with Jon.

'I don't want you going anywhere near him, who knows what he might do to you in a drug-crazed stupor, he's no longer my brother, he hurt Dad and Mum, and I'll never forgive him for that. He's lost. Gone. Let's just accept that and move on.' Jon was bitter at the way his twin had treated his parents.

'We don't know he uses drugs, Jon, all we know is that he's moved in with that girl he met after our wedding, he might need us, Jon, we've got to do something.'

'The matter's closed. I forbid you to contact him, is that clear?' Jon turned and finished dressing for work. He had to travel to Birmingham to attend a conference and would be gone overnight. He hoped that Cathy would forget about Andy. He sensed that Cathy was not happy though. *I'll talk to her when I get home,* he thought.

Cathy stared at her husband. For once she did not recognise him. He had changed. She knew he would never admit it, but the way Andy had fallen in with bad company and then stolen from his parents had knocked

Jon for six. She knew it was a world he couldn't understand. Cathy couldn't either, but she wasn't prepared to give up on Andy so easily.

'Rachel is that you?' Cathy said after Jon had left. 'I must see you, I've found Andy, and I need your help.'

'Help? With what, Cathy? Andy and I are history, and I'm up to my eyes in this new corporate account, I can't get away from the office and I'm due to fly to New York tomorrow. If you really need someone's help, why not ask Mel? She's back from Majorca and still on sick leave after her episode with Vince so I'm sure she'd love an excuse to get out and I know she'd love to help you.'

'OK, I'll do that. I hope you have a great trip,' said Cathy as cheerfully as she could. 'I envy you, but I can't go flying around the world in my condition. I'd be a liability and who knows what nationality the baby might end up with.'

'I'll be back in plenty of time for your due date next week, Cathy. No worries there. Now you take care of yourself and your precious cargo and don't worry about Andy. He's a big boy and can look after himself. I must dash – there's another meeting in five minutes and I can't be late. Love you.'

'Love you too. Good luck.' The phone went dead. Cathy sat on the bed and thought. She had to do something, but could she really defy her husband. She knew her mother would never have done. She thought about her mother and her father. She missed them both but for different reasons. *I must try to visit Dad in prison when the baby's arrived and take some photos. I'm sure he'll fall in love with the baby, babies are so adorable after all.*

'I'll talk to Jon when he gets home,' Cathy said out-loud as if hearing the words would help her come to terms with the situation. She busied herself around the house for a while. The increasing size and weight of her bump was starting to make it difficult for her to do some things. She sighed and sat down. She felt a twinge in her abdomen and Baby O kicked her fiercely. 'Ow! Why you little tinker, just you wait until you come out,' she said to her unborn child confident in the knowledge that he heard and understood every word. 'What shall we do about your Uncle Andy? I must do something, but Daddy said not to. Oh, dear. I can't cope with this. Should I go and see Uncle Andy?' The baby in her womb lashed out at her body, and it startled her. She felt her bump. 'So, you think I should go then?' She felt a strange feeling in the pit of her stomach and was sure that her baby was trying to tell her something. 'I'll go then. Good decision, Baby O. I'll go now and the whole thing will be sorted out before Daddy gets home tomorrow. I'll ask Auntie Mel if she can come with us.'

Mel was pleased to help. She agreed to pick Cathy up from her house so that they could go together.

'Glad you asked me, I'm going stir crazy in the flat on my own, Gill works such crazy shifts, I hardly ever see her. How's Baby O coming along anyway?'

'She's fine, I don't feel that special today, but I must get this matter sorted out with Andy, I've only got another week to go, and I can't wait, it's getting a bit uncomfortable getting around and I've had strange churning feelings in my tummy today, I think Baby O is impatient to see her Uncle Andy. Thanks for offering to drive, I can't get behind the wheel anymore.'

'You'll be back to your usual skinny self in no time, life's just not fair. It's taken me ages to lose all my weight but then again, I had been carting it around a lot longer than you and I didn't have the excuse you have for a bulging waistline.'

'You look great now, Mel. How did you get on with your trip to see Iain?'

'Well, it was interesting to say the least, but I think things will be just fine from now on, I'm thinking of moving out to Majorca to be with him, I've got no reason to stay here now, Mum and the house are gone. I really feel alive when I'm in Majorca, there's something in the air I think, it's such a beautiful place and now I can speak some Spanish I think I'll fit in easily.'

'And there's Iain, or doesn't he figure in all this?' said Cathy coyly.

'Oh yes, he figures alright,' Mel's smile on her face said it all, 'but I will miss Gill and Rachel and you.'

'I know you will, but you'll cope. Gill and Rachel haven't been around as much as we'd both have liked sometimes. But when Rachel isn't here, I sometimes feel stronger not weaker.'

'I feel the same about Gill, I love her dearly and want the old Gill back but in a way, it has made me stand up for myself more and I feel better about myself because of it.'

Mel drove through the area where Cathy had said Andy now lived. It was an area she had never had any reason to visit before. She'd heard it was full of large old, terraced houses that were now past their best and let out mainly in bed-sits. The house she stopped at looked neglected and run down. Its windows were hollow and empty like an old person forgotten by their family and left to decay slowly and alone. She parked her car and made a point of putting the security lock on then she helped Cathy out of the car. They made their way gingerly up the steep steps and looked at the numerous doorbells by the front door.

'Which one is it?' said Cathy.

'Didn't they tell you which flat he was in?'

'No. The detective only said the address, I assumed it was a house not a block of flats, I only know the name of the girl he's moved in with…'

'Sorry I'm late,' a voice called out to them from the bottom of the steps. 'Traffic is always bad at this time of the day, and I got stuck on the Edgeware Road. Some hold up or other. Have you been waiting long?'

'No,' said Cathy truthfully, wondering whom this man

was. 'Do I know you?'

'I'm Matthew Price from the property agents, he gave Cathy a business card, 'I'm here to show you around the apartment.' He used the word apartment despite the absurdity of the grandeur the name gave the place. 'Shall we go in. I've got the keys.' He fumbled with a huge set of keys, which Mel guessed must open most of London. 'When's the baby due then? You're lucky the landlord allows children. But then he allows most things in his properties, the truth be known.' He realised he had perhaps said too much and having found the right key ushered Cathy and Mel inside the front door.

'We're not actually looking to move in, thank you. We're looking for someone,' Mel thought she had better explain herself before the eager man had signed them up for a three-year tenancy or something.

'To be honest, you didn't look like you should be in a place like this.'

'I was looking for a Hayley Mills,' Cathy said.

'Not THE Hayley Mills?' he said, 'Gosh, I didn't know she'd moved in as well, but then it takes all sorts I suppose, never thought she'd end up here though.'

'What? I don't understand,' Cathy said even more confused than her usual self. *This man is talking nonsense*, she thought.

'Sorry, just my little joke. Why would THE Hayley Mills be here unless she was researching for another version of Tiger Bay or something, bit late for that I'd have thought.'

Cathy and Mel stared at him. They had no idea what he was talking about.

'Sorry, I'm a film buff, always rabbiting on about old film, but yes, let me see,' he took out a book and started to thumb through the dog- eared pages. 'Yes, here we are, try number 3, just go up the stairs and it's on the right. I'll just go and um... wait outside again till the real appointment arrives, I think, nice to have met you,' he disappeared outside completely embarrassed by his mistake.

'Thank you,' said Cathy relieved that this man was being helpful but still confused about Tiger Bay wherever that was. She saw the stairs straight ahead of them.

'Gosh, they're so wide and sweeping,' she said and looking around her for the first time she noticed other features. 'This house must have been very grand at one time, and I expect it was cared for so well by its inhabitants, I wonder how many families have lived here over the years?' She could imagine the sounds of children laughing and the smell of home cooking wafting around the hallway, which was in stark contrast to now. Now there was only arguing couples, daytime TV shows at full volume and the distinct smell of boiled cabbage.

'Not as many as now, that's for sure,' Mel said, 'they haven't painted these walls for ages, and the carpet's a disgrace. The lighting doesn't help either, what wattage is that bulb? It can't be more than 15watt at best, God, it's so dreary, how some people live amazes me sometimes, but then perhaps they have little choice.'

The stucco mouldings on the ceiling in the hall were partly remaining and it was evident how beautiful it all must have been once, but otherwise the bastardisation of the building was almost complete. Cathy climbed the stairs slowly. She held the banister to help her, but it grasped her hand with a kind of adhesion she was not expecting. It seemed to be covered with years of grime from sweaty, dirty fingers that had held it before her. She noticed that the stair carpet also had a viscous property that made her expend more energy than she would have liked to break free from its grasp with each step. It was as if the building was crying out to her to take it with her when they left.

The level of light started to diminish the further they moved from the hall light by the front door, it was an eerie feeling to ascend into the darkness. They could still see enough to read the numbers on the doors and found number 3 on their right just as the estate agent had said. Cathy took a deep breath and holding her bump she said, 'wish us luck, Baby O, here we go.'

Mel knocked the door loudly. The emptiness of the hall reverberated the sound around them and Cathy felt like running away, but she thought that the carpet would have probably clawed her back anyway.

After several minutes the door opened a chink. An eye appeared from behind the peeling paintwork and stared at Cathy and Mel, looking them up and down.

'Oh shit!' a voice accompanied the eye, 'you're not his wife, are you? I can't stand it when wives turn up, leave us in peace. If you did your job, he wouldn't need us, would he?'

'I'm not his wife,' said Cathy.

'Well girlfriend or whatever. Bugger off and leave us alone.'

'No. I need to see him and I'm his sister-in-law actually.'

'Is that his then?' the voice chuckled. 'Should have been more careful, love.'

'No, this child is my husband's. Is Andy there? Can I see him, please?'

'You want to see Andy? Oh well, come on in, I'll see if he's in.' Cathy and Mel entered the flat as if they were entering another world. The smell of stale food and staler humans was almost unbearable. It was as if all the waste of the world had descended into this one space.

Cathy turned around to see the woman. She was dressed in a dirty wrap that was far too short to be decent. Her hair was matted and her make up smeared and blotched. The most shocking sight for Cathy however was that underneath all this neglect, the resemblance of the woman to herself was unnerving, it was almost as if she was looking at her own double, but a younger version. The colour of her hair and the shape of the face were identical, her height and the colour of her eyes matched in an uncanny way. The girl was also shocked by the similarity of their appearance.

'God! You look just like me, well, bugger me, that's something, isn't it?'

'Yes, uncanny,' said Cathy dazed. 'We could be twins.'

'Yeah right, I got the bum end of the stick though looking at you. What's your name, anyway?'

'Cathy.'

'Cathy? I've got a client who likes to call me Cathy sometimes, bit of a pervert really, if you ask me, I haven't seen him in ages though, don't know why and I don't care either, he liked to preach to me, bloody nutter if you ask me. But it takes all sorts to make a world, don't it?'

'Yes, very true. I don't want to inconvenience you, but can we see Andy now, please?' This girl was disturbing Cathy, she was saying things which niggled at the back of Cathy's mind, and she thought that somehow this girl and her were in fact connected somehow, but she couldn't for the life of her work out how.

'Sure, I'll see if Hayley and him are in.' The girl walked over to a door and knocked it loudly. 'Hey, Hayley, someone here to see Andy, says she's called Cathy, his sister-in-law or something.'

The door opened abruptly. There stood Andy, unshaven and only wearing a pair of dirty jeans. 'Christ, Cathy, what the hell are you doing here? You shouldn't have come here. Did Jon send you?'

'No, he doesn't know I'm here. He said I shouldn't come but when we found out where you were, I felt I had to come and bring you home, Andy. Please come home, everyone misses you, I'm sure we can sort out any problem you might have but please come home.'

'Cathy, go away and forget this place, you shouldn't have come, I can't go back, not after what I did to Mum and Dad, anyway, I've got a new life here now…with Hayley. We love each other. We're going to get married.

It's not only you who can be happy you know, I can too even if that bitch Rachel doesn't think I'm as good a screw as some dyke, but that's her loss not mine,' Andy drifted back into the bedroom and slammed the door.

Cathy looked at Mel who didn't know what to say. Cathy went over and shouted through the door, 'Andy, don't be so stupid, Rachel is still unsure, I'm sure you can get back together but not if you stay here, stop throwing your life away. You're worth better than this.'

The door opened again but this time it wasn't Andy. A girl stood in the doorway looking at Cathy.

'Who the hell do you think you are talking about this place like that? Andy and I are good together, if you want him then you'll have to go through me to get him and from what I've heard about you, Little Miss Perfect, you haven't got it in you.' Hayley stepped towards Cathy who felt very intimidated by this girl.

Cathy instinctively stepped back and lost her balance, falling awkwardly over the arm of a chair onto the coffee table, which promptly collapsed underneath her. She doubled up as pain seared through her abdomen. The girl came over to Cathy, bend down and whispered in her ear.

'No one's going to take away the best meal ticket I've ever had without a fight, you'd better understand that, Little Miss Perfect.'

Mel rushed over to where Cathy lay and pushed the girl away.

'Help me!' cried out Cathy. 'I'm scared.'

Mel put her arm around Cathy and tried to help her to her feet, but a searing pain coursed through Cathy's body, and she doubled up in agony. Andy came out of the bedroom and looked at his sister-in-law. 'What the hell have you done to her?' he shouted at Hayley, who just shrugged her shoulders.

'Nothing. The silly cow fell over the chair, not my fault, she shouldn't have come here in the first place, we're happy and we don't need her meddling, remember, you said you didn't want anything more to do with them. She's alright just play acting to get your sympathy.' she went over to Andy and started to lick his neck.

Mel stared in disbelief at the callousness she was hearing.

'Andy! She needs help.'

Andy pushed Hayley away from him. 'I've got to help her, she's innocent, she can't look after herself like you can. Jesus, I hope she's alright.' He went over to Cathy and bent down and together Mel and Andy managed to get Cathy onto the sofa. Mel dashed into the kitchen to get a glass of water as Cathy winced in pain and the tears ran down her cheeks.

'Call an ambulance!' Andy shouted to Hayley.

Hayley walked slowly over to the bedroom to get his phone. She came back and threw it at him.

'Call them yourself, loser, and call a taxi at the same time, if you'd rather a fat leso like her then you can go to hell, I can make more money from my regulars than you'll ever have. Loser!' she screamed at him then went back into the bedroom and slammed the door.

'I'm sorry, Cathy, what the hell have I done to you. I was so jealous of you and Jon and now look what's happened.'

'I'll be OK but what am I going to tell Jon? He told me not to come to see you and now he'll know.' She began to sob uncontrollably. Andy had never seen her cry before. She always seemed so happy and easy going. Crying wasn't something you ever connected with Cathy. Andy held Cathy tightly. 'Andy, you're crushing me. I can't breathe. How long before the ambulance arrives? I need Jon. Please ring him.'

Andy backed away from Cathy. 'I can't ring him.'

'Please Andy. I'm so scared. I need him with me.' Cathy creased up in pain and Andy noticed that her clothes were wet and streaked with blood. 'My baby! I mustn't lose my baby, I'll die if anything happens to her, help me, Andy,' Cathy winced at the pain. Andy just stared back at her as if in a trance. He couldn't help her. All he could do was think what Jon would say or do when he found out Cathy had come to see him. He also found himself thinking about Hayley. Had he lost her? Was she really kicking him out – but he needed her, he needed her body next to his, he couldn't survive without her – she was his life, he loved her.

He started to pace around the room holding his head in his hands. He had to think but the sobs and cries from Cathy were getting unbearable.

'Oh, for Christ's sake, shut up, I've got to think,' he screamed at her and immediately realised what he'd done. Mel came back into the room and rushed over to Cathy.

'What the hell are you doing? Have you called for an ambulance? Have you called Jon? She needs him.' Mel was shocked at Andy's behaviour.

Andy lashed out at the wall and smacked his fist hard against the solid structure. The pain brought him back into reality and he picked up the phone and rang for an ambulance. Cathy was breathing very shallowly, and her muffled screams were echoing around the room. Hayley's flat-mate, Karen, came out of her room and looked at Cathy.

'How did this happen?' she said. 'Have you called for a doctor? Christ, she's in labour, get some blankets and a pillow from my room, where the hell's Hayley?

'She did this,' said Andy as he rushed around the flat trying to get the things she had asked for.

'What! Hayley, did you hit this girl? You bitch!'

'She fell over, I didn't touch her, hasn't she gone yet? I don't want either of them in this flat, get them out,' her voice was vicious.

Karen went over to Hayley's room and went in. Andy and Cathy heard shouting and shrieks, then Karen came back in and threw Andy his shirt and personal items including his key ring after she'd taken off the key to the flat.

'You're leaving I take it? First go and check where the ambulance is and then bugger off.' She turned to Cathy and Mel, 'I'm sorry this happened to you, but you shouldn't have come here, you had no business coming here, all you've done is made it worse for everyone, don't ever come back here again, understand?'

Mel nodded and held Cathy as she cried softly in her arms. The pain was only intermittent, and she was gaining control over it in her mind. She just wanted to be out of that revolting place and safely in Jon's arms. Perhaps her mother had been right all along as Cathy remembered what had happened to Martha when she had stood up and defied her husband for the first and only time.

CHAPTER 48

Andy gathered up his belongings and after the ambulance had arrived and checked Cathy and whisked her off to the maternity hospital, he followed Mel out of the flat. The windows of the house looked on them as the rain, which had started to fall earlier, trickled down the walls from the broken drainpipes like tears as the house just seemed to know it had been left behind yet again. Arriving at the hospital, they took ages to find a parking space. As they rushed up the corridor, they saw a nurse coming towards them and feared the worst.

Mel went to phone Jon again whilst Andy stood just inside the delivery room as the midwife was calming Cathy down after her ordeal.

'No need to worry now. The baby's signs on the monitor are showing everything's fine and Doctor's happy that you can deliver naturally,' she said, 'so it's over to Mother Nature to do what she does best. Let's just work through this together. How about something for the pain?' and handed Cathy a mask for gas and air.

'Thank you, I'm so scared.'

'Let's focus on baby now, just take a few deep breaths,

you'll be fine, babies are born all the time and yours will be so beautiful, you'll forget all about this bit, trust me, I've had three of my own.'

'I want my husband,' Cathy started to cry when she thought what a mess she had made of everything,

'Here's hubby now,' the midwife said.

Cathy noticed Andy by the door.

'He's not my husband. I want Jon.'

'I'm sorry,' said Andy, 'he hasn't arrived yet. Mel's ringing him again. He'll be here as soon as he can, I'm sure. Did you want me to leave?'

'No,' Cathy said quietly. 'No, I don't want you to leave us ever again.' She held out her hand and he grasped it and kissed it softly. As the next contraction started, Cathy squeezed Andy's hand so tightly he was sure that all the pain of the last few months was wrung out of him and, as a result, he felt closer to his family then than he had done for ages.

Several hours passed and Cathy coped better than anyone expected. Mel and Andy took it in turns to hold her hand. With the final push, Baby O came into the world just as Jon arrived in the delivery room. They held their baby and kissed her soft wet head. Jon looked at Andy but knew that this was not the time for retributions but a time for the new member to be welcomed into their family and an old member to be reunited with it.

CHAPTER 49

The birth of Cathy's and Jon's baby was the catalyst which the Owens family needed to build new bridges and heal old wounds. Andy and his parents had a long talk and several boundaries and plans for the future were laid down. Andy started to get himself back on track and agreed to pay back his parents. He managed to buy back several of the items he had stolen from them including the treasured picture of his mother's family. She could have forgiven him most of the other things, but that picture was very precious to her. Getting it back seemed to close the rift between them and the family started to function properly again.

Baby O was named Martha Catherine Owens. Her christening was held in June when Baby Martha was three months. Rachel was asked to arrange the reception, and she took on the task with her usual relish and surpassed herself. The hotel she chose was a blaze of colour as the flowers in the gardens and rooms filled the air with a fresh heady scent and a feeling of well-being and hope for the future.

Mel, Gill and Rachel were stood together, simply taking in all the atmosphere when Cathy came over to them.

'Thank you, Rachel. You've excelled yourself again.'

'Anything to make you happy, Cathy, you know that.'

'I'm so happy, I have everything I've always wanted. A loving husband, a beautiful baby and marvelous friends. What more could I ever want?'

'More babies,' said Gill, 'and lots of them, you were born. to breed.' The others laughed and Cathy started to blush.

The group had changed over the last year, and they realised that they were all much happier. Their lives may not be perfect, but they were at least making their own mistakes. They did not have to rely on others to make their decisions, to ask for permission or to guide their lives.

Mel had opened her heart to someone and found that she was loved in return. She knew there were no guarantees, but she also felt that with true friends behind her she could cope with most things in life and in fact had already done so.

Gill knew that getting help from others did not mean abdicating responsibility for herself. She knew it was important just to remember that someone was there should she have a bad day or if she needed some advice. Her new strength was to ask for it.

Rachel knew that being in complete control of her life wasn't the only consideration she needed. Just going with the flow sometimes still made her feel vulnerable but somehow, she felt calmer for it. She held out her hand to Cathy in a gesture of love and friendship. Cathy squeezed Rachel's hand, and the two women looked at each other. They had grown up together not as children but as women and they now faced the world with fresh optimism and hope.

Over the past year the women had all changed. This had been scary, but they knew that the world took no prisoners and guaranteed nothing and yet expected everything.

'Let's toast something,' said Mel. 'Let's look forward to our futures.'

'To our futures,' the group joined in unison.

'What are our futures then?' Gill asked.

'Well,' Rachel said, 'I've started dating a really fabulous girl I met at a conference last week, she's just a dream, you should see her…'

'We get the picture,' Mel interjected remembering the scene in Majorca only too well. 'How about you, Cathy?'

'Jon and I are moving into our new home next month. We can afford something a bit bigger now that Jon's got promotion.' She was so full of enthusiasm that she almost fell over her words in her excitement.

'Oh Cathy, that's great,' said Gill. 'You two are so good together.'

'I'll second that,' said Mel, 'and you all know what I'm doing. Staying with Iain in Majorca until we decide where to make our new base. We'll keep the villa of course but he's away from there so much, it would be best to have a place in Madrid, or somewhere, either way I'm learning more Spanish so I'm ready for anything.'

'Well, I've just heard that I've got funding to pilot that scheme to help victims of violence I wanted to set up, which will be based at the Trauma Centre, so we'll be able to open 24/7. Exciting times but it's going to be bloody hard work,' said Gill, 'I can't wait to get started though.'

'That's brilliant news,' Mel said, 'you've worked so hard to get that idea off the ground, well done you.'

'Here, here,' The others all hugged Gill.

'Thank you, I couldn't have done it without you.' Gill took in a deep breath and smelled the wonderful summer flowers which were all around them. 'I feel so alive now, I've got a purpose helping others to regain their lives they may have thought were lost forever. This last year has been phenomenal, don't you feel it too?'

'I do,' said Cathy, 'I actually have a life now, but it took a lot of courage, and I've got to thank all of you for giving me that courage. Going on that holiday changed my life. Standing up to my father was awesome but it was also really tragic in the end. You lot didn't realise just how vindictive he could be. Why do you think my brother Luke never came home after he left? I will always remember the night he rowed with my dad. Luke just took my dad's abuse, turned around and went upstairs without saying a word. The next morning, he'd gone. I cried because he'd gone, but more because he'd left me behind. Meeting you lot gave me the strength to think about leaving too, but it was the holiday that gave me the catalyst I needed. Thank you, guys. I shall always love you for being there.' Cathy hugged her friends in turn.

'We're such a soppy bunch at times,' Mel's eyes started to glaze over a little. She looked at her friends and thought how all four of them had built up over the years a protective barrier around themselves. *Our very own cloaks of peacock feathers, hiding our true feelings and keeping everyone that little bit further away,* she thought, *but we don't need them now, we've got more power and strength than all the armies of the world, because we've got each other*, Mel looked around at her friends, *well, that's enough emotion for one day, old girl*, and she swallowed hard.

They stood in silence as each relived the hours they had spent together. They thought about the holiday and the bar on that first night in Majorca. They forgot things such as the state of the toilets, the poor quality of the food, the dirty floors and rickety chairs. They only remembered the people, the sounds of talking and laughter, the colours of the lights from the disco and the exhilaration of dancing until their heads reeled. That evening was one of those times which they would all remember with mixed feelings, but most of all as an evening with good friends.

The sun suddenly streamed in through the high windows of the function room, the vivid greens, blues and purples of the stained-glass dancing over the women, melting, swirling and enveloping them and then, just as suddenly, the sun went behind a cloud and all that remained were four young women at ease at last.

EPILOGUE

The same sun, that shone so long ago, beats down on the golden sand of a Mediterranean shore until it hurts the feet to walk on. The deserted beach is clean and smooth, like a landscape from paradise. Four sets of footprints meander across the sand, making their mark in the emptiness. There are no other signs of life, for the lives, which made them, have moved on.

USEFUL CONTACTS

If you, or someone you know, has experienced any of the issues contained in this story, here are some useful contact points. The list is not exhaustive, so it may be good to check out local organisations in your area as well.

https://www.nhs.uk help for all medical issues including mental health, rape and sexual assault.
https://www.samaritans.org chat online to listening volunteers, or phone them on 116 123 from anywhere in the UK.
https://rapecrisis.org.uk 24/7 support line, call 0808 500 222 or chat online.
https://www.cruse.org.uk trained bereavement volunteers offering emotional support to anyone affected by grief.
https://www.victimsupport.org.uk call 0808 1689 111 or chat online.
https://www.gov.uk/victim-crime-abroad for details to get help if you are a victim of crime aboard.
https://www.nhs.uk/better-health/lose-weight/ for advice on losing weight and eating healthier.
https://www.slimmingworld.co.uk to find a group near you to start a healthy weight loss programme with support from a local friendly group (other weight loss organisations are available).

ABOUT THE AUTHOR

Clair was born in Croydon, Surrey but grew up in Pontypool in the South Wales Valleys. After graduating, she started her career as a commercial estate manager and valuer working in Bristol and London before returning to Wales to set up her own property company. Getting bored with the world of property, she studied for an MBA at Cardiff and stumbled into becoming a university lecturer and course director. She eventually became the Entrepreneurship Champion for Wales as part of the multimillion-pound Knowledge Exploitation Fund project but exasperated by the level of bureaucracy she had to deal with, she escaped to Hampshire where she has devoted her new life to her husband and two children. Just to keep herself out of mischief though, she sells vintage books and puzzles which she is pleased to say involves hardly any bureaucracy at all.

Printed in Great Britain
by Amazon